The Morning Chronicle

LONDON, THURSDAY, NOVEMBER 27, 1817

MATRIMONY—A YOUNG LADY of superior education, and person above mediocrity, who in a few months comes into possession of a considerable fortune, being urged to a connection which she abhors, from the avaricious disposition of her Guardian, wishes anxiously to meet a Young Gentleman of good person and disposition, settled in any respectable situation (no matter how distant from town), who would free her in an honourable way from her present distressing situation. Letters (post paid to insure delivery, as the advertiser is not known) addressed to Miss H., No. 7, Church-passage, Picadilly, will be attended to as soon as difficulties experienced allow of.

THE
SUBSTITUTE
BRIDEGROOM

Jeanne Abbott

FAWCETT CREST • NEW YORK

A Fawcett Crest Book
Published by Ballantine Books
Copyright © 1985 Diane J.A. Monarch

Library of Congress Catalog Card Number: 85-90694

ISBN: 0-499-20804-4

Manufactured in the United States of America

First Edition: August 1985

To Reynolds, who made me finish

CHAPTER ONE

The reformation of a rake has ever been the highest ambition of all virtuous women. And Lady Jane Tiverton, despite having achieved her sixty-second year, was not immune to that particular form of folly; she desired to reform her nephew.

This aspiration of her ladyship's was not a passing fancy that would be discarded at the first sign of opposition. In fact, if she had not been of a particularly persistent and tenacious personality, she might have become discouraged at the lack of cooperation her nephew displayed. Not less than two weeks ago, she had sent him an invitation to visit her at his earliest convenience. Still, he refused to appear. If the season had been in full swing, she would have found excuses for his neglect. November of 1817 did not, however, promise to be a month that would make a great many demands on anyone's social calendar, least of all, a young man neither addicted to ton parties, nor partial to sporting activities. So it was with feelings both of delight and disgust that she greeted the news that her recalcitrant nephew had finally arrived to pay his visit.

When her dresser Jenkins, a sour-faced creature, brought the message that her ladyship's nephew was downstairs in the blue drawing room, Lady Jane leaped out of her velvet-draped bed with an energy that belied her years. Unfortunately, it also caused her to spill a good deal of her morning chocolate. Reproaching her maid, Lady Jane impatiently waved away the anxious Jenkins, who was trying ineffectually to sop up the mess.

"More important things concern us!" Lady Jane announced as Jenkins left off her attempts to remove the stain from the satin counterpane and came to lend her support to the more urgent question of choosing a gown.

Jenkins assured her ladyship there was no need to rush as her ladyship's nephew had come not in his own carriage but in a hackney.

"A hackney? How odd." Smiling, with a grim glint in her eye, her ladyship continued, "But it will serve. Now he will not have the excuse of not wishing to keep his horses standing. Yes, yes, Jenkins, there is no need to fidget about me so! It will be of enormous benefit to Lord Shalbourne to be left kicking his heels for a moment or two."

Forty-five minutes later, leaning upon the arm of her butler, clutching an ebony cane, Lady Jane, an impressive figure of black silk and black jet, entered her drawing room and prepared to do battle with her profligate kinsman.

"Well!" Her ladyship conveyed her displeasure with him in that single utterance.

His lordship did not appear disconcerted by her mode of welcome. But, then, Gaylord Edmund Leighton, fourth Earl of Shalbourne, was not easily intimidated. Rising awkwardly from the settee by the fireplace, his lordship smiled with affability. "My dear Aunt Jane, what is this?" He indicated her props with a sweeping gesture. "I had hoped to find you well."

Her ladyship was annoyed as much by his amiable attitude as by the fact that her tactics had been so transparent. Shooing away her servant, she instructed that long suffering retainer as to the proper adjustments to be made to the embroidered firescreen. She then signified that he was to return with the Madeira that Sir John, her late husband, had laid down some years previously. Only then did her ladyship acknowledge her nephew's greeting. As soon as the butler had softly closed the door, Lady Jane interrupted her nephew's response to her polite inanities in order that she might complain. "Took your time in coming, Shalbourne. I might have been on my deathbed."

His lordship was all solicitude. "My dear Aunt Jane, I had no idea the case was so desperate! Should you be up? Ah, but how stupid of me, I should have guessed when you entered upon Chilton's arm. My dear aunt, please forgive me! I have been remarkably uncivil."

She raised her gnarled hand and said, "Enough! Enough! Pray be seated, Shalbourne. I have something of import to say to you."

"I had suspected as much." As he spoke, Shalbourne lowered himself painfully upon the settee and extended his foot toward the grate.

"If you suspected it was important, you might have presented yourself when I requested you to," the elderly lady said tartly.

"Requested?" He frowned and lifted one dark brow. "I had thought it tantamount to a royal summons."

Her ladyship was not used to being addressed in a tone such as her nephew had adopted. Although small and frail, that gray-haired lady had been accustomed to being the terror and tyrant of her family for most of her adult life. Whether the deference her relations had given her over the years had sprung from natural fear or simply from a wish to ingratiate themselves with a lady who had a good deal of money to bestow upon the most obliging of her subjects, her ladyship neither knew nor cared.

"How much have you borrowed upon your expectations, Shalbourne?" her ladyship asked abruptly.

"Why do you ask, my dear aunt?" his lordship inquired.

"Had it from Lady Fairfax that you're dipped pretty badly. In the hands of the cent per centers."

"My dear Aunt Jane, with such a reliable source to inform you, why ask me?"

"You are evading the question, Shalbourne. I can only assume it is therefore true." Whatever else she might have added was interrupted by the return of her butler.

"Ah," Shalbourne sighed as Chilton walked in softly with the Madeira and two of her ladyship's crystal glasses. "Almost, Aunt Jane, I doubted you."

Lady Jane refused to acknowledge this slur on her graciousness as a hostess and the sly reference to the fact that he had not been offered refreshment earlier while awaiting her appearance. Maintaining a stony silence while her servant was in the room, Lady Jane took the opportunity to study her nephew.

Although Shalbourne was tall and pleasingly proportioned, he was neither the athletic Corinthian nor the exquisite dandy. In fact, aside from his war wounds and his unusually dark complexion, there was little to distinguish Shalbourne from his fellow man. Or so it seemed to the casual observer. Shalbourne *did* have a pair of dark, almost black eyes that could be disconcertingly penetrating and fierce. They had caused more than one gentleman to think twice before insulting his lordship. His pronounced limp might have given the impression that he would not, *could* not, be a formidable opponent, but those deep-set eyes revealed to all that he would not give over easily. It was this air of assurance and ease that most galled Lady Jane. If he had appeared at all conciliatory or relenting, she might have forgiven his exploits.

As soon as Chilton had softly shut the door, Lady Jane said bluntly, "I cannot understand your attraction to women, Shalbourne."

"Ah, Aunt Jane, you are beautifully frank, are you not?" There was a note of amusement in his voice. "No, I am not considered a handsome fellow. Oh, I was not so ill-favored before the war, as you might recall, but the Colonial backwoodsman who laid open my cheek with his knife did a remarkably fine job."

"Damned silly war, that one was."

"I couldn't agree with you more. Especially since the one and only battle I participated in occurred *after* the peace treaty had been signed."

She snorted. "That's what you get for fighting in some outlandish spot in the back of beyond. Frenchie name, wasn't it?"

"Yes." He sounded bored. "New Orleans."

"Still," she reflected, "I'd understand the appeal if you'd been a hero."

Shalbourne ground his teeth and hissed, "I may not have been a hero, but I assure you, I in no way acted dishonorably."

Lady Jane continued as if he hadn't interrupted. "And it ain't the scar. I dare say any number of silly gooses think it lends character."

"Then, decidedly, it is the limp. Had one mistress who said cripples gave her palpitations." His lordship poured two glasses of the amber liquid in the decanter at his elbow, his hand displaying a slight tremor. "I, on the other hand, gave her jewels. It seemed to make up for any inadequacies in my person." His lordship swallowed the Madeira in a single gulp.

"Don't be bitter, Shalbourne. I meant only that you're too dark for my tastes."

"Too foreign by half, eh?"

"It's not a style I admire. Why your father must needs marry a Spaniard, I'm sure I couldn't say." Her ladyship fell into a reverie as she considered the picture her words had conjured. "But enough of this. I didn't ask you here to discuss your mother, God rest her soul. Although how she can be peaceful, knowing the life you lead, I'm sure I can't imagine."

"She was never one to care or worry about my exploits, my good aunt," his lordship said. "I'm sure she's still quite peaceful."

Lady Jane decided to change her tactics. "Shalbourne, I will not allow you to dishonor the name of Leighton."

"I was not aware that I had," his lordship said blandly.

"Then you deny that you are in debt to the Jews?"

"No, of course not," he stated calmly.

"Don't be impertinent!" She brought her fist down upon the arm of the brocade upholstered wing chair she occupied. "You're a profligate and a wastrel. They call you the Gay Lord, don't they?"

"And what is so astonishing in that? It is my name, after all." He leaned back as if in thought. "It is interesting that you should mention this. Most of my friends knew me when I was merely Mr. Gaylord Leighton, but even they persist in naming me Shalbourne now. As for my more recent acquaintances, I'm sure they would not be so bold as to address me as Gaylord."

"Don't be deliberately obtuse! You know perfectly well what my meaning is." Her ladyship was cross. She was not a lady who endured defiance from any source. With an air of finality, she stated, "Shalbourne, I am very displeased with you."

"I had guessed as much," his lordship answered with suppressed amusement. "You would not have wanted to see me otherwise."

An answering gleam crept into her ladyship's eye. "Another glass of Madeira?" she asked with deceptive sweetness.

He extended his glass. "Thank you."

She poured his drink and then snuggled back into her chair. "I do not like the life you are leading, Shalbourne."

His lordship, seated on a small horse-hair couch that had looked comfortable but proved to be full of prickly springs, was becoming impatient. "My dear aunt, I have another appointment this morning and my horses cannot wait forever at your pleasure. So let us come to the point."

"Don't try to bamboozle me, young man. I happen to know you arrived in a hackney coach."

My Lord Shalbourne had the grace to blush.

"Had to sell your horses, didn't you?" she asked with a malicious satisfaction. "But enough of this. Shalbourne, you are the last of the Leightons. When do you plan to marry?"

"The last of the Leightons, ma'am?" He stopped midway in the act of bringing the glass to his lips. "Surely not. Leighton is a common enough name. I cannot credit that I am the last of so commonplace a surname." His lordship was stalling. His aunt's question came as the first real jolt to his composure that morning. He had steered clear of any entanglements which might have led to the altar. His mistresses had all been of a class of women who expected nothing of him beyond his monetary consideration and the occasional amorous attention.

"Don't be tedious, my boy," Lady Jane admonished. "I have come to the conclusion that it is time you set up your nursery. Your owe it to your name. If you die, the title of Shalbourne dies with you."

"Come, aunt," his lordship said shrewdly. "Admit that you really think that if I am busy getting myself an heir, I shan't have time for my other less savory pursuits."

"I will admit I am somewhat motivated by a desire to see you engage in more genteel pursuits."

"I had no idea that you considered it genteel to get some lady with child ere I would have done it before."

"Your crudeness is unbecoming, Shalbourne." Her lady-ship met his challenge with an unwavering eye. "I have decided that you shall marry, Shalbourne."

"Have you, indeed?" he inquired with chilly formality. "And do you have any particular young lady in mind?"

"As to that, I shall allow you to choose the young woman yourself."

"How kind, madam."

"Yes, but I have some requirements."

"I'm sure you do." His lordship's sense of humor was returning.

"She must be respectable and reasonably well educated. As for appearance, I'm sure you have your own thoughts and preferences in that."

"Most certainly." It was all his lordship could do to keep from laughing aloud.

"I will not accept any creature like the one I saw on your arm at the opera in June." Her ladyship pursed her lips.

"My God, aunt, you have led a retired life!" His lordship was now so completely amused that even the settee's springs were beginning to seem ridiculous rather than annoying. "Annabelle decided Wrexham was more to her taste three months ago."

"You take my meaning, though, I'm sure. I will not have such a creature as Countess of Shalbourne. And this is no laughing matter, nephew! Have you no sense of what you owe your name? I am advising you to marry. Not for my sake, but for your own."

"My dear Aunt Jane, as much as I appreciate your very worthy advice, I must decline to take it. And now, if you're finished with me, I shall take my leave." His lordship finished his glass, then bent to pick up his cane.

"Not so fast, Shalbourne." Her ladyship clutched the arms of her chair with white knuckles. She knew her nephew was capable of leaving without hearing the rest of her counsel. "Nephew, I know you are in debt. I know that you have borrowed upon your expectations, and I know, too, that as much as you would like to tell me to go to the devil, you will not. I have decided you shall marry."

His lordship paused to consider. He had never been a cautious man, but he knew this was not the time to let his temper get the better of him. So, as he sat there, he put a clamp on his rising anger and tried to consider dispassionately the veiled threat his aunt had just delivered.

"You don't deserve my consideration, Shalbourne," her ladyship stated.

His lordship was not at *point non plus*, but he was chary. "But I'm sure you'll give it to me nonetheless."

"Don't be too sure, Shalbourne." Her ladyship resembled a cat who had cornered a particularly juicy prey. "I sent for you to tell you that I have drawn up a new will."

His lordship felt as if his high collar and tight cravat would choke him. He thought of the debt he had incurred only last night at White's.

"Have you, indeed?" he asked quietly.

"I have." Her ladyship was enjoying this moment. She wished to lengthen it and savor the feeling.

"And am I to congratulate someone on their good fortune?" His lordship refused to allow any of the annoyance or fear he was experiencing to creep into his voice.

"I have left the Tiverton fortune to a foundling hospital in Grantham!" Her ladyship almost laughed aloud at the painful expression that crossed her nephew's face. Oh, she was most definitely enjoying this!

"A foundling hospital, ma'am?" He set his jaw and took a few deep breaths. "Then there is nothing more to say between us." He arose to go.

"Unless you marry, Shalbourne," her ladyship added casually.

His lordship stopped in mid-flight. "Unless I what?!"

"If you marry, I shall revoke the will and write a new one. Of course, there is no guarantee that I will live long enough to revoke the will. So, I suggest you marry as quickly as possible." Her ladyship sipped a bit of Madeira.

"But I have no wish to marry, madam!" Leaning upon his cane, his lordship took a step closer.

Her ladyship shrugged her shoulders. "Then you can have no wish for my money."

Shalbourne pounded his ivory cane into the oriental rug. "But I don't know anyone! That is, not anyone respectable. I mean . . ." His lordship's famous address had deserted him.

"Oh, did I mention, Shalbourne, that I expect to see a child from your union as well? You must prove to me that you are indeed serious in your intention to carry on your title and name."

His lordship was at a loss for words. Turning on his heels, he began to limp out at a quick pace.

"Shalbourne," her ladyship's voice stopped him momentarily. "I suggest you begin to find yourself a respectable wife immediately. The will stands until the birth of a child."

"You are ridiculous, madam!" His lordship turned to face her. His anger caused him to regain some of his eloquence. "And even if I should marry this mythical respectable female, I cannot guarantee the birth of a child before you have opportunity to change your will."

"Why then, I suggest, nephew, that you waste no time." Her ladyship set her glass upon the table next to her and rose to her full height of five foot one. "I am not yet on my deathbed, but I am sixty-two, and even I shall not live forever. At my age, one is liable to depart this veil of tears at any moment. Don't take any chances, nephew. Marry as soon as you can."

His lordship hesitated as if he would speak again, thought better of it, and turning quickly, he wrenched open the door and began his erratic descent of the steps. He would have been little comforted by the expression of self-satisfaction that was planted on his aunt's face as she uttered, ''Good day, Shalbourne. I'm sure a wife will be the making of you.''

CHAPTER TWO

When a young lady whose taste is inclined toward the Gothic or the Romantic finds herself struggling through a ponderous volume, any interruption is welcome. Therefore, when Mirabelle's soft knock came almost simultaneously with the appearance of her blond curls peeking around the door of the bedchamber, Isolde's reply was immediate and eager.

"Isolde?" called Mirabelle, a remarkably pretty girl of seventeen.

"Come in, come in, Mirabelle." Isolde laid aside her book. The picture she made as she reclined on the chaise longue was the direct antithesis of her younger cousin. Where Mirabelle was light, Isolde was dark; where Mirabelle was round, Isolde was trim; where Mirabelle was delicate, Isolde was statuesque. While Isolde would never be labeled a beauty, her countenance was pleasing and her proportions becoming. Her hair was a rich chestnut and her skin, although pale in winter, had a lamentable tendency to darken in the sun. Her nose was long and straight, her demeanor a charming combination of worldly wit tempered with unsophisticated innocence. Her disposition was generally cheerful, although at the moment, a frown marred her features.

"I'm not disturbing you, am I?" Mirabelle asked anxiously.

"Good heavens, no! It's never a disturbance to be taken away from such rubbish." Isolde indicated the book with a disdainful gesture. "Sermons! That's what that idiot gave me to read! Oh! I beg your pardon, Mirabelle."

Her cousin giggled. "Don't." She closed the door after herself in a conspiratorial manner. "I shall be the first to agree that it was idiotish of my father to try and force such fustian on you. He has tried time and again to improve my reading in much the same fashion. Especially when he feels I need a reminder of a daughter's duty."

"Hmm. Well, this time, it is a lesson in the duties of a poor relation."

"Pooh! You're no poor relation. Father may be your guardian now, but when you come of age next January, I daresay you will have a fortune as great as Papa's."

"That may be true, but until that time, I can't help feeling like a poor relation. In the two years I've made my home here, anytime I should need some pin money or find I need a new dress to replace the rags I wear, I must apply to your father. If I spend so much as a shilling, Uncle Wendall makes me feel as if I were snatching food from his mouth."

"I quite understand," Mirabelle said sympathetically. "It's worse for me, you know. He's only your uncle, but he's my father! What is this book you have?" Mirabelle picked up the leather-bound volume and gazed at its back. She read aloud the title found there in gold letters. *"Reflections Upon the Behavior Most Becoming in a Young Lady of the Christian Faith.* Oh, dear, you must have been very bad indeed. This is Papa's favorite! He reserves it for the truly wicked."

"Quite edifying, I'm sure." Isolde frowned. "But I doubt even the good Reverend Hamilton, who penned this work, can persuade me to change my mind in this instance.''

"Maybe the Reverend Hamilton can't change your mind,'' Mirabelle remarked as she tossed the book onto the bed, ''but perhaps I can.''

Isolde's eyes narrowed suspiciously. "I suppose he sent you up here to wheedle me.''

Mirabelle chewed thoughtfully on her lower lip and rubbed a finger along her well-shaped nose which turned up ever so slightly at the tip. "Well, not exactly.''

"Then why are you here? Exactly.''

"Oh, please, Isolde, don't be cross with me. It's just that Papa told me that you won't go and I thought I might be able to convince you otherwise. You see, Mr. Rutherford is going, too.''

"Oh, Mirabelle!'' Isolde gave a groan and then a deep sigh. She had suspected that Mr. Rutherford was besotted with her cousin but had never realized that the case was so desperate with Mirabelle. Isolde could very well understand the young apothecary's fascination with Mirabelle. Her enviable complexion, tinted with just a bit of color as it now was, made her look like a porcelain doll, too fragile to hold and too exquisite not to try and touch. She inspired in men's breasts a desire to protect her small person from the ravages of a wicked world and the feeling that in her, a man had found womanhood's ideal. What Isolde did not understand was Mirabelle's infatuation with Mr. Peter Rutherford.

"Now we come to the crux of the matter, I suppose.'' Isolde nodded her head wisely. "Uncle Wendall told you that if I didn't go, you couldn't go either, am I not correct?''

"Yes'' was Mirabelle's simple reply as she pleaded eloquently with her spaniel brown eyes.

"But don't you see, my dear cousin,'' Isolde pointed out, ignoring the appeal of those pleading eyes. "If I concede these minor skirmishes, I shall surely lose the war!''

Mirabelle giggled. "You mean my father's scheme to marry you to Harold, I assume."

"It is all very well for you to giggle, dear Mirabelle. But if my uncle has his way, I shall soon march down the aisle with the most odious man in all of London! If only your mother were more resolute, I might turn to her for help." Isolde moaned, then added hastily, "Oh, dear, Mirabelle, I beg your pardon once again."

"You needn't," Mirabelle reassured her at once, "I have often wished for just the same sort of thing from Mama." Mirabelle gave a sigh of her own. "But I fear Mama is as afraid of Papa as I. It really isn't fair to ask her to stand up to him when I would never do so myself!"

"Then surely you can see why I must!" Isolde begged for her cousin's understanding.

"Yes . . . but," Mirabelle began hesitantly, biting her lip as she considered what tactics of persuasion to use.

Isolde cast a cold eye in Mirabelle's direction, killing her argument before it was born. "I suppose this proposed outing to the theatre is why you're all decked out in your new finery."

"Oh, Isolde, you know you always like going to the theatre!" Mirabelle coaxed.

"Yes, but not in the company of Mr. Harold Biggelswade!"

"Oh, cousin, I know you don't want to attend, but it's my first real evening gown and if you don't go, I shall probably never spend an evening in it!" she wailed.

"Never is a very long time," Isolde observed drily.

"Yes," Mirabelle readily agreed as she sank to her knees next to her cousin's chair. "So is forever and it's not as if I am asking you to endure eternity in Harold's company. Only this one evening! Please, Isolde!"

"What a goose you are!" Isolde threw off Mirabelle's

hands. "Oh, do get up, do! You're quite ridiculous, you know. And I shouldn't give into you."

Mirabelle's dimple emerged. "But you will! I know you will!"

"Only because I know that by acts such as these, I shall undoubtedly achieve martyrdom at a very young age." Isolde struck a pose. "There is no sacrifice too great for your happiness, my dear cousin."

Mirabelle giggled. "Now who is being a goose?"

"I am," Isolde said with exasperation. "I know I shall live to regret this."

"No, you shan't. You shall have a wonderful time and enjoy the play immensely. Did you know that Papa has managed to procure a box for this evening?" she exclaimed.

"A box? What new conceit is this? How did he manage that, I wonder?"

"Oh, one of Papa's associates—that Sir Henry Something-or-other, who was knighted for his accomplishments in the East India Company—procured it for the season and couldn't go tonight, so he gave Papa permission to use it. Anyway, it's quite a delightful prospect, isn't it? A box all to ourselves!"

"Mighty high notions, if you ask me," Isolde said sourly. "Why is it that we need a box?"

"I suspect it is to impress our friends of our consequence."

"Ridiculous!" Isolde snorted. "Trying to ape the ways of our betters."

Mirabelle smiled. "Why, Isolde, I never realized you were such a snob."

"Not a snob, my dear. Just realistic. It never did anyone any good to try and rise above his station."

"Oh, good heavens!" Mirabelle was disgusted with her cousin's attitude. "It's only a box at the theatre!"

"What does Uncle Wendall want to impress that mushroom for anyway?"

"You mean Harold?"

"Do we know any other mushrooms?"

Mirabelle giggled again. "No, I suppose not." She rose from her place on the floor and danced about the room. "Oh, Isolde, it will be wonderful!" She stopped in mid waltz and cocked her head at her cousin.

Isolde's one remarkable feature was her eyes. Almost clear, they were a pale shade of violet that sparkled humorously below well-shaped brows, a reflecting pool for her various moods, darkening in anger, becoming light in good spirits. Mirabelle tried to read them now as she asked the all-important question. "What will you wear? The teal blue?"

"Sack cloth and ashes."

"Oh, come, be serious."

"I am serious. Oh, all right, all right. I'll dress if I must, but I do this under protest! I hope you realize that, Mirabelle."

"Oh, I do, I do!"

"Here now, isn't this jolly?" Wendall Hackett boomed as he thrust his rather large bulk to the front of the box. "Here, Mary, sit in this one. And, you, Ann, next to her there. What do you say, John? Dare we sit next to our wives, eh, what?" His deep laugh echoed around the theatre.

The party consisted in all of eight people—Wendall and Mary Hackett, their daughter Mirabelle, their niece Isolde Marsh, Mr. John Rutherford, his wife Ann, their eldest son Peter and, of course, the inevitable Mr. Harold Biggelswade. Crowded elbow to chest in a box that was meant to hold a maximum of six, Hackett in his avuncular mood had managed to place his rather large person next to his timid wife, with Mrs. Rutherford on Mary's other side. Mr. John

Rutherford pulled up his chair on the far side of his wife and thus the group pressing up against the front rail of the box was complete. This also meant that in order for the two older gentlemen to carry on a conversation, they had to do it over or around their spouses. As for the ladies themselves, Mary sat quietly, hands folded in her lap, eyes downcast, emitting only an occasional murmur to indicate that she was hearing Mrs. Rutherford's running monologue. Given the manner in which those four had commandeered the places against the front rail, it was going to be difficult for the rest of the party to see the play over them.

"You young people can stand on your strong, young legs behind us once the play begins." Wendall remarked when he saw the predicament that his seating arrangement had created. "We need a place to rest our bones. Don't we, John, old boy, eh, what?"

Actually, considering the notice the box was getting, Isolde was just as glad to be able to draw her chair back out of the line of vision into a dark corner near the door.

Once the play had begun, the talk at the front of the box did not cease. This in itself was not unusual, but, the volume and quantity did not lessen, as was customary even among the most uninterested of playgoers. It was virtually impossible to catch the dialogue above Mr. Hackett's and Mrs. Rutherford's conversation and, of course, the view for those in the back of the box remained impaired.

As the play progressed, Isolde's back stiffened and the look of mortification on her face became more pronounced. She knew it was unkind to be self-conscious about the antics of her companions. What's more, if they had been in their customary place in the gallery or on the floor, she would not have cared. But from the moment she entered the theatre, she felt she had had cause to be put to blush by the loud, boisterous behavior of at least half of her party.

"Miss Marsh . . ." Harold Biggelswade, a young man

whose conceit was exceeded only by his complete lack of savoir-faire, pulled up his chair, scraping it loudly on the wooden floor.

Isolde felt that if he got much closer, he would be sitting in her lap. His coarse features—brows that were thick and unruly, a nose that gave all the appearance of having been broken, a broad and insensitive mouth—were thrust within inches of her own more refined countenance. In order to compensate, she leaned in her cousin's direction.

"Hush, Mr. Biggelswade! The play has commenced, you know." Isolde turned her eyes front and fanned her heated cheeks vigorously.

"But, Miss Marsh . . . Isolde . . ." Harold's whining voice interjected once again into the leading lady's speech.

Isolde's frown deepened. She turned her cold, clear eyes on him and whispered fiercely, "I do not recall, Mr. Biggelswade, that I have given you leave to make free with my name."

"Oh, excuse me, Miss Marsh, if I grow too bold. It is only that I have been on such good terms with your uncle's family for many years now. Ever since I became chief clerk at your family's business, in fact. And if I have come to regard you in the light of but a sister to Mirabelle, it is not to be wondered at. I apologize if I have offended you but since I have named your sweet cousin by her Christian name this past age, I had hoped you would not object to that same liberty in regard to yourself." Harold Biggelswade had decided that Isolde held him at arm's length from maidenly modesty and an attempt to appear interesting. It would never have occurred to him that she found him repugnant. Therefore, while Harold had been making this rambling speech, he had managed to grasp Isolde's hand under cover of the darkness in the box.

For his pains, Isolde rapped him soundly across the knuckles with her fan. Through clenched teeth, she uttered hoarsely, "The play, Mr. Biggelswade! Kindly turn your attention to the stage."

At the interval, having shushed the young man to her right on four separate occasions, Isolde came to the conclusion that the only way to avoid further conversation with him was to begin one herself with someone else.

"Well, Mirabelle, do you like the play?" Isolde tapped her cousin's shoulder to get her attention. "The play, cousin. Do you like it?"

"What? Oh!" Mirabelle started and tore her eyes from their rapt gazing at the lanky Mr. Peter Rutherford. "Oh, yes. Quite lovely."

"Quite," Peter piped in, hearing only the word "lovely" and thinking it referred to Mirabelle.

Unfortunately, Isolde had no answer to their astute observations, and so she fell victim again to Mr. Biggelswade's conversation. Trying a new tactic, she interrupted Harold. "Mr. Biggelswade, do you think you might go and procure a drink for me? I declare, I am quite parched."

Biggelswade beamed. "Delighted, my dear Miss Marsh. How about you, Rutherford? Care to help me find a drop or two for the ladies?"

"What? Oh. Oh. Yes. Should have thought of that myself. You'd like a drink, wouldn't you, Miss Hackett?"

Mirabelle blushed and looked downward. "Oh, yes," she breathed. "If it's not too much trouble, Mr. Rutherford."

Once this course had been decided, the two young gentlemen felt politeness dictated that they make the same offer to the older generation.

"That's right. A good idea, my boy." Wendall Hackett gave Harold a hearty slap on the back. "A drink is just what we all need. Watching plays is a thirsty business. You young fellows run along and get something for everyone. Now, there's the ticket, John. Always bring along some young people to wait on you, eh, what? Much nicer to sit and let them do the work, eh?'' Wendall noticed the woman in the next box. ''Ain't that right ma'am? You agree with me, don't you?''

The woman looked down her haughty nose at Hackett and then turned her back to him as if he hadn't spoken.

Isolde opened her fan, hid her face and sank down in her seat. Mirabelle, who had watched Peter until he left, now turned back to her cousin.

''Isolde? Whatever is the matter? Why are you hiding behind your fan?''

''Did you see that woman? She looked at your father as if he were a nasty insect that had somehow landed on her dinner plate. Oh, Mirabelle, we should never have come!'' she wailed softly.

''Why not?'' Mirabelle asked without rancor. ''I'm having a lovely time. Aren't you?''

''I'm sure you are, dear.'' Isolde lowered her fan. ''That's because you're oblivious. You and Mr. Peter Rutherford sit and stare and stare. But only at each other. Unfortunately, everyone else in this theatre is staring at us!''

This might have been an exaggeration except that at that moment, something struck Wendall Hackett as remarkably funny. He burst into loud guffaws and slapped his thigh, then pounded his hand on the box's front railing. Mirabelle turned her exquisite countenance to consider the crowd at large, seeing that they were indeed the center of attention.

Isolde whispered in her ear. ''Haven't you noticed? They all seem to know each other. They talk and visit among themselves. And laugh behind their hands at us. Oh, Mirabelle, I knew this would be folly!''

Before Mirabelle could frame a suitable reply, the door at the back burst open, revealing Harold and Peter followed by a man in livery with a tray of drinks.

"Look what we found," Harold crowed proudly as he waved the servant forward. "Ain't this something like?"

Mirabelle, like the others, was impressed. "Imagine that, Isolde."

"Probably the management thought that the best way to keep us from contaminating the halls was by confining us to the box," Isolde muttered.

"Oh, don't be such a spoilsport!" Mirabelle admonished. "Do you have the headache or something?"

Isolde sighed. "I must, mustn't I?"

By the time the second interval was upon them, Isolde's discomfiture had turned into a very real headache. She wished she had her Aunt Mary's ability to remain tranquil and unaffected. However, with Harold constantly badgering her with questions and sly attempts to touch her when the box was dark, she found she could not ignore her surroundings and neighbors as she might have liked.

Finally, she closed her eyes and leaned back in her chair, in the hope that the others, and most especially Harold, would leave her alone. She was therefore startled when her uncle addressed her unexpectedly, since he had ignored her heretofore.

"Here, what is this? What is this? Going to sleep, niece?" He called loudly, as if she were across a ballroom rather than in the close confines of a theatre box.

"I'm sorry, Uncle Wendall. I didn't mean to be rude, but I have developed the most intolerable headache."

"Ah," her uncle sympathized with uncharacteristic solicitude. "Feeling poorly, are you? What a shame! Well, I see no reason to break up the party because you are not feeling quite the thing. But I'm sure you'd like to go home, wouldn't you?"

Isolde replied cautiously, "Yes . . . that would be nice."

"Well, then, that settles the matter. Harold shall take you home. You don't mind, do you, boy?"

Isolde's gasp of consternation at this offer was ignored. Harold jumped up. "No, no, of course not. Be happy to oblige." Feeling as poorly as she did, Isolde could not bring herself to object when Harold helped her into her cloak and opened the door for her.

"Here, boy, take this to pay for the hackney coach," Wendall said in another lapse from his normal character as he produced a number of coins from his pocket. She missed the broad grin and quick wink that passed between her uncle and Mr. Biggelswade along with the money.

Isolde did not speak to her escort as they traversed the corridors and emerged from the building. She noticed that there were a few other people milling about outside the theatre and was not surprised to see that they seemed to fall into only two categories: departing patrons, richly attired, and the ragged hawkers of various wares. The surrounding neighborhood was more in keeping with the latter, being in a sad state of disrepair, which caused the theatregoers to hail hackneys and private vehicles hastily in an attempt to depart as quickly as possible. It was one of those rare occasions when she could be thankful for Mr. Biggelswade's escort. Although he could never be described as stout, his thick neck flowed quite naturally into his broad chest and had caused him to earn the epithet of brawny from more than one source. His was the physique of the pugilist and for this reason, the various characters gathered around the warming braziers kept a respectful distance. No one wanted to approach the young man with the crooked nose who looked like he could easily be Gentleman Jackson's current protégé. The others of the small crowd were not so fortunate— they were offered everything from warmed chestnuts to a lady's favors.

Although Isolde was not keen on getting into a closed carriage with Harold, she could see no other course open to her. Her only option, if she wished to end the evening early, was to accept Harold's company.

She allowed him to hand her up into the hackney he had just hailed and settled into the far corner. She heard him murmuring something—presumably directions—to the coachman before he alighted beside her and pulled the door shut.

"What are you doing?" Isolde asked in a panicked voice as Harold turned down the wick of the lantern swinging inside the coach's interior.

"Just dousing the light a bit." Harold opened his eyes wide and assumed a bovine expression.

"Why?" Isolde asked suspiciously and then was immediately contrite as he replied, "Your headache, Miss Marsh. I thought the light might be too harsh for you in your present condition."

"Oh. That's very kind of you, but I assure you, it is quite unnecessary," Isolde said with forced politeness.

The carriage's curtains had been closed by a previous customer and Isolde was of two minds as to whether she should open them or not. While she hesitated to draw them, thus exposing Harold and herself to the eyes of the curious, she was also wary of the intimate atmosphere created by the closed shades. She decided that as long as Harold maintained his respectful distance, she would leave them as they were.

"Is something the matter, Mr. Biggelswade?" Isolde inquired, having noted a vast amount of fidgeting, nervous coughs and sudden shifts in position on the part of her companion. She wondered if perhaps he was as nervous as she about their present situation. That thought caused her to thaw toward Harold a bit. She sent him her first sincere smile that evening.

"What?" a startled Harold squeaked in reply to her question and her unexpected smile. "Oh, nothing. Nothing at all."

"Do public conveyances make you nervous?"

"Oh, no, no. Not a bit." He then wiped his sweaty brow with a large, spotted handkerchief.

"Well, something has you worked up into a tizzy."

"Only your sweet presence, my dear Isolde," he exclaimed, grasping her hand in his sweaty paw.

"Let go of my hand!" Isolde hissed as Mr. Biggelswade lost what little ground he had gained with her. "And if you recall, I have not given you leave to call me by my Christian name."

Harold gulped nervously as Isolde snatched back her hand. "Sorry," he muttered. "Are you going to sleep?" he asked anxiously after a few moments of awkward silence.

"No," Isolde snapped. "I am resting my eyes. My headache, you know."

"Oh, yes."

Silence fell once again. The gentle swaying of the coach, combined with the darkness and the quiet, rocked Isolde into a deep sleep.

Chapter Three

After what had seemed only a few moments, Harold's unwelcome voice penetrated the fog inside Isolde's head. Shaking her roughly, he pulled her from the coach before she had had a chance to recover her wits. Isolde, who had never been at her best when first awakened, yawned broadly as the coach pulled away. She vaguely heard Harold whine, "I thought I should never awaken you!"

Isolde, still too sleep-befuddled to think clearly, much less answer this very astute observation, somehow managed to register a certain foreboding even in her clouded mind at the implications of the dark, deserted square, the retreating coach and Harold's expression. When she looked up into the open doorway next to where they stood, she recognized that the woman whose large shape was silhouetted there was not her uncle's friendly maid. In her present state, it was a full two seconds later before she realized that the doorway was not even that of her uncle's house.

She gave an exasperated cry. "Mr. Biggelswade, where is your head? This is not my uncle's house! Quick! Catch the coach before it goes farther! The stupid man has set us down in the wrong square altogether!"

Harold's hand gripped her elbow. "That shan't be necessary, my dear."

Isolde, standing firmly by the fence at the foot of the stairs, could see, and smell, that the woman standing in the doorway was three-quarters drunk. Turning on Harold, she demanded, ''What is the meaning of this, sir? This is no more my uncle's house than . . . than it is Kensington Palace! I demand that you call back that hackney and take me home!''

''No need to play the innocent, my dear Miss Marsh. You knew well enough when we descended from the coach what my intentions were. Come. The bawd is waiting for us.''

''Don't be an even greater fool than nature intended, sir! You know perfectly well that I was half asleep when we arrived. I certainly had no indication that you would be so dead to all propriety as to attempt this, this . . . seduction! Let us return at once to my uncle and I shall say nothing of your ridiculous charade to him. He would be most unhappy, sir.'' Isolde was not at all frightened by her present predicament, only remarkably indignant.

''Oh, yes, he would be most unhappy.'' Harold concurred and took a strong hold on her arm. ''This little 'charade,' as you so charmingly put it, was his idea!''

''Uncle Wendall!'' Isolde gasped. ''I don't believe you!''

''Alas, it is all too true.'' Harold began to pull her up the steps. ''Since you refused my most proper offer of marriage, an offer which had your uncle's full approval, and since you said nothing would prevail with you to change your mind, your loving uncle hatched this scheme. A night or two in my company and I expect you will be as anxious as he for me to make an honest woman of you.''

''What?'' She grabbed the spiked decorative top of the iron railing to steady herself. ''Unhand me this instant! I don't believe that my uncle can approve this scheme!'' Isolde pulled her arm from his grasp and turned to run after the fast retreating hackney. Much to her chagrin, her long skirt became entangled in her feet and she tripped ignominiously, falling forward upon her hands and knees to the pavement. Immediately, Harold's hands were lifting her off the ground.

Harold's bovine expression was gone. In its place was a lecherous grin. "I don't know why your uncle should so favor my suit as to suggest this very improper method of bringing it about. But far be it from me to object. Come, my love, the lady of the house awaits us."

"No!" Isolde struggled against his grasp. "Let me go or I shall scream!"

"I shouldn't try that if I were you," Harold began only to be interrupted by a piercing screech. "Shut up, you stupid bitch!" Harold swung one hand and hit her. The blow landed squarely on her left eye. Isolde gasped.

"Be quiet or I shall hit you again. Do you understand, Isolde?" Harold shook her.

"No! No! I don't understand!" Isolde cried. They were once again at the bottom of the steps and she noticed the dark shape still standing in the doorway. She appealed to it for aid. "Madam, you cannot wish to be a party to this! I am being forced against my will . . ."

"Ain't no concern of mine, miss. The gentleman said I was to let you stay for a night or two. I don't ask no questions. Especially when I gets paid in gold," she answered grimly.

For the first time in her twenty years, Isolde cursed. She turned a horrified gaze to Harold. "You can't mean to do this!"

"Of course I do, my dear Isolde. So now, if you will condescend to climb the stairs. Or shall I be forced to carry you?" Harold asked and slackened his hold.

In that brief moment, Isolde tried to pull away and let out another scream. Harold raised his hand to hit her again. From out of the shadows, another dark shape hurtled itself upon the couple. Before Harold had time to gain his bear-

ings, a cane descended mercilessly on his back. The new assailant beat Harold so fiercely that he could do little more
than try to ward off the blows with his hands.

The bawd, seeing that the young man was being routed,
the young lady rescued, opted for a full retreat. She ran up
the last step and into the house with an alacrity that belied
her enormous bulk and advanced years, to say nothing of her
drunken condition. She slammed shut the door, threw the
bolt, and doused the lights.

Isolde, her eye throbbing uncomfortably, was still able to
discern that Mr. Biggelswade lay senseless on the ground.
She put a restraining hand on her rescuer's arm and said
gently, "That's enough, sir. He's quite unconscious and
perfectly harmless now."

The stranger stopped with his cane in midair, his breath
coming in gulps, and turned his head to consider her. Although it was dark, and Isolde's eye was beginning to swell
shut, she could still discern a bloodlust in his attitude that
was disconcerting. "As much as I would like for you to
murder that pig," she explained in dignified and level accents, "I should greatly dislike for you to have to stand trial
for his demise. I fear the judge would not take such a lenient
stand as I am inclined to assume."

"Good God," came the deep, refined voice, "is he your
husband then?"

"Oh, no!" Isolde was quick to deny. "Thank God, he is
not!"

She perfectly understood the stranger's question. After
all, a man had an unalienable right to beat his wife without
expecting interference from any source. "On the contrary,
he is the last man I should accept in that or any other capac-
ity. And since he knows that to be the case, this was to be his
method of persuasion."

"A rape, then?" he inquired politely.

"Just so." Isolde raised a tentative finger to her eye. "Ouch!"

"Here, let me see." The stranger moved closer and took her chin into one hand. He turned her face so that her eye was in the pale moonlight. "I fear, madam, that you are destined to sport a black eye in the not too distant future."

"How vexatious!" Isolde exclaimed.

He grinned down at her. "Vexatious? It occurs to me, Miss . . . ?"

"Marsh. Isolde Marsh," she supplied helpfully, not knowing quite why she told this stranger her name so willingly.

"Miss Marsh. It occurs to me that most young ladies of my acquaintance would have thought a black eye a disaster of no mean order and yet, you find it merely 'vexatious.' I don't suppose you'd care to swoon or go into strong hysterics?" he asked, an edge of amusement to his voice.

"I should say not!" she replied indignantly.

"I didn't think so." He tried to sound disappointed.

"And don't be ridiculous, sir." Isolde smiled back at the gentleman. "I'm sure you should hate it if I chose to indulge in some sort of histrionics at this moment."

"You are undoubtedly correct," he replied. Bending to retrieve his hat, which had fallen off in the scuffle, he momentarily checked Harold's inanimate form. "Unfortunately still alive. But, as you say, an inquest into his murder would be most inconvenient." He straightened up and crooked his elbow. "Allow me to escort you back to your home."

"Oh, I couldn't put you to so much trouble," Isolde demurred and did not take his offered arm.

"I insist," he replied. "It is not the part of the knight errant to save his lady from the dragon, only to desert her by the corpse."

Isolde giggled and then cried, "Oh, you mustn't, sir! It hurts abominably when I laugh."

"I fear you shall find it isn't laughter but rather simply a smile which causes your eye to pain you. We shall study to be grave and solemn."

The momentary silence that followed was broken by Isolde advancing a step with her hand extended. "I am much in your debt, sir."

"I was glad to be of service," the stranger replied as he took her cold little gloved hand into his own large one. He lifted her hand, pushing the glove back slightly so that his lips made contact with her skin.

Isolde was glad for the darkness as she felt a blush creep across her cheeks. The gentleman's action had been most unexpected.

He spoke again, "Although I must say I find it very odd that a young lady of your obvious, ah, attractions should be in the company of such a bounder."

"I, too, find it a source for amazement, sir, that I ever allow myself to be in Mr. Biggelswade's company."

The stranger let out a sharp laugh. "Biggelswade, did you say? What an extraordinary name!"

Isolde found herself smiling again at the man. "I've often thought so. Oh, dear!" she then exclaimed.

"What is it, my dear?" the gentleman asked solicitously.

"I have just thought of something. Since I have a blackened eye and my dress is quite dirty from falling down, I shall look an awful fright and be the object of a good deal of amusement and speculation should I return to the theatre." Isolde was too forlorn to notice his raised eyebrow. She would have been horrified to know that her statement confirmed the suspicion in his mind that she was an actress of some sort.

"I was going to ask you to return me there, you see, since it can't be that far." Isolde, who had not previously felt inclined to tears, was utterly cast down by the thought that she dare not return to her uncle's party in her present condition. The gentleman found it necessary to produce his handkerchief and present it to her.

"You mustn't cry, my dear," he admonished gently, wiping the tears from her face. "Remember your eye."

"I am sorry, sir," Isolde said. "Quite stupid of me. Please forgive me."

"There now, nothing to forgive. After all, I did say we should study to be grave. Although not, perhaps, lachrymose." He returned the handkerchief to his pocket and continued to gently wipe her cheeks with his fingers. She smiled bravely at him. "You are quite right, of course," he said, "we should be remarkably conspicuous if I were to return you to the theatre. I have a house not a step or two away, if you should care to go there first."

"No." Isolde acquitted him unjustly of any ulterior motives. "No, thank you. If you would help me find a hackney, I shall return to my own home."

"If you insist," the gentleman sighed. "We can use the one I have hired for the evening. It is only on the other side of the square. I was in it when I heard your screams. Shall we go and endeavor to find the way to your lodgings? I would deem it an honor to escort you there."

"Oh, I couldn't. It would be much too far out of your way. Especially if your own home is so close." Isolde began to protest, and then stopped short as Harold moaned.

"Ah, the dragon stirs," the gentleman remarked. "Come, now. I'm sure neither one of us has any desire to be here when he returns to his senses."

"No, of course not," she agreed. Then, laughing nervously, she added, "In truth, sir, I have no idea where in London's vast reaches I might be. So, if you are certain it's no bother, about taking me home, I mean. It could be an awfully long trip, you see."

"No bother at all, my dear."

As Isolde and the gentleman began to walk across the small square toward the parked vehicle, Isolde supplied the gentleman with her direction. She did not see his reaction to this information and so did not know that he found it odd that her "protector" had chosen to set her up in so profoundly middle-class a neighborhood as Burton Crescent. As it was, she was more concerned when she noticed that he was walking with a decided limp. "Oh, sir, are you hurt? I hadn't realized, I mean to say, I didn't think Mr. Biggelswade had had an opportunity . . ."

"There is no need to fret." He frowned and continued walking, pulling her along. "'Tis an old injury. A souvenir of the Colonies, you might say." His bitter tone served to increase Isolde's embarrassment.

"I'm sorry. I had no idea. Please forgive my stupidity." She was glad now for the lack of light—not only because of her eye but because she could feel the blush progressing over her cheeks once again. She did wish, however, that she might have gotten a better look at the tall, dark stranger who had rescued her. His voice and what she could discern of his clothing all indicated a refinement that bespoke money and breeding. Little else could she say for certain.

They were silent for the rest of the short walk to the coach. Helping Isolde to enter, the stranger relayed her address to the driver and then pulled himself into the coach, sitting beside her on the seat.

As the coach began to move, Isolde said, "I want you to know, I greatly appreciate this."

The stranger interrupted her, "Think nothing of it. It would never do to let you ride the streets unattended, my dear Isolde." Again he took her hand and raised it to his lips.

"But . . . how did you know my name?!" Isolde's heart beat in a most alarming fashion.

"You told me yourself. Don't you remember? It is most unusual. I am not likely to have forgotten it so soon," he explained.

"Oh." Isolde was on uncertain ground. The man's manner toward her was hard for her to comprehend, but she suspected him of flirting with her. "Sir, as much as I appreciate the sentiment behind your thought, I don't think it proper for you to be using my name so freely. I don't even know your name."

"I could wish for your sake, lovely lady, that 'twere Tristan. But, alas, it is not. My parents were not so farsighted. As for proper introductions, our method of presentation did not lend itself to such niceties. So, my lovely Isolde, I would ask you to think of me as a worthless fellow of no importance who languishes for no greater honor than to be your *preux chevalier*. Sir Tristan, if you will. If only for tonight."

"You are being absurd, sir!" Isolde laughed. "Lovely lady, indeed! With a black eye surely on the way!"

"Ah, but I can see past such trivialities."

"It's surprised I am that you can see past my imperfections. Especially with the lights being so very harsh as they are. It makes little faults so much more noticeable than normal." Sitting in the darkened carriage, she teased him in return, and didn't know how to account for her reactions. It was somehow exhilarating to be alone with this stranger who was so remarkably charming. She had thought Peter Rutherford had a pleasing manner, but this man's was even more so; Peter treated her as Mirabelle's cousin, this man, as a lady who interested him. And although Harold was only too aware of her charms, his methods were crude and odious. She did not move in that social sphere where such compliments as he was paying her were a way of life; she only knew that it was different and provocative.

"Even in this brilliant glare, my sweet lady, no imperfections do I discern."

She knew the man's compliments were false and exaggerated, even though he would have had a clear view of her before the bawd had slammed her door and doused her lights. Isolde attempted to retreat from dangerous ground. "You still haven't told me your name, sir."

"You insist upon an introduction? Sir Tristan will not serve for now?" he asked. "Isolde is enough for me. No! Don't remind me of the rest. I know you told me once." He raised his hand as she started to speak. "But 'twould ruin the spell."

"I see, sir."

"Sir Tristan, if you please," he admonished.

"Sir Tristan. You are quite right. Mundane considerations such as proper introductions are utter nonsense, of course. How unchivalrous of me to have suggested that you tell me your name." Isolde felt that she might regret her lapse from propriety later, but, for now, in the dark coach, it didn't seem to matter.

"That's much better," he said. "And, now, fair lady, having slain the dragon . . ."

"Dragon?"

"The terrible dragon Biggelsbait or whatever his name was," he answered, feigning surprise at her question. "Having placed my life in peril for your sake, I would claim my reward."

"Reward?"

"Yes. It is customary, you know." He slipped his arm around her shoulder and gently pulled her closer. Lifting her chin with his other hand, he leaned down and kissed her. Isolde made a halfhearted attempt to push him away and then found herself responding despite a resolve to the contrary. At first, his kiss was tender, but as he felt her response, it became gradually more intent and impassioned. It was as he deftly untied her cloak and moved his lips over her cheeks to her throat and the base of her neck that the enormity of what he was doing finally dawned upon Isolde. Pulling away slightly, she laughed nervously and said in a whisper, "You mustn't do that, sir."

His lips were on hers again as he asked softly, "Why not, sweetheart?"

Wishing to turn the mood back to the lighter one of only a few minutes before, she smiled shakily and said, "Whatever will my Lord Cornwall say?"

He gave a faint laugh as he realized she was referring to the legendary Tristan and Isolde; Cornwall had been Isolde's cuckolded husband. So, he thought, the doxy was at least as educated as her voice had indicated.

"Would you not take pity upon a poor, wounded man, my love?" he asked.

"Wounded? Did he . . ." Isolde tensed and clung to his lapels, worried that somehow Harold had hurt him after all.

"Indeed," he whispered, "the arrow shot from your *beaux yeux* has struck me fatally in the heart."

She relaxed and replied in a bantering tone, "Then let me pluck it out, Sir Tristan, and ease your pain."

"'Twere fatal to remove it so. I should bleed to death, I fear. There is but one way to ease my pain," he answered. Then as if to demonstrate to her what he meant, he bent once again to press his lips against her skin.

Isolde started and backed away, placing her hands against his chest as if to hold him off. With an anxious smile on her lips, she said, "Almost, sir, you make me afraid."

"Never for your life, I hope," he answered. "For 'twere as precious to me as my own."

"Not that, sir." And then, before she had given proper consideration to her words, she added, "For my virtue."

He advanced toward her on the seat and tightened his

hold. "Come, come. Surely young Cornwall has had that from you ere now."

Isolde felt as if he had slapped her. He thought her a woman of easy virtue! The tears stung her eyes as she acknowledged bitterly that her actions of the last few minutes could not have led him to think otherwise. She should have slapped him; protested when he first kissed her. This time, when she pushed him away, he sensed she meant it. Struggling to pull her cloak about her as some sort of shield, the tears began to fall and try as she might, she could not stop them. When she attempted unsuccessfully to retie the strings on her cloak, she felt his hands once again on hers.

"Here. Let me," he said in what sounded to her ears as an exasperated tone.

Searching in her reticule for a handkerchief, Isolde was now sobbing in earnest. Quietly, the man handed her his for the second time that evening.

"What's the matter?" he inquired politely. "Why the tears?"

"They are for the folly of a maid who did not look carefully to the fragility of her reputation," Isolde answered miserably.

It was at this moment that the coach stopped. Quickly, grabbing her reticule, Isolde leaped out of the carriage before her companion could stop her. She addressed him briefly, her head bowed in mortification. "I doubt we shall meet again but I wish to express my gratitude for your kind offices on my behalf."

She could not look at him or meet his eyes as he took her extended hand. He kissed it once more, this time palm up. Isolde snatched her hand away. It was as if his touch had burned, even with the protection of her soft kid glove.

Without further words, she turned and lightly ran up the stairs of her uncle's townhouse. As she searched in her reticule for the latchkey, she heard the stranger giving the driver directions to take him to Shalbourne House in Mount Street.

Letting herself inside with the key dug out of the bottom of her bag, she heard the sound of the vehicle's steel-rimmed wooden wheels on the cobblestones as it pulled away. It was then that she looked down and discovered that she still held his handkerchief. It was a beautifully embroidered, lawn one, infinitely more elegant than any she owned. As she gazed abstractly at the graceful "S" worked upon it, she bethought herself of the fact that the gentleman had asked to be taken to Shalbourne House. Undoubtedly, her erstwhile rescuer was named Shalbourne. She assumed he owned the house in Mount Street—a very fashionable address—which would account for his dress and accent.

Mount Street, she mused. So much for his assertion that his house was near the scene of the crime. Slowly, she ascended the stairs as something in the back of her mind continued to bother her. Something about that name. But she didn't think she had ever met any Mr. Shalbourne before. And, certainly, she did not know anyone living in Mount Street. Where had she heard that name?

Once in her room she rang for the maid, Jenny. Hiding the handkerchief in a drawer, she sat at the dressing table and began abstractedly to remove the pins from her hair. She was just considering a closeup view of her bruised eye when Jenny arrived.

"Miss, your aunt and uncle and Miss Mirabelle ain't yet come through the door. Whatever are ye doing here without them? And, Lord have mercy, child, what have you done to your eye?"

Briefly, Isolde explained that she had developed a headache at the theatre and had come home early. She further explained that there had been a slight accident on the way home and she had hit her eye on the opposite seat of the coach's interior. Jenny was skeptical, but she knew it was not her place to question this explanation.

"That Mr. Biggelswade brought you home, I suppose?" she said darkly.

Isolde did not deny it and so Jenny came to her own conclusions about how Miss Isolde had acquired her black eye. Well! She never did like that cad, Harold Biggelswade, anyway!

Isolde did nothing to stop the flow of chatter Jenny engaged in as the maid combed out her tresses. Lending only half an ear to what the maid was saying, Isolde's attention was caught as Jenny mentioned the name Shalbourne.

"What was that?" Isolde demanded.

"Shalbourne, miss," Jenny explained. "That Earl what's so wicked. My Aunt Ida has a friend who is married to the brother of his second footman. And *she* says that the story I just told is the gospel truth. Monstrous, isn't it?"

Her heart seemed to have leaped into her mouth. Of course! The Earl of Shalbourne! Oh, Lord! The most notorious rake in all of London! She covered her face with her hands.

"There, now, miss," Jenny said as she patted Isolde's shoulder. "We'll just get a bit of beef to put on that eye and some laudanum drops for that headache of yours. That'll do the trick, it will. Never you fear."

But Isolde very much feared that it would take more than a few drops of physic to ease the pain that now pounded in her head.

CHAPTER FOUR

Mirabelle, who was not yet privy to a full accounting of the previous evening's events, bounced into Isolde's bed-chamber and disturbed her cousin's slumbers at an hour much earlier than Isolde might have otherwise chosen. Calling as she came, Mirabelle made her way to her cousin's reclining form and began to shake her mercilessly.

"Yo-hoo, Isolde! What's the matter with you, Sleeping Beauty? It's after ten o'clock! I've been up for *hours*! And you were sound asleep when I got home last night, so don't try and tell me . . ." Mirabelle gasped. "Isolde! What ever have you done to your eye?"

Isolde yawned, blinked, grimaced, and then placed a light finger to her eye. "Oh, dear, Mirabelle, it was to be a surprise. I have decided to take up a career as a prizefighter. Alas! You have found me out!"

"Isolde!" Mirabelle whined in impatience. "Be serious, do! Now, tell me what happened this instant or I shall scream."

"Ah, well, we can't have that, can we? Whatever will the servants think?" Isolde swung her feet to the floor and began to shrug into her dressing gown. "Well, to put it in a nutshell, it seems I had a difference of opinion with Mr. Biggelswade."

"What?"

"Yes. When he and I left last evening to go home, we wandered a bit far afield."

"You were lost then?"

"No, we . . ."

"Did you meet with an accident?"

"Mirabelle, you mustn't interrupt. No, we were not lost, although I must confess that I thought we were at the time. And, no, I don't think it could be described as an accident. I believe it was quite intentional. You see, we found ourselves in a most disreputable part of the city where Mr. Biggelswade was determined that I should visit an even more disreputable old hag. I declined the invitation into her house and Mr. Biggelswade took exception to my decision. Perhaps he thought me impolite." Isolde sat at her dressing table and began to loosen the braid that fell to her waist.

"But, but . . ." Mirabelle sputtered in wide-eyed astonishment. "Never say Mr. Biggelswade actually struck you!"

"As you please." Isolde began to brush her hair. "I shan't say it. But it is true, nonetheless."

"Why, that horrible old bully!" Mirabelle was outraged. "Who was this woman he wanted you to meet? Why should he make his visit at that hour? Oh!" Mirabelle gasped as a thought occurred to her. "Do you suppose it was his mother?"

Isolde began to laugh. "Oh, dear, Mirabelle, you are an innocent, aren't you?"

"What do you mean?" Mirabelle was confused. "Is there more to this tale than you're telling me?"

"Alas! That is all too true!" Isolde exclaimed. "There is a great deal more to this tale than I have so far told. You see, the invitation into the old woman's house was for the night."

"For the night?" Mirabelle questioned. "You mean there was a party in progress?"

"No, there was no congenial company to dance and play cards with into the small hours of the morning. No, indeed. What she and Mr. Biggelswade intended was for me to spend the night in one of her bedchambers."

"You mean to sleep there?"

Isolde gave a bitter laugh, jumped up from the dressing table, and began to pace the floor with agitated movements.

"But why?" Mirabelle asked, still not comprehending. "There was no need for that, surely. You could easily come home to your own bed. It's not as if you were a long ways off and forced to break your journey at an unknown inn."

"My dear, sweet, innocent Mirabelle, their intention was not that I spend the night alone. Mr. Biggelswade was to accompany me."

"What?" Comprehension dawned on Mirabelle. "But you're not married! How could you sleep in the same . . ." Mirabelle was unable to finish the sentence as she turned beet-red.

"Exactly." Isolde stopped her pacing to look directly at her cousin, a grim expression on her face.

"This is an outrage! Have you told my father yet?"

"No."

"Then you must!" Mirabelle interrupted. "At once! He shall know how to deal with such a scoundrel! That he should dare! You must know my father would never countenance such scandalous conduct! Why, I'm sure he will discharge Mr. Biggelswade from his post this very day once he finds out about last night! My father will never let this go unpunished!"

"I very much fear, my dear cousin, that my uncle's wrath is more like to fall on my hapless self than young Mr. Biggelswade."

"Isolde, you don't mean that! You are distraught! I know

my father has been promoting a match between the two of you, but he would *never* allow Mr. Biggelswade to go to such lengths as that!''

Before Mirabelle could continue her tirade, the door of the chamber was pushed open slightly and Mary Challoner Hackett stepped by timid degrees over the threshold into the room. An older, grayer version of her daughter Mirabelle, at one time Mary Hackett had been an acknowledged beauty. Life, however, had not been kind to her. She was a shy, retiring creature of delicate constitution and gentle disposition married to a man who had not cherished her but, rather, had dominated and abused her good nature. At the present moment, it was easy to see that Mary Hackett was laboring under some strong emotion. Her hands fluttered and gently shook as she pressed a white lace handkerchief to her lips. As she closed the door after herself, she uttered, ''Oh, dear, oh, dear, oh, dear,'' and then gulped at her temerity in expressing her emotions in such strong terms.

''Aunt Mary, are you not well? Please sit down. Shall I ring for Jenny?'' Isolde asked as she walked to the distressed woman's side. It was at moments such as these that Isolde found it most difficult to believe that her own mother, Susan Challoner Marsh, and this woman had been sisters.

The only surviving offspring of Enoch Challoner, Susan and Mary had been as different as it was possible for sisters to be. Mary, the eldest by a year, had excelled in the domestic arts, becoming the mother of the household when Enoch's wife died of childbed fever following the birth of her third stillborn son. As for her sister, Susan, it was apparent that her talent lay in organization and business. If she had been a man, she would have been the natural successor of her father, taking over Challoner's Spice and Tea Importers and making as much of a success of it as her father had. As it was, Susan went on to organize her husband's parish instead and at the time of her death, had almost organized her husband into being a bishop. Wendall Hackett, an ambitious young clerk at Challoner's, had recognized this strength of character in Susan and had opted for marriage with the elder, quieter, and more biddable Mary, even though Susan was Enoch's favorite.

"Oh. No, so kind. Thank you, my dear. I'll just rest here a moment." Mary Hackett sank into a heap on the small, satin-covered settee. A kindly soul, Mary looked a great deal older than her fifty odd years since her blond hair had faded to white and her soft skin had already begun to sag and wrinkle. She reminded her niece of a timid dormouse. Her thin figure was virtually overwhelmed by lace and cotton voile as her morning dress settled in billowing waves about her. Taking one of her niece's hands into her own trembling one, Mary said earnestly, "Jenny told me last evening . . . your eye. Oh, dear, so painful, I'm sure . . . I know just how humiliating."

"Mama," Mirabelle interrupted this incoherent speech impatiently. "Mr. Biggelswade is responsible. He struck Isolde! Papa should be told at once!"

"Oh, dear . . . how shocking . . . oh, dear . . . your papa . . . oh, my . . . he knows all about it, child." Mary waved her handkerchief in a languid attempt to stir up a breeze on her heated cheeks.

"There!" Mirabelle said to Isolde triumphantly. "Now you shall see justice done!"

Mary turned her concerned countenance toward her niece. "Your uncle, my dear . . . most distressed. He, oh, dear . . . ah, he . . . that is . . . Mr. Biggelswade . . . that is . . . he didn't, did he?"

"Didn't what? Strike me? I fear he did." Isolde explained with more emphasis than patience.

"No, no, no, I mean, he didn't . . . oh, dear, your uncle is most unhappy. The banns have been arranged, never fear." Mary patted Isolde's hand reassuringly and looked at her with sympathy.

"The banns!" Isolde rocked back on her heels.

"But, Mama! Whatever for?" Mirabelle demanded.

Mary turned her tearful gaze at her daughter. "Oh, dear, Mirabelle. You shouldn't know, that is, you're still such an innocent. Isolde *must* marry Mr. Biggelswade now."

"Must? Why must?" Mirabelle asked.

"Poor dear." Mary patted her niece's limp hand which remained still in her lap. "Isolde knows, don't you, my dear?"

Isolde snatched her hand away. "No! I'm afraid I do not!"

"But you've been compromised, Isolde," Mary explained in a quiet voice. "Your uncle explained it all to me. Harold was such a naughty boy to . . . ah, oh, dear. But your uncle explained how great was the temptation for the boy."

"To strike me?" Isolde asked, shocked and indignant.

"Oh, no, oh, no, oh, no!" Mary hastened to reassure her. "You mustn't think he meant to strike you! I expect he just became carried away. Gentleman are apt to, at such a time, you know. Why, even your uncle . . ." Her voice faded as she stuffed her lace handkerchief in her mouth to stop further revelations.

"Aunt Mary," Isolde asked grimly, "just what is it that my uncle has told you?"

"Why!" Mary's eyes grew round as two saucers. "He told me that Harold and you . . . last night . . . before you came home . . . well . . ." she lowered her voice to a whisper. "He told me all about that woman's house, my dear. And how you and Harold . . . very naughty of him. But Mr. Hackett seems to think it for the best, so we mustn't argue."

Her face red, her mouth set, Isolde hissed through

clenched teeth, "I don't know what you have been led to believe, my dear Aunt Mary, but I am *not* compromised! I was home long before you were last evening, so there was hardly time for anything untoward to have happened!"

"Then—" Mary looked at her niece, a confused questioning expression on her face—"Mr. Biggelswade. He didn't . . . you didn't . . . I mean, the two of you . . ."

"Mama, " Mirabelle interrupted. "Whatever are you talking about? Harold Biggelswade hit my cousin and for that you want him to marry her? How can that have compromised her? I should think, rather, you would want to bring charges against Mr. Biggelswade!"

"Oh, no! Quite disastrous, I'm sure," Mary hastened to inform her daughter.

The door to Isolde's bedchamber flew open for the third time that morning.

"Oh, miss," Jenny announced. "Your uncle's sent for you. Right away, he says. And you not even dressed yet!"

"Oh, dear, oh, dear, oh, dear." Mary rose from the settee. "You must go to him at once, Isolde. Mirabelle and I . . . leave you to dress. As soon as you've seen him . . . will have to go over wedding plans. Oh, dear, oh, dear, it's all so soon." With those cryptic words, she exited the bedchamber with a protesting Mirabelle in tow.

When Isolde entered her uncle's study half an hour later, he began by shouting at her as he waved a piece of paper in her face. "What is the meaning of this?"

"Since I have not yet read its contents, I hardly qualify to give you an interpretation as to its meaning," Isolde pointed out reasonably as she settled into the chair opposite him.

"Don't use that impertinent tone with me, young lady!" her uncle admonished. Knowing that he seldom appeared to advantage in conversation with his niece, his tack was to put her on the defensive from the onset. Assuming an injured air, he continued, "Your aunt may brook that kind of behavior from you, but I shan't! I take leave to remind you that you are a guest in this house and I expect you to act accordingly!''

Isolde maintained a discreet silence in the face of this statement. Whenever her uncle was displeased with her, he took the opportunity to remind her that it was only through his very generous nature that Isolde was able to make her home with his family in Burton Crescent. Until two years ago, Isolde had lived under her parents' roof—a small country parsonage in Lincolnshire. Her parents had been killed in a carriage accident while they were on their way to collect their daughter from a visit with her Grandfather Challoner. Enoch Challoner, who had stood in the position of guardian to his granddaughter following that unexpected tragic accident, did not live long. His heart had never been strong, and with the death of his favorite child, Isolde's mother, he lost the will to live. Isolde lost her indulgent guardian and found herself in the hands of the tyrant who now stood before her.

''I have had the most disturbing note from Harold,'' Wendall Hackett began, hands clasped behind his back as he paced before the desk in his study.

Isolde merely folded her hands demurely in her lap and cast her eyes downward. ''Indeed?'' she mumbled.

''There is no need for coyness, niece.'' Wendall narrowed his eyes. ''We both know to what I refer. You had best resign yourself to being Harold's wife, because I have arranged for the wedding to take place four weeks from Saturday and the calling of the banns will begin Sunday next.''

''What?'' Isolde's eyes flew back up to his. ''Are you mad? Harold did not compromise me, if that is what he has led you to believe in his note.''

''You needn't remind me, my dear niece, how badly bungled last night's affair was!'' Wendall pounded his fist on the desk, rattling the cups and plates left there from his breakfast and causing more than one of the volumes on top to advance precariously close to the edge. "I would procure a special license and have the ceremony tomorrow, but I do not want tongues to start wagging unnecessarily."

"Good Lord!" Isolde gasped as the meaning behind his words sunk in. "He didn't lie, did he? That wretched scheme *was* your idea!"

"Of course it was!" Wendall said in an exasperated voice. "What with you vowing you would never marry Harold, no matter what the advice of older and wiser heads than yours, what other course was open? I knew from experience that if he'd bedded you first, you'd be anxious enough to wed later."

"From experience?" Horrified, the full perfidy of her uncle's character was beginning to dawn on her. "You mean that you and Aunt Mary . . . ?"

Wendall gave her a knowing look. "I was very ambitious, and I knew that old goat, your Grandfather Challoner, did not appreciate my worth. As his son by marriage, however, I rose very rapidly in the ranks of Challoner's Spice and Tea Importers. It also guaranteed me a half interest in the company. Unfortunately, when you come of age next January, I shall lose control of your half. I should greatly dislike that, my dear Isolde. It has been most rewarding these last two years to be in full command of the firm. Harold would never dream of usurping my authority."

"Is that what this is all in aid of?" Isolde asked. "Just some plan to give you continued mastery over Challoner's?"

"Only in part, my dear, only in part. My reasons are my own. However, I hope you begin to see that I am in earnest. I have decided, Isolde, that you are to marry Harold."

"I shall never consent!" Isolde exclaimed defiantly. "If it is my money you want, why, then, you may have it and welcome. But I shall never consent to marry Harold Biggelswade and that is my final word!"

"Your consent is irrelevant, my dear girl. And, please, no more melodramatic offers of turning over your fortune. You and I both know that is impossible. Any other girl in your position would be glad for such an offer. Harold is a nice enough lad. He's not unhandsome."

"He is an uncouth pig!"

Wendall's jaw tightened in anger. "Isn't my . . . my clerk good enough for you, Miss Hoity-toity? Do you think because your grandfather was some obscure baronet that you're too good for the likes of Harold?"

"No, of course not. That has nothing to do with this."

"Just like that old bastard, Sir Randolph, you 'ere! Think you're bettern' the rest of us! Well, you think Sir Randolph would have given a tinker's damn who you married or why? Humph, the high and mighty old bastard cut your saintly papa out of his will without a shilling! Disowned him, he did! And all because of that pretty piece of baggage—Miss Jessamina Thorpe!" Wendall sneered at his niece.

Isolde grimaced distastefully, "If you will recall the facts, Uncle, it was my Uncle James she was engaged to and not—"

Thrusting a pudgy finger at his niece, Wendall interrupted, "You might profit by Miss Thorpe's example, my girl! Now, there was a young lady who disobeyed her guardian's wishes and look at the trouble it caused!"

"I hardly think . . ."

Wendall chuckled softly to himself, "Although it would have been a good joke on that old bastard, Sir Randolph, and his bloody, snooty son James if she had succeeded in passing off her bastard as the next baronet."

"I cannot find anything amusing in the circumstances surrounding my Uncle James's murder!" Isolde informed Wendall indignantly.

"Murder?" Wendall looked surprised. "Your father's brother died in a duel!"

Isolde snorted. "When has a duel—a supposedly fair and honorable fight—ever taken place in a man's own apartments? And when has a man ever been killed in a duel by taking a ball in his back?!"

"Sound just like that sanctimonious ass, your father, when you say that!" Wendall sneered. "But I knew those two, your father and his brother James. Just like Cain and Abel, they was. Your father was jealous of his brother, always hated him 'cause he could see their Pa favored James."

"You cannot mean to imply my father had anything to do with his own brother's death?" Isolde cried.

Wendall, who knew the present subject was the only one likely to disrupt his niece's sangfroid, jabbed the knife a little deeper. "Why, even James' fiancée, the beautiful Miss Thorpe, let slip before she disappeared that she had met the father of her child and James' murderer in your father's house. Hardly the right company for a Reverend, I would say."

"My father knew nothing, I tell you! Nothing!" Isolde jumped to her feet as she hotly denied his charges.

Wendall shrugged his fat shoulders. "It makes no difference to me if your father lead the girl down the path of temptation or not. What concerns me is your own defiance regarding *my* wishes. A girl of your advanced years, on the shelf like you 'ere, should be grateful for any offer! Especially one as flattering as Harold's!"

"I am not on the shelf! I shall only be twenty-one in January. And I am *not* flattered by Mr. Biggelwade's attentions!" Isolde's voice shook with temper. "Furthermore, you know perfectly well that my father had no hand in his brother's death! Why everyone should choose to take the word of a woman like Miss Thorpe who was no better than she should be, I shall never know! If my father said he did not know who the man was who seduced her and then killed her fiancé, then he *did not know*!''

"Insolent hussy! It is beyond me why I even attempt to be polite to you!'' Wendall turned his bulk, stalked to the other side of the desk, and lowered himself into the chair found there.

"Polite?'' Isolde seethed, throwing herself back into her own chair in disgust.

"There is no use in further protest, Isolde. Wed Harold, you will. And if need be, to gain your cooperation, I shall arrange another evening like last night. Only this time there will be no mistakes made. And you shall come away with more than a blackened eye. Even if the boy must make you''—he coughed delicately—''*enciente* first, I shall certainly encourage him to do so. Do I make myself understood? Or perhaps you *want* to end up like Jessamina? With child? Without a father for your bastard and nowhere to go? Shall we see just how defiant you are once Harold is finished with you?''

Isolde glared ineffectually at her uncle. Challoner's had provided her mother with an easy competence which her father, a proud man, had insisted throughout the years be for his wife's exclusive use. Through the scruples of one parent and the economy of another, Isolde stood to be the possessor of a comfortable independence in only a few weeks' time. She had no wish to share that fortune with an unwanted husband! She could not, however, see any way to prevent it from happening.

Wendall wondered aloud as he leaned back in his chair. "Perhaps I should arrange for a special license, as I mentioned earlier. I'm sure I can guarantee Harold's agreement.''

"I doubt you shall find Mr. Biggelswade in any condition to agree to any of your nefarious schemes.'' Isolde took great pleasure in telling him. "I don't know what he may have told you in his note, but he was caned quite thoroughly last night for his impudence and I doubt he shall be rising from his bed anytime in the near future."

"Eh? What is this? What is this?" Wendall sat up and stared at his niece. "What do you mean, caned for his impudence?!"

"Yes," Isolde explained, her caution deserting her in the face of her uncle's latest threats. "A gentleman—which I take leave to suggest that Harold Biggelswade is *not*—perceiving my distress, came to my aid and caned Harold quite thoroughly."

"No wonder that boy's note made no sense!" Wendall pounded his fist on his desk a second time that morning, this time dislodging the books, which crashed to the floor unheeded. Rising and coming to her side with a speed that was astonishing in a man of his bulk, he gripped her arm in a most brutal fashion and pulled her up from her chair. His eyes narrowed suspiciously. "Perhaps you are more like Miss Thorpe than I suspected. Planning to make a cuckold of your fiancé as well, eh? Who was he, missy?"

"I, I don't know . . ." Isolde lied.

"Don't lie to me, girl. I want to know who he is!"

"I don't know, I tell you!" Isolde was determined to keep the knowledge to herself. "He didn't tell me. He put me in a hackney coach for home and that's the last I saw of him!" She hoped none of the servants had seen her arrival or her uncle would know her story was not completely truthful.

He threw her back into the winged chair. "Very well. Just so long as he doesn't conveniently arrive to rescue you a second time. For the wedding will take place as I have arranged, niece, and I will tolerate no interference from any source. Especially strange 'gentlemen'!"

Isolde smiled wanly. She knew only too well that her "Sir Tristan" was not likely to appear so opportunely a second time. And even if he did, he was more likely to offer her carte blanche than any honorable means of escaping her present dilemma. She allowed her uncle to dismiss her without further protest against his arrangements. She even nodded and answered at the appropriate time when cornered by her aunt full of wedding plans a short time later. But she attended with only half a mind. The rest of her consciousness was concerned with the more pressing question of why a world could be so unfair as to introduce a knight in shining armor only to reveal that his coat of mail was tarnished and dented quite beyond repair. Groaning inwardly at the shabbiness of an unkind fate, Isolde resigned herself to the fact that she was soon to be Mrs. Harold Biggelswade.

Chapter Five

When a man sets out to find a wife, he is apt to have several ideas about the type of creature he is willing to consider for such an exalted and honored position. If he has had the misfortune to fall in love without first laying down rational and carefully considered principles, he is likely to overlook small faults and imperfections of personality which may later prove irksome. However, if he sets his mind firmly on certain ideals and specific traits, his chances of future happiness are greatly increased. Or so it seemed to Lord Shalbourne.

Therefore, immediately upon quitting his aunt's house, he sought out his friend, Lord Denbigh, so that they might discuss the matter. The theory being, that whereas one mind might produce a list of names and ideals, how much better and more complete such a list must be with the thoughts of two.

Viscount Denbigh proved, however, to be a difficult prey to run to ground. Having first sought that volatile young man at his lodgings in Jermyn Street, Shalbourne was greeted with the intelligence that my lord had driven out his chestnuts to tool Miss Forrester around the park. Yes, my lord, answered Denbigh's long-suffering valet cum butler and general factotum, he did believe Hyde Park was the destination mentioned. Return? He was sure he couldn't say, as my lord had said that he would be dining away from home and not to expect his return very early that evening.

"Damn it, man," Shalbourne exclaimed. "What about his horses?"

"As his lordship will no doubt recall, my Lord Denbigh stables his horses rather distant from his lodgings." Whatever else that patient gentleman might have added was lost as Shalbourne turned in disgust and limped hurriedly away. Finding a hackney, he decided that he was unlikely to find Denbigh anytime soon, so he would take care of some other "important" business instead.

The next afternoon saw him once again searching for his friend Denbigh. Reassuring his mistress that marriage would not interfere unduly with their relationship had been a pleasant way to spend the previous evening. It was on his way home from that rendezvous that he had rescued the young actress, Isolde What's-her-name. At least, he assumed she was an actress. She had been so concerned about returning to the theatre and only an actress of consummate skill would have attempted the performance of outraged virtue she had given, much less succeeded as well as she had. Ah, well, he shrugged off the incident. She had been a pretty enough piece but he needed to concern himself at the moment with finding a wife, not seeking a young actress.

Arriving at White's about mid-afternoon, Shalbourne found the club relatively quiet. Although there were still the inevitable hardened gamesters who arrived at noon and left in the wee hours of the morning, Lord Denbigh was not in evidence. Shalbourne, determined to wait for a moment or two and see whether his friend would put in an appearance, sat in a quiet spot beside one of the many fireplaces and made as if to read that day's papers. Just half an hour had passed, and Shalbourne was beginning to become restless, when Denbigh, an expression of gloom on his face, sauntered into the room. His many-caped Garrick was open negligently, a few whip points thrust through a large button hole. An unobtrusive individual followed Lord Denbigh, holding his hat and gloves and waiting patiently for him to divest himself of his coat.

"Gay!" Denbigh called out. "By all that's wonderful! You here?"

"Knew I'd find you here. Wouldn't have set foot in this Tory bastion otherwise."

"But, I mean, you *here*? Thought you were at your Aunt Jane's deathbed!"

Shalbourne looked a good deal startled. "Deathbed? The devil, you say?"

"Your coat, my lord," said a soft voice at Denbigh's elbow.

"What? Oh, yes, here you are, my good man." Denbigh allowed himself to be helped out of his driving coat.

"George!" exclaimed Shalbourne as he struggled to his feet. "Forget your damned coat! What is this you hear about my Aunt Jane's deathbed?"

The unobtrusive individual regretfully quit the room, as the conversation had all the earmarks of proving very interesting indeed.

Denbigh stood before the fire warming his coat tails. "Well, isn't that where you went yesterday? Heard you had some sort of summons to your aunt's house. Heard she was dying and had sent for you. Egads, when you think about it, it's remarkably ironic in view of today's news!"

Shalbourne groaned in a mixture of relief and exasperation as he sank back into his chair. "Good God, man!"

"What's the matter? Thought it might be a good thing for you if the old lady did stick her spoon in the wall." Denbigh was puzzled. "Isn't she the one with all the money?"

"Lord, yes. Rich enough to buy an abbey, I should think." Shalbourne took a sip of the drink at his elbow.

"But she ain't ready to cast up her accounts yet. Personally, I hope she lives to be a hundred."

Denbigh was surprised. "What's this? Ain't she the one you said was an autocratic, interfering old battleax of a woman who always acts as if *she* were head of the family?"

"Did I say that?" Shalbourne asked drily. "How very perceptive of me, to be sure."

"Now, look here, Gay. Either she's a termagant and should depart as quickly as possible from this world or she's an angelic old lady and everyone benefits enormously from her presence. Now, which is it, old boy?"

"Both," muttered Shalbourne gloomily. "That is, she's a shrew who I hope lives to plague me more than I deserve."

Denbigh grinned. "Out with it, Gay. There's more here than meets the eye and you're itching to tell me. What's more, I'm agog to hear. So tell me, what has your aunt done now?"

"Changed her will. In favor of a foundling hospital at Grantham," Shalbourne growled.

Denbigh let out a bark of laughter. "No, really, old boy, doing it rather too brown by half. Come now, the truth."

"That is the truth," Shalbourne said as he poured himself another glass from the decanter next to him. "What's more, she delivered an ultimatum to me. She'll only change the will in my favor if I settle down and begat myself an heir. Now, what's sent you off into whoops?"

"No, really, Gay! You'll have to do better than that!"

"You may choose to disbelieve me," Shalbourne said sourly. "But I intend to find a suitable bride at the earliest opportunity."

Denbigh, an arrested expression on his face, asked, "You're serious, aren't you?"

"Never more so."

"But who? Gay, you can't *want* to marry, surely?" Denbigh was shocked at Shalbourne's calm and felt it necessary to express all the outraged sensibilities that his friend seemed hesitant to voice. "Good God, man! This is the outside of enough! The old bitch can't serve you such a turn as this! It's outrageous! It's intolerable! It's unreasonable! It's Gothic!"

It was now Shalbourne's turn to grin at his friend. "I wonder if you realize what a comfort you are to me, George? Yes, it is outrageous, intolerable and whatever else you said. But what choice do I have? I can't afford to snap my fingers at Auntie Jane's fortune. And I know the old shrew. As much as it would go against her grain to leave her fortune away from the Earl of Shalbourne, she has no great love for me personally and would not hesitate to cut me out altogether if I hadn't had the bad taste to succeed to the title."

"But you can't want to marry!" Denbigh repeated.

"No. But, then, who of us ever does? However, I suppose that eventually I would have married. After all, I am the last of the Leightons, as my aunt pointed out. I admit that I would have preferred to put off such an inevitability, but that is out of the question now. I must secure Aunt Jane's fortune and if marrying will do that, I shall marry. The only real objection I have to Auntie Jane's scheme is her method of execution. I should have preferred to take my time and married when I saw fit, not at her instigation."

"Well, I suppose you're right. I cannot like it, though." Denbigh shook his head.

"I cannot say I am happy about it myself," Shalbourne said. "Care for some of this brandy, George?"

"What? Oh, yes." Denbigh wore an abstracted air. "But who, Gay?" Denbigh seemed to be taken with this home question. "Who to ask?"

"Been trying to decide. It's not as if I've set out to fix my interest with any particular young lady. Can't say I've been to Almack's since I got back from the Colonies three years ago.'' Shalbourne settled back to consider the issue comfortably. He added, ''Not that I could have gotten vouchers if I had wanted to enter those hallowed halls. At least half the patronesses have been at odds with me since that affair in '13.''

''Well, you would have been heartily bored, old boy.'' Denbigh, alarmed at the bitter tone in his friend's voice, was eager to make excuses. ''Nothing but dancing and gambling for chicken stakes. And you wouldn't credit it, for one must concede they have a decidedly fashionable air, only serve orgeat and lemonade! Shocking. Isn't even good lemonade. And what's more, don't even dance the waltz much anymore. Too many of the starchier ladies found it too forward by half.''

''Guess they thought all those sweet young girls would be too excited by actually finding themselves being held around the waist by their partners. Corrupting influence.'' Shalbourne gazed thoughtfully ceilingward. ''Pity. Waltzing was certainly my favorite dance.''

''Oh, yes, and so partial to dancing that you are.'' Denbigh was the sole member of that class privileged to tease Shalbourne about his infirmity. ''But this is getting us nowhere, Gay. Got to find you a bride.''

''I don't even know the crop on the marriage mart anymore. That's why I came to you,'' Shalbourne stated baldly.

''To me?''

''Know for a fact that you haunted Almack's all last spring. Always seeing you at balls and parties—playing the gallant.''

''*Playing* the gallant, indeed. I'll have you know I *am* the Gallant.'' Denbigh was grinning. ''Of course, that means I have a certain intimate knowledge of several of this year's crop. From occupying myself to good purpose on the dance floor, you understand.''

''Of course,'' his friend agreed cheerfully. ''You know,

George, it's no wonder I've heard more than one matchmaking mama refer to you as dangerous.''

"I raise no hopes I can't fulfill," Denbigh explained.

"Decidedly dangerous," his friend murmured.

"Just what is it you do want?" Denbigh asked. "In a wife, that is."

Shalbourne became thoughtful. "Well, she must be of reasonably good birth."

"How good?" Denbigh interposed.

"Well, I don't demand the daughter of an Earl or Duke, certainly, but I wouldn't want a tradesman's by-blow."

"How about a tradesman's legitimate offspring?" Denbigh asked politely.

"Oh, well, in that case"—Shalbourne was quick to perceive the ironic gleam in his friend's eye—"if she's legitimate, maybe. But only if she stands to inherit at least thirty thousand."

"Oh, indeed, that goes without saying," Denbigh replied. "But, seriously, Gay, do you want a bride with a large fortune?"

"Good God, why should I?" Shalbourne exclaimed. "With Auntie Jane's blunt, why should I need an heiress? Mind you, I wouldn't turn a young lady away just because she was one."

"Oh, no, of course not," Denbigh agreed. "Can't hold that against her, can we? So what else do you require?"

Shalbourne leaned back and stared once again at the ceiling for inspiration. "Her manners should be pleasing but definitely not pert or coming. Reasonably intelligent but, God forbid, not a bluestocking."

"What about person?"

"Hmm," Shalbourne considered. "Doesn't have to be a beauty, mind you, but I don't want some butter-toothed, hook-nosed harpy either. God knows I'm no bargain when it comes to appearance, but I don't think it's too much to ask that my bride be reasonably pretty.''

Denbigh agreed with alacrity and pointed out helpfully that if she was like most women, after a few years of marriage and a few children, it probably wouldn't matter much anyway. ''Why, just look at Lady Damplymare!''

Shalbourne, who had not been attending this dire warning, narrowed his eyes suspiciously. ''What about Lady Damplymare?''

''You'd never recognize her, I daresay,'' Denbigh said in his prosaic manner. ''Grown quite stout, she has. Remarkably ill-tempered, too. Expect that comes of living with Damplymare. Lord, that would make anyone turn sour. Damplymare'd probably be happy if you did succeed in eloping with her this time. I know if she were my wife, I'd be just as happy to see someone carry her off.''

''I'll keep that in mind,'' Shalbourne said sarcastically. ''Are you quite finished now?'' he asked sweetly. ''Because if you are, maybe we could return to the issue at hand?''

''You're the one who brought her up!''

Shalbourne knew it would be useless to deny this charge. And since it would probably result in further discussion, he held his tongue.

Denbigh, upon whom the true spirit of a matchmaker had descended, busily arranged himself in a comfortable chair. Leaning forward, he prepared to put his all into the question before the court.

''Ready?'' Shalbourne asked in the same sardonic tone their schoolmaster at Eton had often adopted.

''Never more so,'' Denbigh assured him. ''What is it, exactly, that you look for in a wife, Gay, my friend?''

''Well, I'd like her to be educated. You know, French, pianoforte, watercolor, all that rot.''

''What about the harp?'' Denbigh asked with deceptive innocence.

"What *about* the harp?"

"Well, you mentioned the pianoforte. I wondered how you were disposed toward the harp," Denbigh explained.

"A harp?" Shalbourne thought about it for a moment. "Don't think I could stand for that, George."

Denbigh sighed. "Ah, well, that leaves off at least one young lady I had in mind."

"Here's an item that should eliminate any number of candidates." Shalbourne leaned forward in a conspiratorial manner. "She must be virtuous."

"Virtuous?"

"Yes, virtuous. You know, religious without being pious. Tolerant and understanding."

"Especially of your pecadillos," Denbigh supplied helpfully.

"Naturally. Without indulging in any of her own. I have no intention of being a cuckold." Shalbourne's aspect became quite grim at the thought of such a possibility. "And, of course, she must be a virgin."

Denbigh was bereft of words momentarily. "Of course," he added shakily and gulped. "You insist on it, I suppose?"

"Oh, absolutely," Shalbourne stated.

"Well, then, I fear you are destined to marry someone straight out of the schoolroom," Denbigh said.

"You're right, of course," Shalbourne added after a thoughtful silence. "Gad! What a fix! I shall undoubtedly be bored to distraction. Ah, well, tell me the worst, George, can you think of any candidates for the title of Lady Shalbourne?"

"Lord, yes," Denbigh readily replied. "Any number of them."

"But will I find one willing to take me?" Using a self-deprecating gesture, he indicated his scarred face and incapacitated limb.

"Don't be such a paperskull, Gay," Denbigh said disdainfully. "Got an earldom now, don't you? Ain't anyone likely to turn Lord Shalbourne away, no matter how much they might have hesitated to take Gaylord Leighton."

With this truism acknowledged, Denbigh got down to more important issues. "Of course, there are only a limited number still in town. And even fewer you might be inclined to tolerate. Picked a bad time for this nonsense, old boy."

"I am aware of the fact that the little season's almost over," Shalbourne commented. "I know most of 'polite society' are headed back to their country estate or someone else's for the Christmas season. Won't be any real parties for weeks. Just a few private soirees and maybe a lecture or two. I'll have to work fast. Those left in town are probably preparing to leave even as we speak. Not that the timing was my choice, mind you." Shalbourne was hot to defend himself. "The old lady just sprang it on me."

"Well, the timing couldn't have been worse!" Denbigh shook his head gloomily.

Shalbourne smiled. "Oh, come, now, George. It can't be as bad as all that, can it? I mean, the papers were full of Princess Charlotte and the new heir this morning. Surely there will be parties enough to celebrate the event where I can meet and court a young lady."

Denbigh turned horrified eyes to his friend. "You haven't heard yet, have you?"

"Heard what?" Shalbourne asked.

"Finding you a bride will be more difficult than you bargained for—the country will be in mourning for weeks!" Denbigh lost what little was left of his jovial air as he recalled what it was he had meant to tell his friend when first he'd entered the room. "Princess Charlotte and her baby died early this morning."

CHAPTER SIX

Isolde had hoped for some kind of a reprieve when the Princess had died so unexpectedly and plunged the nation into mourning. Nonetheless, the banns had been called once already and would be called again the day after tomorrow. Tragedy might come to the lives of kings, but the business of everyday living among their subjects must go on. The day of the wedding was now only three weeks away.

The day of Princess Charlotte's internment was exactly suited to Isolde's mood, being unseasonably wet and cold. Although she had no inclination to join the crowd of mourners and gawkers who would line the streets to witness the pageantry of the solemn event, she did retire to the drawing room for solitude and a chance to indulge her melancholia. Pounding out some dirges, gloomy airs, and other uplifting music on the ancient pianoforte which sat in a corner, her mind wandered and she was able to dwell on her problems to her heart's content.

Leaning into the keyboard, she tried to translate the notes before her into music. As she hit the wrong key for the fourth time in as many minutes, the central figure of her nightmares entered the room.

"Good morning, Isolde," he said as he shut the door. "Your aunt told me I might find you here."

It had been almost two weeks since Isolde had laid eyes on Harold Biggelswade. Not since that fateful night after the theatre, in fact. Flashing him a look of resentment, she noted that he looked none the worse for his adventure. She knew that Harold had been abed for the better part of a week, only recently returning to work. His illness and then his labors had kept him away until now.

"How delightful you look this morning, Isolde," he began as he advanced toward her.

"I . . . I hope I see you well, Mr. Biggelswade," Isolde uttered sweetly and falsely. "Although I am surprised to see you."

"Ah," Harold said. "You mean my being here at an hour when I am usually hard at work at Challoner's? Your uncle, out of respect for the Princess's funeral today, released his staff from their labors. And since I have been unable to do so before now, I thought to myself, what better opportunity to come and visit you, dear lady?" He glared at her meaningfully, his eyes conveying the unspoken circumstances causing his "illness." His expression dared her to defy him as he possessed himself of her hand and tried to kiss it in what he considered an elegant manner.

Isolde stiffened as the picture of a very different man doing the same thing splashed across her mind's eye. Before Harold could complete his purpose, and somehow defile the memory that Isolde kept locked away, she snatched back her hand. Rising from the piano stool, she pulled herself up to her full height and regarded him coldly. She asked in chilly accents just what he thought he was about.

Harold grinned at her. "The cat has her claws bared this morning, I see." He raised his thick hand and thrust his stubby fingers in her dark curls. He murmured, "Nice kitty."

Nauseated, Isolde sought to move away from him. "Your manners are offensive, sir."

Harold smirked in reply.

Isolde, having placed the pianoforte between herself and Harold, tried to speak earnestly to that gentleman. "Sir, there is something of import that we must discuss. As you know, my uncle has gone so far as to begin the reading of the banns."

"Yes, although, for my part, I would just as soon have applied for a special license and not waited the three weeks until our wedding day." Harold's grin reminded her of a character she had once seen in a Hogarth print on the subject of the progress of a rake.

"I cannot believe, sir, that you would wish to marry anyone who is reluctant. Indeed, Mr. Biggelswade, I find I cannot love you," Isolde tripped on the word "love." "It is not reflection on you or your character, I assure you." She blushed rosily at the necessity for uttering such obvious falsehoods. Good manners dictated, however, that she should at least *try* not to hurt his feelings.

"Are you thinking I hold the other evening against you, my dear Isolde?" Harold advanced a few steps. "I must tell you, I never did care for your uncle's scheme and certainly would not have allowed myself to be party to it if I had known your maidenly sensibilities would have been so outraged and offended. Although, I should not be sorry to meet the bloke what so cowardly attacked me! I would certainly enjoy repaying him in kind!" Harold licked his lips as he contemplated tearing his unknown assailant limb from limb.

"Cowardly!" Isolde backed away from him until she was trapped in a corner of the room next to the mantel of the cold fireplace. "If anyone was . . . but, no, I'll not say more on a subject that could only be painful to both of us."

"Painful?" Harold quirked his face. "Aye, it was very painful! 'Course, if you had cooperated a little more, it might have been a pleasant experience for both of us."

"How can you even suggest such a thing?"

"Well," Harold's eyes narrowed lecherously. "Such a sentiment does not augur well for our wedding night, but your uncle assures me that your attitude is the natural reluctance of a young, untried virgin. You shall learn to be more willing and loving in time, I'm sure."

"No!" Isolde whispered desperately as he took another step closer. "I don't want to marry you! And I can't believe you want to marry me! This is all some notion of my uncle's."

"Poor, shy Isolde." Harold smiled and placed a hand on her arm. "This excess of modesty does not become you. Come. Admit that it is not that you don't wish to marry me, but that you are too afraid to marry anyone. Especially with the unknown state of . . . ah, physical intimacy, that such a step implies. See. You flinch even now when I've only touched your cheek. You must learn to be less nervous with me since I am to be your husband."

Isolde tried appealing to any scraps of chivalry he might possess. "Mr. Biggelswade, you must believe me when I say it is not an excess of modesty."

Suddenly, for no apparent reason, Harold reached out and grabbed Isolde by her arms. Shaking her roughly, he shouted at her in a complete reversal of his previous congenial manner, "What's the matter? Ain't I good enough for you? Just because me mum wasn't"—he lowered his voice to a menacing growl—"it's because I'm a bastard, isn't it?"

Isolde, her attention arrested by his rough handling, was as shocked by the revelation inherent in his question as the sudden change in his character. She saw once again the creature who had struck her not so many nights ago and wondered how one man could be two such different people. This time, with fear in her voice, she said, "No, no, of course not. That would never matter to me." She thought, but did not add aloud, "If I loved you."

He stopped shaking her and let go of her as abruptly as he had seized her. He grinned at her. Isolde wondered if perhaps Mr. Biggelswade was a bit mad.

"Just wanted you to know who will be master in my house," Harold explained. "I'll endure no insolence from any woman, let alone one who is to be my wife."

"Why, then, I should make you a terrible wife, Mr. Biggelswade. We should never suit. It is not in my nature to hold my tongue and I fear we should come to cuffs continuously."

Standing so that she could not escape from her corner, Harold remarked, " 'Twill serve to make life more interesting. At least until I've broken you to the bridle."

"I do not appreciate being referred to in such terms, sir. I am not a horse," Isolde stated flatly.

"No? But you've a decidedly coltish nature, Isolde." Harold took her chin in her hand. "I find it a most appropriate analogy."

She attempted to remove his hand. However, Harold was not to be put off. He wound his arms around her and pulled her close. As she struggled to escape, he tightened his hold and laughed softly as his superior strength became apparent.

"No one to save you now, Isolde," he said in a self-satisfied tone. "Oh, no, my dear! Don't do that! How would you explain a scream! After all, what's a kiss between an engaged couple?" With that, his head advanced toward hers and despite pulling back as far as she could, contact was inevitable, since the wall was directly behind her. As he pressed his lips against hers, Isolde began to feel faint. She fought off her dizziness and redoubled her struggles when he forced his tongue into her mouth.

Just when she thought she must surely swoon, Mirabelle tripped into the room calling her name. Stopping short on the threshold, her mouth agape, Mirabelle gasped in shock. "Mr. Biggelswade! Isolde! What are you doing?"

Harold let go of Isolde, who leaned against the wall in an attempt to remain standing despite the weakened condition of her legs. Harold turned to Mirabelle, "Good morning, Mirabelle, Your cousin and I were merely placing the seal on our bargain."

Mirabelle was surprised, but rose to the occasion, "You are truly engaged then? I . . . I wish you both very happy, I suppose." She shot a puzzled look at her cousin. Isolde had vowed only that morning that she would never willingly marry Harold.

"Thank you for your wishes, cousin. May I call you so now that we are to be related?" Harold asked as he politely bent over Mirabelle's hand.

Mirabelle's hesitation was only momentary. "Oh, of course."

"And now, if you ladies will fetch your coats, I should be more than happy to escort you for a step or two down the street. Indeed, it was with just such a delightful commission in mind that I came this morning," Harold said as he straightened and let go of Mirabelle's limp hand.

"No!" Isolde managed to say. Recovering some of her composure, now that a third party in the room protected her, she added in stronger accents, "I really have no interest in exposing myself to the elements this morning. Thank you just the same, sir. I find I do not feel quite well."

"Ah, well, another time perhaps." Harold smiled benignly at her.

It was all Isolde could do to retain her composure as Harold took his leave of them. Her replies to his civil leave-taking were less than enthusiastic and as soon as he had left the room, she sank onto the bench at the pianoforte.

Mirabelle looked at her cousin with questioning eyes. Advancing hesitantly into the room, she began, "Don't misunderstand me, I'm very happy you and Mr. Biggelswade seem to have come to some sort of agreement.''

"Agreement?'' Isolde rubbed her bruised arms. "There is no agreement between Mr. Biggelswade and myself. It all seems to be between him and my Uncle Wendall. In fact, I wish that Uncle Wendall could marry Harold Biggelswade! I am of the opinion that we should all be happier with such an arrangement!''

Mirabelle giggled. "If Mr. Biggelswade's behavior when I entered the room just now is any indication, I should think he is quite content with this match.''

Isolde scowled at her cousin. "Very humorous, Mirabelle,'' she said drily. "Personally, as the object of Mr. Biggelswade's unwanted attentions, I do not find such a thought either comforting or diverting.''

"But, Isolde, don't you want to be a married lady?'' Mirabelle asked. "I know that I should love to run my own establishment, make my own decisions, and have children to occupy my time. I quite envy you.''

"Envy? Why, then, you can marry Harold and with my blessings, too! But, I warn you, Mirabelle, you must consider that although you may run your household, your husband will still be your lord and master, and your desires to make your own decisions would be set aside soon enough. As for children. Please, Mirabelle, do but consider for a moment. If I do indeed marry Harold Biggelswade, he shall be the father of my children. My God, every feeling must revolt at such a thought!''

"Yes, I suppose it would be a shame if they should take after their father in appearance.''

Isolde gave a derisive laugh. "It is not so much the thought that my children would be like Harold that is disconcerting—although that alone is enough to cause palpitations in even the most strong-minded of individuals—but the . . . the thought of the process of . . . well, begetting those children is most repugnant!''

Mirabelle cast a conspiratorial glance about the room, pulled her chair closer to her cousin, and asked in an urgent whisper, ''Do you know, Isolde, exactly what that, ah, process is?''

''No. What?''

''No, no, I'm asking you.''

Isolde looked down at her hands and nervously twisted her skirt between her fingers. ''Well, I'm not quite certain. But, I believe it comes about from sleeping in the same bed with only one's nightclothes on.''

''Only sleeping?'' Mirabelle sounded disappointed.

''Oh, well, I suppose kissing would be obligatory as well,'' Isolde added impatiently.

''Oh, dear. I quite understand your reluctance to engage in such an activity with Harold. I should not like it above half myself.''

''Anyway, my mother always told me that when the time came, my husband would explain the details to me. Oh, but Mirabelle,'' Isolde wailed. ''I should almost rather take any man off the street as husband than spend the rest of my days as Mrs. Harold Biggelswade. He's so . . . so . . .''

''Coarse?'' Mirabelle supplied helpfully.

''Well, yes. But it's not only that, I can't quite explain my feelings. I think—no, I take that back—I *know* Harold would not hesitate to beat a woman. Witness the fact that he has already struck me. In fact, he is much like my Uncle Wendall in that he uses his superior strength to win any argument. I should infinitely prefer a man of wit.''

''Yes. Harold, like Papa, seems to have a most violent temper,'' Mirabelle agreed.

''Especially when he is thwarted,'' Isolde added. ''That's not the worst of it, though. I suppose I could learn to avoid any situation that might cause him to become violent if he were a rational being. But I'm convinced, dear cousin, that he is quite mad!''

"Mad?''

"Yes. Anyone who changes as quickly and as wholly as he does from being quite jovial to being completely incensed is not a man in control of his faculties. I thought his attic to let this morning when he laughed at me and then attacked me by turns. I know I am not explaining this well, but the expression on his face, the complete change in character. Well, all I can say is I think he should be in Bedlam rather than at large on London's streets!''

"There is no help for it then,'' Mirabelle said practically. "You mustn't marry him.''

"Oh? Mustn't I?'' Isolde's voice dripped with sarcasm. "And what do you suggest, cousin?''

"Why, you must defy Papa!''

"Please understand, Mirabelle, it is not a want of resolution nor even a lack of courage on my part that makes such a course impossible to follow. It is that I have no other choice,'' Isolde said. "Short of running away, I don't see what—''

"But that's the perfect solution!'' Mirabelle exclaimed excitedly. "Why, in two months time, you shall be of age and able to do quite as you like. You have only to avoid marriage with Harold until that time!''

"And, what, pray tell, do I do in the intervening weeks?''

"Perhaps the Rutherfords—''

"You know perfectly well,'' Isolde interrupted, "that the Rutherfords or any other of our family's friends would support Uncle Wendall in this. They would not think it proper for me to ignore my guardian's wishes in such a fashion. I can hear them all now—'But, my dear,' '' Isolde mimicked, '' 'your Uncle Wendall knows what is best for you! Your objection is only the natural nervousness of a new bride.' ''

Mirabelle chewed her lip. "Yes. I suppose you are right. Perhaps one of your father's old parishioners . . ."

"Don't be absurd! First of all, they would probably all take the same position as your family's friends. Secondly, it's been two years since I laid eyes on any of them. Why should they become involved in what can be best described as a private domestic quarrel? And, thirdly, how should I ever get to Stretton on my own without funds?"

Mirabelle fell silent for a moment, cast down. Suddenly she lifted her drooping head and snapped her fingers. "I have it! You shall become a governess!"

"For somewhat more than eight weeks?" Isolde asked politely.

"Yes, of course!" Mirabelle said excitedly.

"Under an assumed name, no doubt."

"Oh, perfect, Isolde! Quite brilliant of you to have thought of that!"

"Without references, I suppose."

"Oh, dear. I hadn't considered that." Mirabelle was only momentarily put off her scheme. "But, surely they aren't necessary. Not with your superior qualifications! Why, you know such difficult things, like Greek and Latin."

"Yes, but my watercolor painting and sewing are indifferent at best. My performance on the pianoforte is adequate for my own pleasure but hardly remarkable."

"But, your French . . ."

"Is not up to most people's expectations of a governess. You must remember, Mirabelle, that I learned my French from the village seamstress, who happened to be one of my father's parishioners. Actually, if a young man desired to make the grand tour, I should be better qualified for his tutor than for a governess."

"Well?"

"What?" Isolde asked blankly and then burst into laughter.

"Oh, Mirabelle, what a goose you are! I believe there is one qualification for a tutor where I fall miserably short."

An indignant Mirabelle began to protest.

"Most tutors are men" was Isolde's simple reply.

"Well, a lady's companion, then. I'm sure you could . . ."

"You forget again, Mirabelle. No references."

"A milliner's assistant."

"You forget my sewing."

"A shop assistant."

"And run the risk of meeting my aunt or a family friend? They would be sure to reveal my whereabouts to your father."

"A maid."

"And begin at the bottom? For I would have to, you know, with no previous experience. The life of a tweenie is not one that appeals, thank you. Up at four to black the grates and set the fires, haul water for the kitchen, assist the cook, do all the worst jobs in the establishment from dawn to dusk. Ugh!"

"But there must be something . . ." Mirabelle was finally becoming discouraged.

"Yes. There is. I shall advertise for a substitute bridegroom in the *Chronicle*," Isolde said in a serious tone with a straight face.

"Isolde!" Mirabelle breathed in awe. "That's absolutely brilliant!"

"Yes, isn't it? Can't you see it now? 'Matrimony'—I think I should state quite clearly from the outset that I will accept nothing less. Then, I suppose I should describe myself. Something like 'a young lady of superior education.' You do agree, don't you, that I have had a most superior education?"

"Oh, yes, of course. As I said, you know such difficult things!"

"After, I shall mention that I will be coming into a fortune soon. Not when or how much, mind you. I shall then explain that my guardian is urging me to make a match that I abhor. Maybe even throw out a slur to the effect that my guardian has a most avaricious disposition and that is why he is promoting the match. I should then perhaps reiterate that I wish to meet with a young gentleman—only gentlemen need apply—who would do the honorable thing by me.''

"Oh, yes. You don't want anyone to get any mistaken impressions,'' Mirabelle agreed solemnly.

"I should then arrange that the letters would be sent to an address other than this one, as I doubt my uncle would approve my machinations.''

"Oh, no.'' Mirabelle nodded in agreement. "You're quite correct, I'm sure. Papa would most likely burn any replies first and he would be most angry at you for indulging in such a step.''

"Most angry,'' Isolde said drily.

"Oh, but it's a lovely scheme!'' Mirabelle enthused. "I especially like the idea of emphasizing that you will accept only an honourable solution to your problem.''

"Do you?'' Isolde asked. "Yes, that is a nice touch, isn't it? There is only one problem with the plot.''

"What's that?'' Mirabelle asked cautiously, ready to have this idea shot down like all the others.

"The whole point of this exercise is to find a way to deliver me from my uncle's tyranny before he can force me to marry Harold. And, yet, how am I to marry my liberator without my uncle's permission?''

"Lie.''

"What?'' Isolde was confused.

"Lie.'' Mirabelle frowned and explained seriously. "Find a parish where you are not known and when the rector asks your age, lie. After all, by the time my father found out what you had done and could begin to set measures afoot to have the marriage annulled, you would be of age and there would be nothing he could do.''

Isolde sat in awe. "Mirabelle! I would never have

thought it of you! That's quite incredible! I take my hat off to you! Splendid! Brilliant! I shall marry another. It will be quite easy. Except for one small detail.''

''Pooh!'' Mirabelle waved her hand. ''What could be of any consequence now?''

''A minor detail at best. Forgive me for even mentioning it,'' Isolde said, ''but, who, I wonder, shall I wed?''

''But the advertisement . . .''

''Oh, don't be ridiculous, Mirabelle!'' Isolde was weary of the game. ''You know it is quite impossible.''

''Surely there is someone you could marry.''

''Who do you suggest? Peter Rutherford? Ah, I thought not. I can tell from the expression on your face that such a plan does not sit well with you. And yet he is the only eligible young man of my acquaintance. Aside from Harold Biggleswade, of course. Besides, can you really imagine any gentleman you might be inclined to put forth allowing himself to be a party to this idea of yours?''

''It wasn't my idea!'' Mirabelle bristled. ''You're the one who first mentioned advertising in the *Chronicle* for a husband! Though I must admit I think your idea of an advertisement is the best. You are no doubt correct in your assessment of our chances of finding anyone among our acquaintances who would be willing . . .''

Isolde rose impatiently from the piano stool. ''Oh, really, Mirabelle. This is becoming tiresome. Three weeks from tomorrow, I shall marry Harold and there's not a single thing anyone can do about it! Now, if you'll excuse me, this room is far too cold to spend another minute in, and, besides, your mother will be expecting us to join her for luncheon soon and I should like to lie down for a moment or two before I have to face her talk about the latest additions and inventions for my wedding.''

''Isolde!'' Mirabelle stood and followed her cousin to the door where she laid a restraining hand on Isolde's arm.

"Just answer me this; if I should find a young gentleman who would be willing to marry you before this marriage with Harold is to take place, would you do it?"

Isolde laughed bitterly. "Of course, my dear. I should marry the devil himself! Provided, of course," she added humorously, "he were young (that is, under the age of senility), of good person (I mean, his cloven feet are only noticeable without his shoes) and of a good disposition (or only slightly less disagreeable than Mr. Biggelswade). I should like him to be in a respectable situation. I wouldn't want to find myself married to a professional pickpocket or highwayman. Quite unnerving always to be wondering if he would return or end up arrested and subsequently transported. And, of course, he would need to be free of any entanglements. That is, it would be most embarrassing to have another wife and several children put in an appearance soon after the wedding."

"Let me understand this. Young, good person, good disposition, respectable situation, and no entanglements?"

"Yes, I would say that sums it up very nicely."

Mirabelle smiled widely. "Why, then that shouldn't be too difficult! I'm sure to find someone before these three weeks are up. Never fear, Isolde! I shan't fail you!"

"Thank you, my dear." Isolde patted Mirabelle's hand as she stepped out of the room. "I rely on you completely." Then, rolling her eyes, she mounted the stairs to her bedchamber.

Mirabelle skipped across the hall to the library where she pulled out a sheet of writing paper and mended a pen. It took her the better part of two days before she had everything set down to her satisfaction. It took her still another morning to find out how to go about setting her plan in motion. But by Monday afternoon, the arrangements were complete and Mirabelle was sure she would soon have the solution to her cousin's dilemma. All that was required of her was a little patience and of fate, a little kindness.

CHAPTER SEVEN

Shalbourne had been drinking deep and losing consistently at cards. There was a morose, querulous air about the earl. He was ripe for a quarrel, his normally stormy aspect being even more tumultuous this evening. When Grey's ill-timed remark about being able to best Wentworth's walking feat, even if he were forced to limp quite as much as the Gay Lord himself, wafted across the room just as the conversational din had momentarily subsided, Shalbourne was up from the table and across the room before Lord Denbigh was able to give voice to his hesitant suggestion that Shalbourne was perhaps playing a bit recklessly. Pulled off by his friends as he attempted to choke the life out of Grey, Shalbourne demanded satisfaction and magnanimously gave Grey the choice of weapons. Gray, knowing himself to be in an untenable position, since he had not previously realized that the Gay Lord himself was in the cardroom, began a much garbled and hoarse apology. In disgust, Shalbourne shook off his well-wishers, told Gray in no uncertain terms what he thought of him, and limped out of the room before his shocked audience had time to breathe a sigh of relief.

Once on the street outside of Brook's, where the deplorable incident had taken place, Lord Denbigh was able to catch up with his friend.

"Gay? Gay! Wait for me, damn you!"

His lordship turned swiftly.

"Don't give your black looks to me, old man," Denbigh exclaimed. "I expect nothing but gratitude from you. After all, I've brought you your coat and hat."

Shalbourne grabbed the two articles, growled at his friend, and began to walk away.

"Oh, no, my lad, not so fast." Denbigh took hold of Shalbourne's elbow and began to stroll along beside him as if nothing untoward was to be seen in this midnight sojourn down St. James with a man who was known never to walk anywhere. "I'm not going to let you off so easy as that, old boy. You've been looking for a fight all evening and if you must needs have one, it had best be with me. I, at least, am not afraid of your dark looks and your ugly disposition."

Shalbourne ground his teeth and shook off his friend's hand as he tried unsuccessfully to put on his coat.

"Let me help you." Denbigh, not to be put off by the vulgar epithet hurled at him, remarked, "Just so. And, now, if you have quite vented your spleen, here."

Shalbourne stared at my Lord Denbigh in indecision. Deciding that a scuffle for his topcoat in the middle of St. James Street would be far more undignified than the occasion warranted, he allowed himself to be helped into it without further comment. They continued their sojourn in silence for a few yards until Denbigh said, "As much as I enjoy a soothing stroll on such a clear evening, and as much as I am sure you are quite capable of marching to your apartments without the least assistance from either me or anyone else, I do hope you find it in your heart to take pity on me, Gay, and allow me to call a hackney."

Shalbourne muttered his reply. Denbigh, seeing that his lordship did not find favor with this suggestion, proposed an alternative. "Then, perhaps, you will come home with me for a small drink to fortify you on your way. My lodgings are just a step from here and as I have no desire to walk all the way to Mount Street with you, you would do well to avail yourself of my invitation.''

Shalbourne ground his teeth again.

''Really, Shalbourne, I cannot believe that is good for you.''

''Leave me alone, you interfering—'' Shalbourne began furiously.

''Oh, I have no intention of doing that. In your present state, I should be a very poor friend, indeed, if I were to let you wander the streets of London on your own. You would be bound to commit murder before the sun came up and I would so dislike the scandal. After all, Shalbourne, I am one of your dearest friends. It would undoubtedly reflect upon me.'' Denbigh stopped suddenly to consider. ''Perhaps your only friend, after tonight. Really, Shalbourne, as much as Grey deserved that setdown, you must admit it was remarkably bad ton to name him what you did—and at Brook's, too! Really, I am quite shocked,'' he stated calmly as they resumed their walk.

Shalbourne smiled tentatively. ''Like hell you are.''

''Oh, but I am,'' Denbigh assured him at his most urbane. ''There, now, that's much better. How badly are you dipped after this night's work?''

''Denbigh, do you never lose your good humor?''

''No, I don't think that I do. One of my best traits, I should say.'' His lordship was proud of his accomplishments.

''One of your most exasperating ones,'' Shalbourne stated.

''Oh, no, how unjust of you to say so! When I have been at such pains for your sake. It has become quite exhausting, though, old boy, and I shall demand satisfaction of you shortly. Ah, here we are. Now you must, you shall, join me for a brandy.''

So it was only a few short minutes later that Shalbourne found himself ensconced in a chair by the fire in his friend's apartments. Like most bachelors living on the town, Denbigh lodged in a few rooms on the second floor of a house in the fashionable quarter of the city. He kept one servant, and as soon as that gentleman had brought their brandy, Denbigh dismissed him to his bed, saying that they would fend for themselves that night.

As soon as the two friends were alone, Denbigh demanded, "Well, Shalbourne?"

"Well, Denbigh?"

"Are you going to tell me why you set out this evening to lose what little money you have left, to drink yourself into a stupor, and to murder one of the pillars of society?"

"Pillars of society, George?" Shalbourne grinned for the first time that evening. "Coming it a bit too strong, my lad."

"Well, we shall allow that Grey is perhaps not one of the pillars of society, but, despite his actions to the contrary, he was *bred* a gentleman. Hipped, Gay?"

"Blue-deviled." Shalbourne tossed off his glass.

"Helena Forrester?" Denbigh asked quietly.

Shalbourne laughed bitterly. "Who else? Accused me of being a fortune hunter!"

"She should be so fortunate!" Denbigh poured his friend another glass from the decanter. He had been worried for days about Shalbourne's state of mind; ever since the afternoon they had made their list of possible brides. Enough brandy might serve to loosen Shalbourne's tongue and provide Denbigh with a full accounting of the events of the last three weeks. "You may as well know that your search for a wife has become common knowledge. Unfortunately, rumor has it that you're hanging out for a rich one."

"Rich? Ha!" Shalbourne said. "Egad, I'd be glad for any wife at this point!"

Denbigh was startled. "Any wife? What of our plans? Our list of candidates?"

Shalbourne smiled grimly. "You know my aunt's ultimatum. No wife. No money. I should be as rich as Croesus once I inherit Aunt Jane's fortune, but unless I find myself a respectable wife, I shall get nothing."

"Yes, yes, we discussed all that before!" Denbigh was impatient for a full explanation. "As for finding a wife, you know there must be plenty of women willing to share Auntie Jane's fortune. Mustn't give up just because Forrester was fool enough to turn you down."

"She's not the only one, Denbigh," Shalbourne explained wearily. "She wasn't my first choice, you know, even if she was yours. Didn't ask *her* until today."

"Not the only one . . . ?! You mean, you offered for another female first and she turned you down as well?" Denbigh, being prejudiced in his lordship's favor, was much shocked.

Shalbourne did not voice his reply. He merely lifted his hand and indicated the number four.

Denbigh nearly choked on the brandy that he had brought to his lips. "Four? You mean to tell me that three other women *and* Helena Forrester turned you down?"

"No," his lordship began.

"Well, thank God for that! For a moment—"

"No. Helena makes five," Shalbourne interrupted. "Four others besides her."

"Good God!" Denbigh swallowed his drink in one gulp and quickly poured himself another.

"Almost, Denbigh, you begin to restore my faith in myself." Shalbourne tossed off another glass of brandy. "I should have come to you sooner. You hearten me immeasurably. I had begun to wonder if perhaps I had become so hideous that no one could find me palatable."

"But, Gay! I don't understand it." Denbigh was a good

deal confused. "Egad, I didn't think there was a woman alive who could resist your charm when you chose to turn it in their direction. Why, that Woodbridge woman left Leyland for you! I mean, Leyland! I didn't think anyone had a chance against his romantic sop!"

"The Woodbridge woman was ripe for the picking. Leyland can be a dead bore after a few weeks of his poetry." Shalbourne smiled wryly at the memory of that dubious female.

"You mean to tell me," Denbigh asked, his voice incredulous, "that in the last three weeks, you have proposed to no less than five ladies and been rejected by all of them? I find that incredible!"

"I fear I misled you, George. Only one of the young *ladies* actually turned me down—Miss Forrester."

"What do you mean?"

"Why, only that Miss Jenkins' papa, being a Methodist, found he could not stomach my past. Miss Grant's mama, a close friend of my aunt I might add, was tempted by my expectations, but did not think them sure enough. And despite the fact that Lady Anne was found locked in my embrace in her father's study, my small earldom was not exactly what his grace had in mind for his darling daughter. Are you getting my point, Denbigh? As much as the young lady herself might find me to her taste, her parents like not my reputation, my unsure future, or my unimportant title. Ah, but you are thinking, mayhaps I have set my sights too high? But even Old Winslowe had objections to me—"

"Winslowe! Why, the old goat positively smells of the shop! Don't tell me he objected to your title! It's common knowledge he'll pay through the nose for a baronetcy, much less an earldom!"

"Ah, so I thought, my dear George," Shalbourne answered. "But it seems that a man of my unsavory ways could not possibly be expected to make his little girl a suitable husband. Who would have thought the old man actually had his daughter's happiness at heart?''

"Gay, I cannot believe there is no one!''

"Oh, perhaps if Princess Charlotte had not died so unexpectedly or if this were during the season, I would have had better luck. However, town is a bit thin of company. And, now, with the funeral over, most have gone to the country for Christmas.''

"Then, there's no help for it, you shall have to attend Almack's on opening night next April and see what's being offered as the new crop,'' Denbigh spoke philosophically. "I'll arrange vouchers, never fear. Your feud with Princess Esterhazy . . .''

"Is irrelevant. You forget, there is some urgency involved here, George. The longer I remain unshackled, the greater the chance that Aunt Jane will die without having made me heir,'' Shalbourne explained, his face regaining some of its dark, brooding look.

"Is there really any danger of that? She seemed healthy enough,'' Denbigh began.

"Like a horse, as far as I can tell. However, I received this in the post three days ago.'' Shalbourne pulled a dog-eared and crumpled bit of vellum from an inner pocket of his coat. "Listen to this. 'Dear nephew, I was most pleased to hear from Lady Fairfax that you have taken my words to heart, etc., etc.' '' Shalbourne flipped the sheet over and scanned for the sentence he wanted. "Ah, here we are . . . 'Am very happy to inform you that I find I will be able to spend the Christmas season with you and your fiancée at Shalbourne Manor . . .' '' Shalbourne crumpled the note. "Faugh!'' he exclaimed in disgust.

"So?'' Denbigh shrugged. "Put her off. Explain you haven't found the right girl yet. She shouldn't be that difficult to stall. You're a clever fellow. Surely you can think of something.''

"Haven't met my Aunt Jane, have you, Denbigh?" Shalbourne asked. "I swear the woman is positively too clever by half. Won't be so easy to fob off. Lady Fairfax won't be the first to tell my aunt what the odds are that I shall be producing a fiancée for her inspection over Christmas. I'm sure Mrs. Grant will delight in telling her firsthand just how well my campaign to find a wife is progressing." Shalbourne ran an agitated hand through his hair. "Good Lord, George! The last thing I want to do is to have to face her without some female in tow when she'll soon know I've already asked at least one young lady. I can't let her think that no one will have me! My God, *that* would really drive home the nails in my coffin!"

"Then, there is nothing else to do, old boy. Have to marry the Woodbridge woman," Denbigh stated flatly.

"The devil you say! My dear George, I may be a ramshackle fellow with no reputation to speak of, but I do know what I owe my name! Woodbridge?!" He spoke her name with distaste. "She's nothing more than a common prostitute! Woodbridge to be Countess of Shalbourne? Even *I* would not stoop so low."

Denbigh interrupted his friend before he could continue. "No need to shout, old fellow. I understand. Just a joke, really. I would never seriously entertain such a suggestion."

"I may be a profligate and a wastrel, but my wife shall be both respectable and chaste!" Shalbourne barked at his lordship.

Denbigh roared with laughter. "My God, Shalbourne, you should hear yourself! I can't believe you of all people. Chaste, you say! Egad! You demand chastity!"

Shalbourne had the grace to turn a slight red underneath his tan. "I've told you before—they'll be no brats not of my parentage in my household! I don't think that's a great deal to ask. Oh, come, Denbigh, be reasonable. A man may be a rake with the morals of a Lothario but he wants his wife's virtue to be unquestioned.''

"Naturally." Denbigh grinned at his friend. "Oh, you are quite in the right on it, Shalbourne. A man may have as many mistresses as he pleases, but his wife may have only one master.''

"Find that hypocritical, Denbigh?" Shalbourne inquired politely.

"What do you think?" Denbigh replied.

"Then why don't you make Eileen the Viscountess Denbigh?" Shalbourne asked in a bland tone, gazing intently at his brandy glass.

"Eileen? The woman's a trollop!" It was Denbigh's turn to color. "Ah, Shalbourne, your trick I believe."

The two gentlemen fell into a brooding silence.

"There's no help for it, Gay," Denbigh sighed. "I fear you shall have to lower your standards a bit if you demand a wife in the next three weeks."

"Mayhaps I should take an advertisement out in the *Times*." Shalbourne was beginning to feel the effects of overindulging. "Wanted. A wife who is personable and presentable; a good knowledge of pianoforte and French a must. Cleanliness and wit also desirable. Apply no. 13 Mount Street."

Denbigh grinned. "You forget, Shalbourne. Only ladies of first respectability need apply."

"Nice touch, Denbigh. One must certainly add that line. I warrant you I would have any number of applicants." Shalbourne reached down and picked up one of the many newspapers that adorned Denbigh's sitting room. "Why, you can see that one advertises for any number of things. Here's a young lady seeking a position as a governess. And look this ad seeks a manservant who 'understands the business of the house and taking care of a horse and chaise and can generally make himself useful.' I wonder if I might add that as well, generally able to make herself useful around the house. Why, it stands to reason, Denbigh, somebody must read these advertisements, else there wouldn't be so many printed.''

"Oh, decidedly. And, no doubt, you should sign it, discreetly, of course, 'the Earl of S.' I daresay, by afternoon, you would find Mount Street a veritable sea of applicants." Denbigh laughed heartily with his friend at the vision of chaos such a notice would create.

Sitting comfortably in Denbigh's small parlor, they began to weave a ridiculous tale about the young ladies who would doubtless appear on Shalbourne's doorstep. As the decanter emptied and the fire's new coals turned fiery red, the two gentlemen became more outrageous in their speculations and more slurred in their speech. Finally, as the dawn approached, Shalbourne lasped into unconciousness on Denbigh's couch, his many-caped Garrick still on. After an unsuccessful attempt to remove his friend's coat, Denbigh, suppressing his drunken giggles, contented himself with the removal of Shalbourne's shoes and then made his way to bed. There, his lordship, in the act of removing his waistcoat, forgot his planned order of action and lay upon his pallet in what was left of his evening wear.

Well into the next morning, Denbigh's valet, cautiously picking his way through the array of sporting magazines, discarded clothing, and overturned chairs, as he brought his master his morning chocolate, sighed once again. The fact that his lordship, a personable young man and as a kind a master as anyone could wish for, was invariably disorganized and capable of creating shambles out of what had been, when his man retired, an impeccable surrounding, would always be a source of distress for that worthy retainer.

Denbigh groaned as his man ventured to shake his lordship awake. Whispering in kindly tones, Smithson said, "Excuse me, your lordship, but I took the liberty of mixing this for you and his lordship.''

Grateful, Denbigh gulped the brew his man had presented upon a silver tray and than spoke hoarsely, ''Thank you, Smithson. Did I understand you to say that there is someone else here?''

As he drew back the drapes and began to gather up his lordship's discarded garments, Smithson explained, ''Yes, mi'lord. My Lord Shalbourne spent the night, it appears, upon your settee. Needless to say, his lordship's leg is not what it might otherwise be this morning.''

Denbigh was insulted by the reproachful note in his man's voice. ''If you are suggesting what I think, I'd like to know how I was to persuade Shalbourne to take my bed instead of the damned settee! Even if his lordship had been cognizant of his surroundings when I retired (which I take leave to say he was not!), I doubt even my persuasions could have seduced him to take the bed over the delightful prospect of reposing upon the settee. My God, man, you know his damnable pride as well as I do! My guess is that he would have walked home to his own bed before he would have put me out of mine. Not that that course was an option, mind you. You may have noted that despite the fact that Shalbourne had on his coat, his plans did not proceed in the manner in which he had intended.''

''Yes, mi'lord.'' Smithson felt the necessity of acknowledging his lordship's tirade in some manner. ''Now, your lordship, if I might remove your clothing, I'm sure we can find a more suitable, and certainly less wrinkled, outfit for you this morning.''

Denbigh allowed himself to be assisted out of his crumpled garments and into fresh linen before he felt the necessity to speak again.

''Breakfast laid out in the sitting room?'' Denbigh inquired as Smithson helped him into his brocade dressing gown.

"Yes, mi'lord," Smithson answered. "His lordship has already started to partake. I have taken the liberty of lending him our pluche dressing gown as well as some fresh linen while I endeavor to remove some of the creases from his Garrick and evening coat."

"Thank you, Smithson. I shall be out momentarily." Denbigh ran a brush through his golden locks while Smithson silently retreated.

A few minutes later, his hair having been carefully combed into a careless windswept style, Denbigh entered his sitting room to find my Lord Shalbourne already seated at the table, his head obscured from view behind one of the morning newspapers. Shalbourne grunted his greeting as Denbigh said good morning. Denbigh, deciding that his friend was not in need of conversational company this morning, picked up the *Chronicle* as Shalbourne had already laid claim to the *Times*. Glancing briefly at the first page, he began to chuckle silently as he remembered hazily their plans from the previous evening. Glancing over the columns of advertisements, he poured himself a cup of coffee. As he raised the cup to his lips, he noticed a particularly good bargain in horseflesh being offered.

Quite suddenly, his eye was caught by an advertisement near the top of the second column. He choked and spilled his coffee in his lap.

Chapter Eight

It has been said that all things come to he who waits. Denbigh, as he yawned and closed his eyes, was beginning to doubt the truth of that statement. Never could he remember being so bored as he was at this moment.

In an initial burst of enthusiasm, he had taken his curricle to the address given in the advertisement, thinking that a personal communication was more likely to produce results than an impersonal letter. He had been gravely disappointed to discover that the address where the letters were to be sent was not the home of the young lady, the mysterious "Miss H.," but merely a receiving office for her correspondence. As a matter of fact, the address turned out to be a small milliner's shop in a less fashionable quarter of the shopping district, patronized by the wives of city merchants and bankers.

Determined to stay until the young lady put in an appearance, he knew from the harassed proprietress that a Miss Hackett, who had arranged for her correspondence to be sent to the shop, had not yet come to check on her mail. The proprietress shrugged negatively when Denbigh asked if she happened to know the direction of this Miss Hackett's home.

Denbigh, who was discouraged by this response, convinced himself that, certainly, this Miss Hackett must surely come that afternoon to find out if she had had any answers to her advertisement. In a helpful spirit (Denbigh having passed her a few pound notes), the milliner sent two of her assistants to bring down her best chair from her apartments above the shop so that Lord Denbigh might sit in comfort. In fact, his chair had been placed as close as the proprietress had dared to the display window, as he lent a decidedly fashionable air to the shop. Denbigh, unaware that he was being displayed, settled down to wait and enjoy the view.

By now, the edition of the *Morning Chronicle* he clutched in his hand was dirty and worn since he referred to it at least once every ten minutes. He had not told my Lord Shalbourne about his intentions, rudely pushing his friend out the door after breakfast in his anxiety to be the first to answer the ad. That way, if things did not work out, Denbigh would save Shalbourne from being disappointed.

Lord Denbigh speculated once again as he reread the words on the printed page. "Matrimony," the advertisement ran. "A Young Lady of superior education, and person above mediocrity, who in a few months comes into possession of a considerable fortune, being urged to a connection which she abhors, from the avaricious disposition of her guardian, wishes anxiously to meet a young gentleman of good person and disposition, settled in any respectable situation (no matter how distant from town), who would free her in an honorable way from her present distressing situation. Letters (post paid to insure delivery as the advertiser is not known) addressed to Miss H., no. 7, Church-passage, Picadilly, will be attended to as soon as difficulties experienced allow of."

Unfortunately, as the afternoon crept by, the novelty of watching the various customers perform for his benefit soon began to pale. Consulting his pocket watch for the eighth time in less than an hour, he had just come to the conclusion that his vigil was useless when a young lady stepped into the shop followed by an older woman who was clearly her maid.

"Now that's what I call a pretty face!" Denbigh thought to himself as he sat up with the first sign of interest all afternoon.

The young lady, petite, blond, and expensively, if not fashionably, dressed, stomped her feet daintily to remove the snow from her pattens. Denbigh's heart beat quickly when the milliner nodded significantly in his direction. Leaping from his chair, which he knocked over in his zeal, Denbigh grinned excitedly. If this was indeed the young lady who had placed the advertisement in the *Chronicle*, then his friend Shalbourne was in for a bit of luck for a change!

He took a step forward as the young lady handed the milliner a few coins and asked in a soft voice if she had had any mail.

"Miss Mirabelle Hackett!" Jenny said in a disapproving tone. "Just what are you up to, young lady? Are you carrying on a clandestine correspondence? Why, if I'd known . . ."

Before Mirabelle could respond to this accusation, Denbigh caught her attention by politely doffing his hat and said, "Miss Mirabelle Hackett, is it?"

"Yes?" Mirabelle said uncertainly, taking a step closer to the frowning, disapproving Jenny for protection. "I'm afraid you have the advantage of me, sir."

"Miss Mirabelle!" Jenny hissed in her charge's ear. "Just what are you about? Have you arranged to meet this gentleman here away from your father's eye?"

"Oh, sorry," Denbigh said, ignoring Jenny's outburst and addressing himself exclusively to the exquisite creature before him. "Allow me to introduce myself." He bowed politely and continued, "Ashton, George Ashton. Friends call me Denbigh."

"Do they? Denbigh, you say. How . . . singular of them." Mirabelle smiled in pretty confusion, charmed by his manner despite her determination to remain aloof. After all, it would never do to allow a strange young gentleman to accost her in this manner, no matter how handsome or well bred he might be.

"Oh, stupid of me, should have explained myself!" Denbigh exclaimed as he reached into an inside pocket of his coat. "Here, my card." He produced an elegant gold case and extracted an engraved calling card.

Mirabelle glanced briefly at the card he had handed her. What she saw there caused her eyes to widen and her mouth to drop. Her attention was riveted to the last entry. Slowly, she raised her eyes to regard the gentleman standing next to her. Blinking, she gazed in awe at the tall, lithe form, noting the blond curls which were meticulously brushed into a windswept style. His well-cut coat of blue superfine set off to perfection his broad shoulders and small waist. His waistcoat was of an exceptionally fine, embroidered cloth and his biscuit-colored breeches were of the first stare of fashion. His greatcoat sported a remarkable number of capes. The fine beaver hat he held in his hand was matched in elegance by his silver-tipped walking stick and kid gloves.

Jenny grabbed the card from Mirabelle's nerveless fingers and struggled to read aloud. " 'George Archibald Charles Ashton, Viscount Denbigh.' Viscount Denbigh!" Jenny gasped and stared in much the same manner as her mistress at the young man.

Denbigh, who was beginning to feel a bit like a giraffe in a zoo, noticed that all the ladies in the shop were staring. Even the proprietress, who had become inured to his presence that afternoon, was impressed anew.

As she shifted uncomfortably, Mirabelle, too stunned to fathom the reason for his boldness and too overwhelmed to be insulted by it, inquired politely, "What can I do for you, my lord?"

"You could do a great favor for me, Miss Hackett,"

Denbigh explained. "If I could just persuade you to speak with me for a moment or two. Are you on your way to any place in particular? My curricle is outside and I would be happy to escort you wherever you might like to go."

"Miss Mirabelle, you ain't never going to get in no carriage with this stranger, are you?" Jenny exclaimed.

"Jenny, please!" Mirabelle addressed her maid in an undertone. Although aware of the impropriety of accepting such an invitation, Mirabelle was tempted, if only for curiosity's sake.

"You are the 'Miss H.' who advertised in the *Chronicle* this morning, aren't you?"

"What?" Jenny squealed.

Mirabelle blushed a fiery red and bit her bottom lip in consternation. She hadn't wanted Jenny to know that! "Excuse me a moment, Jenny, I would like to speak to this gentleman alone. Let us step outside, sir, where we might discuss this more privately."

"Miss Mirabelle!" Jenny scolded.

"Jenny!" Mirabelle warned. "I'll be right back."

With that, she allowed Denbigh to hold open the door for her and preceded him out of the shop. Standing on the sidewalk in front of the shop window, she and Lord Denbigh provided entertainment and much speculation for the ladies inside. Everyone, including the shop's owner, had halted what they were doing to join Jenny in her vigil at the window. Unfortunately for the audience, the show was a silent one.

Meanwhile, under Jenny's and the others' disapproving eye, Mirabelle addressed my Lord Denbigh. "My lord, I shall not deny that I am the 'Miss H.' of that advertisement, as such denial would be quite useless. However, I don't know what reason you may have had for seeking me out in this manner, since you are obviously a gentleman who does not need to look to such a source for a wife. Well, I take leave to suggest that I doubt your sincerity, and cannot help but think that perhaps you are trying to make a May-game of something that is of the utmost importance to me. Therefore . . ."

"Please, Miss Hackett," Denbigh spoke and took her hand in his. The audience in the shop leaned closer. "You must believe me when I say that you are in a position to do me a great service. However, the street is hardly conducive to serious discussion. Are you sure I can't persuade you to take a turn in my curricle so that we might continue this conversation with a little more privacy? I know we have not been properly introduced, and I am fully aware that a young lady of your obvious breeding would not normally consent to such an action on so short an acquaintance, but you will admit that the circumstances are unique. And really, it is most important that I speak with you. A letter would never have done." Denbigh gazed soulfully into Mirabelle's eyes.

Mirabelle, who had not thought to retrieve her hand during this speech, was completely bowled over by his charm. She knew only a moment's hesitation. The gentleman's sincere tone and the earnest look that had gone with his entreaty convinced her that he had only the purest of motivations. Biting her lip again, she wondered to herself what he would think of her if she willingly went for a ride in his curricle without the benefit of proper introduction. Ah, well, too late really to care what the young gentleman thought. His opinion of her was probably fixed already, for what could he think of a young lady who could place that kind of advertisement on the front page of the *Chronicle*? Besides, it would be too cruel to her cousin, Isolde, if she allowed this gentleman to slip though her fingers. With a quick nod of her head, she consented to his plan.

A displeased Jenny watched from the shop window as Denbigh brought Mirabelle's hand to his lips, turned away and hailed a man who was walking a high-perched phaeton up and down the street with two perfectly matched bays. Since she believed that Mirabelle had dismissed the gentleman and he was setting off, Jenny did not hurry out to join her young mistress. Therefore, it was with horror-stricken eyes that she watched Lord Denbigh hand Miss Mirabelle up to the passenger seat and then climb up next to her. As Jenny flew out to stop them, Denbigh instructed his groom to wait for their return.

"I hope you are quite comfortable, Miss Hackett. There is a rug on the seat if you should require it," Denbigh said politely.

"Oh, no, thank you, my lord," Mirabelle reassured him. "My muff and redingote are quite enough to keep me warm."

"I suppose if I had been thinking, I would have brought my coach instead of a vehicle open to the elements."

"Oh, no, this is much better! I should never have consented to accompany you in a closed carriage!" Mirabelle, as yet unaware that she had left her maidservant lecturing his lordship's servant on all the terrible things that would happen to that young rake Lord Denbigh for his improper advances, added, "Surely no one can challenge the propriety of my riding with you in an open one. Oh, you do have lovely horses! Even Sir James of my late uncle's parish never had so fine a pair. And he quite prided himself on his stables, you know."

"Sir James?" Denbigh prompted, anxious for any information that might shed light on the girl's background.

"Sir James Danforth. Oh, I don't wish to deceive you, my lord. I never had anything more than a nodding acquaintance with Sir James. I doubt he would remember the awkward, ugly little girl that used to visit her uncle in Lincolnshire, but I do remember his horses!"

"Surely never ugly, Miss Hackett!" Denbigh said with great gallantry as Mirabelle blushed and disclaimed. "So your uncle was with the church, was he?'' Denbigh went fishing again after a pause.

"Oh, yes," Mirabelle said proudly. "He was almost a bishop, too!"

"Almost a bishop?"

"Yes. It was quite tragic, really. He and my aunt were killed in a carriage accident just a few weeks before he was to be elevated."

Better and better, Dengigh thought to himself. There was certainly no question of Miss Hackett's respectability. Odd that she should have chosen the medium of the *Chronicle* to find a husband, especially as remarkably pretty as she was. Still, her eccentricity was certainly Shalbourne's fortune!

"Miss Hackett, I am not unaware that there is a certain amount of awkwardness attached to our situation, but I must be frank with you and I hope you will be the same with me."

"Of course, my lord," Mirabelle was cautious. Surely this young lord who gave all the appearance of being possessed of both wealth and position did not need to look for a wife in a newspaper? But what else was she to think? Isolde, a Viscountess! That would surely be something like!

Denbigh continued, "Miss Hackett, if you are still of the same mind you were when you placed that advertisement in the *Chronicle*, I have a proposal to lay before you."

Was this personable, wealthy, attractive young man going to offer for her cousin? It was even better than she could have imagined!

"I have a friend, Miss Hackett, a very close friend who is in need of a wife," Denbigh stated.

"A friend?" Mirabelle was disappointed.

"Yes. My friend needs a wife because of his aunt."

"His aunt?" Mirabelle was confused.

"Damn, I seem to be making a mull of this. Miss Hackett, my friend's aunt is a very wealthy woman. She has decided that for the sake of his family name, and for whatever other reasons known only to herself, that she wants him to marry. My friend"—Denbigh ran his fingers through his hair—"Oh, hell, ah, excuse me, Miss Hackett, I may as well tell you his name so I don't have to keep referring to him as 'my friend.' It's Shal . . . ah, Leighton." Denbigh made a quick decision. If this girl was as respectably middle-class as she appeared, she might not want to marry "the Gay Lord." Damn Shalbourne's reputation anyway! He thought it best to deceive her just a bit. "Edmund Leighton."

The castles Mirabelle had been building in the air had crumpled without a trace. Ah, well, she hadn't really believed she could be so lucky as to produce so wonderful a suitor as a real Viscount. Really, that had been very foolish! she thought. She might have known that he was just like her, acting as a go-between for another. Mirabelle listened as the young gentleman continued.

"Well, Edmund's aunt wants him to marry so he must. There's only one problem. Edmund's too shy to ask anyone." Denbigh stopped briefly to steal a glance at Mirabelle's face and test her reaction to this blatant lie. Besides, he argued with himself, it was all in a good cause and harmless enough. Since he knew his friend to be a paragon, it would be grossly unfair if his reputation should prevent him once again from procuring a suitable bride.

"Is that why he sent you?" Mirabelle asked.

"Sent me? Oh, no, Edmund would run me through if he knew what I was doing!" Denbigh uttered before he had had time to think. "Oh, don't misunderstand me, Miss Hackett! It's not that Edmund wouldn't want you as his wife, it's just that he seems to have some cork-brained notion that he should find one for himself."

Mirabelle, who had begun to giggle quite early on in his speech, set out to rectify his misconception. "Oh, no, my lord! It isn't me who needs a husband! It's my cousin! Isolde!"

"The devil you say!" Denbigh jerked on the reins in his agitation. The next few minutes were spent in bringing his horses back under control. "Your cousin?" he asked, as disappointed as she had been earlier.

"Yes. She is the daughter of the uncle that I was telling you about. My father, who is her guardian, is forcing her to marry the most perfectly awful young man. And, unfortunately, we don't go about in society very much and it seems we never get to meet eligible men! So I thought that if I only advertised in the newspaper, I was bound to find any number of gentlemen to choose from."

Denbigh latched on to this excuse as a Godsend. "Oh, yes, yes, I perfectly understand. Edmund's the same way. Painfully shy, he is. Too shy to even speak to a girl, much less ask her to marry him. And, too, none of his friends are old enough to have daughters of marriageable age. Doesn't get out much. Never sees anyone. Doesn't go to parties. Never takes his nose out of book long enough to notice women, much less ask one to marry him." Denbigh hoped that heaven would forgive him the picture he was painting. More importantly, he hoped Shalbourne would forgive him.

"Oh? Is he very bookish?" Mirabelle asked.

"Oh, yes," Denbigh further perjured his soul. "Quite the scholar he is. Used to call him 'professor' up at Oxford."

"Oh, did you go to Oxford together?" Mirabelle was awed by the possibility.

"Yes," Denbigh answered truthfully for the first time in ten minutes. "I won't wrap it up in clean linen, Miss Hackett. I've already told you that Edmund is too shy to have come to you on his own. I doubt he'd have the courage even to write to you. But he's a good man, a great friend. Always willing to help his comrades. Did I mention he's a war hero?" Denbigh neglected to mention which war. He thought it best to let her believe it was the more glamorous Napoleonic campaigns in the peninsula than the less prestigious tiff with the Colonies. "Would never treat your cousin with anything but respect. Puts women on a pedestal—probably what makes him so shy with them. Never gambles—well, not excessively anyway. Has a house in town and two in the country as well as a personal income of over four thousand a year. And with what he stands to inherit from his aunt, I dare swear his income could eventually rival 'Golden Ball Hughes.' "

Mirabelle laughed. "My lord! You quite overwhelm me! What I can't understand is why this paragon has not been snatched up before? Surely some lady with a bit of resolution in her character should have caught him in parson's mousetrap 'ere now? Come, sir"—Mirabelle's eyes sparkled merrily—"the truth now. What is wrong with him?"

Denbigh blushed and stammered, "Ah, well. You have me there. I see I shall have to make clean breast of it. You see, Edmund received some rather severe wounds in the War. I did mention that he was a . . ."

"A war hero. Yes, you did," Mirabelle finished for him.

Denbigh coughed and continued reluctantly. "Ah, yes, well, Edmund has a rather large scar on his face. Runs from here to here." Denbigh indicated his temple to his cheek. "He has several others as well, but not where they can be seen. And, well, he limps rather badly."

"Limps?" Mirabelle asked with sweet sympathy.

"I don't want you to think your cousin would be tying herself to a cripple. But Edmund can't ride for very long at a time. Has the devil of a time being comfortable in a carriage for more than a few hours. And, he'll never be inclined to escort his wife dancing."

"Oh, the poor dear man!" Mirabelle's soft heart was touched by the image Denbigh had painted. "How sad! I quite see now why he is so very shy. It must be very hard for him to go out into company. Well, you may rest assured, my cousin would only have the greatest respect for the manner in which he received his wounds, and never think twice about them after that. He can get about without assistance, can't he?''

"Oh, lord, yes!" Denbigh was adamant, realizing he might have gone a bit too far in his description. "Just that you won't see him walking when he could ride and no fear of him coming into a room unexpectedly. Always hear him coming up the stairs. And slow at it, too.''

"Is he a young gentleman?" Mirabelle asked anxiously.

"Of an age with myself," Denbigh replied. "And, personally, I don't consider thirty-two old.''

"And you say he has a good disposition?"

"The best.''

"I assume his person is adequate, aside from the wounds you described.''

"Oh, yes. Very handsome fellow, but for those.''

"I should think," Mirabelle added reverently, "that they would add rather than detract from his appearance! After all, one might say they were his medals!''

"Ah, exactly," Denbigh agreed uncertainly.

"And he certainly wouldn't have any entanglements, since he is so shy with women!" Mirabelle was pleased. "So, it sounds as if he were perfect!''

"Well, I don't know if I should go quite that far.''

"Oh, you know what I mean. It's just that he meets all the requirements that my cousin set forth for me," Mirabelle explained.

"Ah, yes. Speaking of your cousin. Do you suppose you could tell me a bit more about her. Not that I doubt she would be perfect for Mr. Leighton!" Denbigh hastened to tell her. "It's just that I told you so much about Edmund.''

"Oh, of course, I quite understand." Mirabelle was happy to oblige. "Well, Isolde's father was a clergyman and she lived in Lincolnshire most of her life. She's lived with my family in London since her parents died two years ago. She's rather tall, I'm afraid.''

"Oh, no problem there. Edmund's almost six foot.''

"Oh, lovely!'' Mirabelle enthused. "Well, my cousin has dark hair and sort of blue eyes and, oh, she's just much prettier than I could ever hope to be!''

Denbigh gave his companion a startled look and was even more surprised to see that she seemed to be completely sincere.

"She is almost twenty-one.'' Mirabelle gave this information reluctantly, as if it were something to be ashamed of. "And she doesn't know how to sew very well or paint watercolors at all. But she can play the pianoforte quite nicely.'' Mirabelle brightened as she spoke of her cousin's good points. "And she can read and write both Latin and Greek. She also speaks French. Oh, she's really quite a nice girl and I truly love her! It's such a shame that we don't know anyone other than Mr. Biggelswade and Mr. Rutherford!''

"Mr. Who and Mr. Who?'' Denbigh asked.

"Biggelswade and Rutherford. Mr. Rutherford is, well, not interested in my cousin, and Mr. Biggelswade is her fiancée.''

"Egad! Then it's no wonder your cousin doesn't wish to marry him! Lord, imagine changing your name to Biggelsbane!''

"Wade.''

"What?''

"Never mind,'' Mirabelle said. "It's of no consequence. Suffice it to say that my cousin is being forced to wed that gentleman against her will, and that she said she would rather wed the devil himself than Harold!''

"The devil?'' Denbigh chuckled to himself, how appropriate!

Mirabelle just then realized that although she had paid for

her letters, she had been interrupted by his lordship before she had actually received them. With a shrug of dismissal and without a pang of regret, she promptly forgot those letters and the gentlemen who wrote them and jumped whole-heartedly into arranging a match between her cousin and Mr. Leighton. "There is just one minor problem," she said.

"What is that, Miss Hackett?"

"Well, the wedding between my cousin and Mr. Biggels-wade is set for Saturday next. The banns have already been called and invitations sent. If she is to escape this match, she must wed by special license before the week is out."

"Ah, I see." Denbigh nodded his head sagely. "Well, it just so happens that Mr. Leighton is anxious to be wed quickly, too, as his aunt wants to meet his bride during the Christmas season."

Mirabelle and Denbigh fell to a discussion of the urgency of the matter. They considered and discarded several possible days, deciding on Friday morning. They agreed that Denbigh would take care of producing a license and that as soon as he had made arrangements with a minister, he would have a note sent around by hand to Mirabelle's home with the information. Halting in front of the milliner's shop once again, Denbigh and Mirabelle took leave of one another, very pleased with themselves and each other. Both were convinced they had gotten the better bargain and felt that any difficulties that might arise between them could be ar-ranged easily enough to their mutual satisfaction. They parted company the best of friends, both looking forward to meeting again on Friday.

Each set out for home with the same thought in mind, though. Now would come the troublesome interview—persuading the principals of the piece to consent to the plot!

Chapter Nine

Although it is not unknown for a couple to meet at the altar, it must certainly be a nerve-wracking experience for the two persons involved. In the case of Gaylord Edmund Alastair Leighton, Earl of Shalbourne, and Miss Isolde Genevive Marsh, spinster, only the direst of necessities and the pressures of a limited amount of time could have induced them to consent to such a program.

"Are you disguised, Denbigh?" had been Lord Shalbourne's incredulous question when the subject had first been broached. "Because only a drunk would seriously expect me to wed this creature you've discovered!" He had gone on at great length at how cork-brained the scheme was, adding as his final objection, "My, God, man, I've never even laid eyes on the woman!"

Denbigh managed to squeeze in the fact that he had gone to all the trouble to investigate the girl's story. "Ingelsides knows the family, I tell you. Oh, I know they're engaged in Trade, but, damn it, Gay, you were willing to take Winslowe's gal! Why not this one?"

"First of all, just who the hell is Ingelsides?"

"Why, my man of business, of course. And I might add the girl will soon be part owner of a very tidy little spice and tea importing company."

"Spice and tea!" Words failed Shalbourne. "Who the hell cares?" he managed after a moment. "Just tell me this, George, what kind of brazen hussy would advertise for a husband in the *Times*, for God's sake!"

"No, no, you've got it all wrong, old boy. It was the *Chronicle*," Denbigh reassured him.

"Oh, well! That makes all the difference in the world, of course" was Shalbourne's biting reply.

Denbigh, inspired by his friend's skepticism, became amazingly eloquent. It took all the powers of persuasion he possessed, but he eventually managed to convince Shalbourne that things were not as havey-cavey as they seemed.

Shalbourne's fate was sealed when Thursday's post brought yet another communication from his Aunt Jane. In it, she expressed displeasure at the fact that she had not heard a word from him in regards to an impending betrothal. Furthermore, she had heard the most scurrilous rumors to the effect that no one would have him. She hoped that when she came to Shalbourne Manor at Christmas he would be able to prove the falsehood of those stories by introducing her to the future Countess.

As he uncorked his third bottle of Burgundy at Watier's that evening, his aunt's letter in hand, Shalbourne was amazed to find that Denbigh's plan had a lot to be said for it. "Would it be asking too much to meet this Elsie Hackett before the ceremony?" he had asked plaintively.

Denbigh, who had lent only half an ear to Mirabelle's prattle and none at all to Ingelsides', had erroneously informed Shalbourne about Isolde's name. "I don't think that such a good idea, old boy," Denbigh refilled Shalbourne's glass. "Especially in light of what that advertisement said about the girl's guardian. Ingelsides, too, wasn't too keen on the fellow." Anyway, he shrugged, Shalbourne was caught either way. Best to get the distasteful deed over as quickly as possible without such unnecessary complications. If Gay would only present himself at St. George's Church in South Audley Street on the morrow, he could meet his formidable aunt with a clear conscience and a lovely wife. "After all, old boy, if Auntie Jane wants to meet your fiancée, think how much more pleased she will be with you if confronted with a fait accompli."

"Lovely?" Shalbourne asked, hopeful, mournful, drunk.

Denbigh, who was sure the gods could not be so cruel as to saddle Miss Mirabelle Hackett with anything but a beautiful cousin, lied without a qualm. "Of course. Ingelsides said so."

Meanwhile, Isolde was every bit as shocked as Shalbourne at the proposed union. She was scandalized that Mirabelle had dared to make arrangements on her behalf based on what had originally been a jest, and wouldn't listen to what her cousin might have to say in recommendation for the scheme.

"It's nothing to me if the man was a war hero, Mirabelle!" Isolde emphatically stated. "I will not wed a man I've never even seen! Have you?"

"Have I what?"

"Have you seen the gentleman in question or only gotten a second-hand description from this Lord Dimwit?"

"I have too seen him!" Mirabelle perjured her soul as easily as Denbigh. "And his name's Lord Denbigh."

"No. It's Lord Dimwit. And you are Miss Halfwit if you think I will lend myself to such an outrageous proposition. In fact, Mirabelle, I cannot help feeling that you are the victim of the gentleman's warped sense of humor. Furthermore, I take leave to suggest that this gentleman is no more Lord Denbigh than I am . . . Napoleon Bonaparte!"

Since she absolutely refused to discuss the issue further, Mirabelle was left frustrated and impatient. On the same Thursday evening that Denbigh was engaged in getting his friend too intoxicated to object, she, too, suffered a veritable stroke of genius. She persuaded her mother to invite Harold Biggelswade to join the family for dinner. By the time Harold departed that evening, Isolde had not only consented to the scheme, she had become even more enthusiastic than Mirabelle.

As the candles guttered in their sockets, Mirabelle sneaked into her cousin's chamber to discuss details. Mirabelle enthusiastically applauded Isolde's decision to go through with the marriage with "this stranger" (as Isolde was wont to call him). And she further pointed out that as far as she could tell, Isolde had but two choices; on the morrow she could marry Mr. Leighton who had viscounts for friends and was a war hero to boot, or she could wed Harold Biggelswade the day after.

Isolde, who had acknowledged the truth of this dismal declaration, further exclaimed, "For as much as I dislike the thought of marrying this stranger, I hate more the idea of being tied to that swine for the rest of my life! This is one time I should rather have the devil I don't know than the one I do! God knows, Beelzebub himself could not be more repugnant to me than Harold Biggelswade!"

It became necessary to take Jenny into their confidence when she burst into the bedchamber in time to hear Isolde's last remark. Once Mirabelle had given an expunged and garbled version of the proposition, Jenny, as relieved as Isolde, announced she was glad that her young lady "wouldna hafta marry that blighter!" They could not have known that Jenny had developed an intense dislike for Mr. Biggelswade on the evening that Isolde had come home with a blackened eye, and so were further astonished when Jenny even went so far as to promise the services of her husband, Jonathan "Coachman," as an escort to the church the next day.

"For the Good Lord knows sich a hole-in-the-corner affair ain't what I would have chosen for you, Miss Isolde," she exclaimed, "but washing floors on Sunday for some heathen wild Indian would be better than marrying that man! And though your uncle may turn me off without a character for helping ye elope in this havey-cavey fashion, the good Lord will surely reward me in the next life fer sich an action. And that's a fact!" Although Mirabelle and Isolde were a bit startled by Jenny's diatribe, they were in complete sympathy with the sentiment she expressed.

When it was mentioned that the bride and groom were to leave immediately following the ceremony for a sojourn in Nottinghamshire, Jenny became quite animated. She bustled about the room, busily packing "bare necessities" for such a journey into two large wicker hampers and three bandboxes. "And what's more, Miss Isolde, I'll be able to take 'em down to the coach tonight while the rest of the house is abed so no one'll be the wiser."

Mirabelle applauded the cleverness of Jenny's plan, since she herself had not previously considered the need for a change of clothing for the bride, much less enough to allow her to be comfortable for a fortnight or two. As Mirabelle threw herself into the spirit of Jenny's task by offering free advice on what to take and vetoing one or two items of her cousin's wardrobe that Jenny wanted to include, Isolde grabbed Mirabelle's arm and dragged her across the room out of Jenny's earshot. "You didn't mention this before!" Isolde hissed angrily.

"If you'd have let me show you Lord Denbigh's note about the arrangements he'd made . . ." Mirabelle started.

Ignoring this very reasonable defense, Isolde stated with finality, "I can't go to Nottinghamshire with a strange man! Alone!"

"He won't be a strange man—he'll be your husband." Mirabelle pointed out reasonably. "There's nothing improper in that. Besides, I think it's a brillant idea to leave London."

"Why, then you may go to Nottinghamshire in my place!" Isolde replied unreasonably. "And with my blessing, too!"

It was when Jenny, in her artless prattle as she folded a morning gown, mentioned the fact that if they planned things well, Mr. Hackett need never know where Miss Isolde had gone, and with her out of London altogether, there was no chance of an unplanned meeting, that Isolde began to see that the groom's desire to whisk his bride off to Nottinghamshire did have something to be said for it.

"Yes. Do you want Papa hot on your heels demanding that the marriage be set aside?" Mirabelle drove the point home further. "If you remain in the wilds of Nottinghamshire until after your birthday in a few weeks time, there will be nothing Papa can do. In fact, I wish I were going with you, for then I should escape his questions!"

The next morning dawned bright and clear with only a bit of a nip in the air to remind one that it was December. Announcing their intention to anyone who would listen, Jenny and Mirabelle left in the family coach for a final fitting on Mirabelle's dress, which was to be worn for Isolde's wedding to Harold Biggelswade. Those who had been informed of this aim would have been somewhat surprised to see Jonathan Coachman pull the coach to a halt some three blocks away and pick up Miss Isolde, who had left earlier, claiming an errand in the opposite direction.

Isolde, who had honored the occasion with her best spencer of lavender-colored velvet and matching wide-brimmed poke bonnet with ribbons and ostrich plumes, was busily wiping the skirt of her matching floral-printed wool challis dress when she entered the coach. "It was fortunate you did not come a moment earlier. Mrs. Rutherford set upon me with that wretched little pug of hers. If she can't control the filthy little beast, I don't think she should be allowed to bring it in the vicinity of decent people!" Isolde was interestingly pale beneath her dark, chestnut curls and her companions allowed her to vent her spleen on Mrs. Rutherford without a murmur. The look that passed between Jenny and Mirabelle clearly showed they understood that Isolde's nervousness was causing her to be uncharacteristically harsh, and both sympathized with how nerve-wracking it must have been for Isolde to try and get rid of the nosy Mrs. Rutherford before the coach arrived.

Isolde was not the only nervous one. My Lord Denbigh was pacing up and down the small portico in front of St. George's Church when the Hackett coach pulled up. Denbigh heaved a sigh of relief, pocketed his watch, and strode up to open the coach door. Before he could carry out his intention, however, Jonathan called to him from the box, "Here, you! You this Mr. Leighton what my Miss Isolde's come to marry?"

Denbigh was as taken aback by the coachman's jaundiced eye as he was disconcerted by the question. "Ah, yes, ah, I mean, no, I'm not Mr. Leighton."

"Ah," Jonathan nodded his head sagely. "Then you must be the bloke what claims to be this Lord Denburgh."

"Denbigh!" He corrected indignantly. "And I don't claim to be him—I am!"

"Whatever." Jonathan remained unimpressed. "You just git one of those lads to come over here and hold these horses heads so's I kin meet this here Mr. Leighton, my lad."

Fortunately, since my Lord Denbigh was too stunned by Jonathan's impertinence to move, one of the "lads" came over of his own accord in the hopes of earning a shilling or two.

While Jonathan negotiated with the urchin, Jenny descended from the coach and caught Denbigh's attention by snorting, "Huh! You!"

Mirabelle's head peeked out and Lord Denbigh was rewarded with his first friendly countenance. "Ah, there you are! I knew you should not fail!"

Denbigh came out of his stupor and rushed to help Mirabelle descend. "Miss Hackett!"

"But where is Mr. Leighton?" Mirabelle looked around as her feet touched the ground.

"He is within, entertaining the worthy priest," Denbigh informed her. "But I might ask you the same. Where is your cousin?"

"Here, my lord," Isolde said as she held out her hand, waiting for him to assist her.

The first feeling that washed over my Lord Denbigh when he laid eyes on the bride was one of intense relief. It was vastly gratifying to know that he had not lied to his best friend when he had reassured him that his wife was sure to be "lovely." Although she could never be compared to her cousin, the beautiful Mirabelle, at least Shalbourne needn't be ashamed to be seen with his bride. He grinned at Isolde as he helped her from the coach.

"Miss Hackett," Denbigh addressed Isolde and bowed over her hand. "I'm very pleased to make your acquaintance."

Mirabelle giggled. "But I'm Miss Hackett, stoopid! This is my cousin, Miss Marsh."

Denbigh was confused. "Marsh?"

"Yes," Mirabelle said.

"Damn!" Denbigh cursed under his breath, then added in a louder voice, "Well, there's no help for it, I suppose. I shall have to tell the priest that I've mistaken the name. Sure it isn't Hackett? You are cousins, after all."

"I assure, my lord," Isolde eyes twinkled with humor for the first time that morning. Good Lord, the gentleman was every bit as half-witted as her beautiful cousin! she thought to herself. "My name is Marsh and has been from my birth. Although after today, I expect to change it."

"Huh?" Denbigh was more confused than ever. "Change it?"

"Yes. To Leighton, of course." Isolde smiled momentarily and then frowned as she wondered if Mr. Leighton were as dense as his friend. Ah, well, she supposed it was better to have a stupid husband than an offensive one.

"Well, if this ain't the whelp, where is he?" Jonathan interrupted, having settled the care of his horses to his satisfaction.

"He's inside the church," Mirabelle told the coachman.

"Well, am I going to see the young pup before these shenanigans start or not?" Jonathan demanded.

"What the devil?" Denbigh muttered to himself.

"This is Jonathan, Lord Denbigh." Mirabelle introduced her servant as if he had been a social equal to his lordship. "He's Jenny's husband. You remember Jenny, don't you? You met her the other day."

"Ah, of course," Denbigh said, thrown off his stride by these unexpected introductions. But not for nothing had he been trained in the social graces from an early age, he tipped his hat politely to the husband and wife, albeit with a somewhat bewildered expression on his face.

Isolde, who found much to her surprise that she was beginning to enjoy the proceedings, explained helpfully, "I think what my cousin is trying to tell you, my lord, is that Jonathan and Jenny insisted upon coming to make sure everything was quite aboveboard."

"Aye." Jonathan cast another suspicious look at Lord Denbigh. "Ye might be takin' advantage of my young ladies' innocence for all I know. Why, Miss Isolde never even had a proper conversation with this here Mr. Leighton as fer as I kin tell and it's clearly me Christian dooty to speak to the young dog before anyone kin make a mistake they might be regrettin' later."

Since Denbigh had no ready reply to this statement, it was

just as well that the verger stuck his head out of the church portal and demanded in a querulous voice, "Here, now, we going to have a wedding or not? The reverend don't like to miss his lunch, no how, and his missus won't keep it waitin' his pleasure or yours, fer that matter!"

The withered old gentleman shooed them into the church's vestibule where the ladies were instructed by Jonathan to wait, as there were certain things he needed to discuss with Mr. Leighton that were best said among men exclusively. He followed the complaining verger and Denbigh into the church hall where they eventually found the priest and Shalbourne in the church office.

If Denbigh had been surprised at the coachman's demands and intentions, a very hung-over Shalbourne was dumbfounded. As a result, the ensuing inquisition between the coachman and the earl did much to bear out Denbigh's rather inaccurate accounting of his friend's character as told to Mirabelle. Apprehensive already at the thought of saddling himself with a wife, exhausted by his trying half hour with the jaded priest, and stunned by Jonathan's impertinence, Shalbourne was hard pressed to give his usual sharp answers to the questions Jonathan was firing at him. However, his hesitant manner did him no disservice in Jonathan's eyes and it wasn't many minutes before Shalbourne had won Jonathan's approval.

Pocketing his watch, the priest interrupted before Shalbourne could regain his wits and say something he might regret. "If you are ready, gentleman, I think we should begin. I assume the bride is here," the priest said in a tone which stated very clearly that he very much doubted that she was.

"Aye, she's here right enough," the verger piped in.

"Perhaps I shan't miss my lunch, after all," the portly priest said, once again leaving his audience with the feeling that he was sure he would miss his meal.

The emaciated verger organized the group into the church

proper, where a stiff-necked Shalbourne stood next to his friend while the bored priest contemplated his lunch. The verger sent Jonathan to escort the bride in and as Jonathan departed on his errand, Shalbourne grabbed Denbigh's arm and demanded in a hushed voice, "What the devil is going on here, Denbigh? Who was that blackguard anyway? Her father?"

"Good Lord, no!" Denbigh was shocked at such an unjust accusation. "Her coachman, of course. I assure you, Gay, she's perfectly respectable."

"Damn it, man! So's the damned coachman, but that doesn't mean I want him for my father-in-law!"

Fortunately for Denbigh, the priest interrupted to ask the bride's name again. A harassed Denbigh glanced furtively at Shalbourne's stormy features and answered, "Marsh. Elsie Marsh."

"Marsh? Damn it, man, you said her name was Hackett!" Shalbourne whispered hoarsely.

"What's toward?" Denbigh asked, his eyes wide and innocent. "It's the same woman I told you of."

The priest coughed to get their attention as the bride was now standing next to them, clinging to Jonathan's arm as if it were the only thing keeping her standing.

Mirabelle and Jenny had followed. Jenny chose to sit in the first pew and Mirabelle stood a pace behind the bride.

A panicked Shalbourne turned to look at his bride only to receive the full force of several ostrich feathers in his nostrils. He sneezed and his mind raced as he realized he was about to marry a woman whose face he had never seen—just the top of her bonnet. My God, what am I doing? he thought to himself. All this, just to satisfy the whim of some old witch that I don't even care for!

Denbigh, whose sixth sense told him that Shalbourne was about to take to his heels, took hold of his friend's arm, smiled blandly at him, murmured "Bless you" in a belated response to his sneeze, and directed Shalbourne's attention to the priest by a nod of his head.

The stout priest, whose fist had been well greased by my Lord Denbigh, began to drone out the ceremony.

Isolde, who was in as bad a state as my Lord Shalbourne, did not notice the small discrepancy in her name when both the priest and Shalbourne said "Elsie" instead of "Isolde," although she did say it correctly herself. As for Shalbourne, his voice shook as he said "I do" and in his terror, he stuttered rather badly over the section where he was to repeat the vows the priest intoned.

". . . now pronounce you man and wife. You may . . ." the bored priest yawned before he could finish the sentence.

Denbigh, thinking the proceedings over, pumped Shalbourne's hand, congratulating him and saying, "Well, we brushed through that tolerably well. Now only have to face Auntie Jane with the news."

Shalbourne refrained from pointing out to his friend that the first female to be faced was this woman he had just taken to wife, for he was still ignorant of her countenance.

Mirabelle, with tears in her eyes, hugged her cousin and kissed her. She whispered in Isolde's ear, "Oh, he's ever so handsome—even if he does have that hideous scar!"

Isolde, who, like her husband, had not yet gotten a good view of her spouse, smiled wanly and fainted dead away.

When she returned to consciousness, she was lying on the hard settee in the priest's office. Someone was chafing her hand, her hat had been removed, and the face that swam into her immediate view caused her to murmur, "Tristan."

Shalbourne smiled with a contemptuous sneer that was at once terrifying and attractive. One of his thick, heavy brows was raised in a gesture of questioning and the other slanted across his forehead in a straight line. He looked like the Corsair himself. "I take it, my dear Isolde, that you are not an actress?"

"An actress?" Jenny spoke indignantly. "I should say not! Why, Miss Isolde's father was a clergyman."

"I'm sure this is all very fascinating," the priest interrupted, his tone saying that he was dead bored with the conversation. "But if the young lady is quite recovered, she must sign the register as her husband has already done."

Isolde struggled to a sitting position, her eyes never leaving Shalbourne's face. The verger thrust a book and pen at her, indicating with a bony finger where she was to sign. She glanced down only long enough to scrawl her name, seeing that Gaylord Edmund Alastair Leighton had already signed. Before she could finish reading the entry, the verger pulled the pen and book out of her grasp since she had obviously already completed her task.

"Are you a friend of Mr. Leighton's?" Isolde whispered hoarsely to Shalbourne.

Shalbourne gave a wicked laugh. "Ha. No, my dear wife, I *am* Leighton."

Isolde's heart stopped beating and she felt faint again. She dug her nails into her palms, hoping the pain inflicted would help her retain consciousness.

"And you are Mrs. Leighton now!" Mirabelle's happy voice chirped in from somewhere behind Isolde.

"No." The color flushed into Isolde's face and then receded, leaving her chalk-white.

"Quite right, my dear," Shalbourne said in a bored voice as he produced a snuff box. "You are *not* Mrs. Leighton."

Several witnesses opened their mouths to protest. Those mouths remained open when Shalbourne continued. "You are Lady Shalbourne now."

"Shalbourne?" Jenny squeaked. "Not that earl what's so wicked?!"

"Gaylord," Isolde gasped as she realized the connection between his Christian name and his sobriquet.

Shalbourne gave an ironic bow. "One and the same."

Jenny swallowed and stared as Mirabelle hastily said, "Oh, I daresay you're exaggerating, Jenny. Anyone can see that Lord Shalbourne is a very nice gentleman."

"Your confidence in me, Miss Hackett, is quite moving," Shalbourne said, his flashing eyes and biting tone belying his words.

"You must go now," the verger whined. "The reverend's lunch."

"Really, don't hurry on my account," the priest said, but they all rose since it was obvious he was anxious for them to leave.

Denbigh handed Isolde her bonnet, which she tied with shaking fingers. He held his arm out for her to take, saying, "Allow me to escort you to your carriage, Lady Shalbourne."

Isolde rose uncertainly, her frightened eyes still on her husband's face. She was too befuddled by events to protest and so meekly allowed Denbigh to lead her outside.

It was when Isolde's luggage was being transferred to the post chaise Shalbourne had hired for the journey that Denbigh tried to lighten the mood by saying, "By jove, Gay, if you don't take a care, I shall be the first to kiss your bride! In your haste, you forgot to, and I shan't be held accountable for my actions if you don't rectify the situation soon!"

Shalbourne shot a dark look at Denbigh and hissed through gritted teeth, "Very well, Denbigh. Since you are determined to turn this farce into a romance . . ."

He limped up to Isolde, smiled sardonically, and whispered, "At least try to appear to enjoy it, my love, or your coachman will probably shoot me where I stand." He then bent and kissed her briefly on the lips. "Smile," he instructed softly as he pulled away.

Jenny hugged her mistress and cried, "Ah, I wish I were going with ye, Miss Isolde. But don't you worry about nothin', I'm sure that story I told ye the other day was just some jealous cat howling at the moon. Anyone kin see that his lordship's a true gentleman. 'Sides, being a ladyship is ever so much better than anything I coulda hoped fer ye and that's a fact."

Jenny went on at some length. Only Isolde, who was not attending to what Jenny had to say, heard Shalbourne hiss to his friend Denbigh, "I could murder you for this, George! My God, to have taken such a creature to wife! Any imbecile can see she would have been better suited to being my mistress! I should never have let you talk me into this! To have such a woman as the Countess of Shalbourne—all feeling must be revolted!"

"It is you who is the imbecile, my lord," Denbigh replied in a dignified voice and then walked away. "Allow me to hand you into your coach, my lady."

Isolde blinked back the angry tears that her husband's words had produced. She cast a nasty look in Shalbourne's direction and then tossed her head as if to point out how beneath contempt he was. Looking back at my Lord Denbigh, she took his proferred arm and replied, "Thank you, my lord. *You* are certainly a gentleman." With head held high, she entered the waiting coach.

CHAPTER TEN

One might be tempted to say that it bodes ill for a marriage when the couple involved have their first misunderstanding within five minutes of exchanging vows. Certainly, both Lord and Lady Shalbourne were inclined to agree with this gloomy prediction as the silence between them lengthened and the distance from London increased.

Isolde was endeavoring to gain a hold on her temper when Lord Shalbourne interrupted her reverie to sneer, "My lady—"

"Oh, have done, my lord," Isolde angrily broke into his speech. "Have done. You mock me each time you address me so and I do not appreciate it. I may have been remarkably naive and stupid to have got myself into this situation in the first place, but I hope I am not unintelligent!"

"Oh, bravo, my dear. And what do you do for an encore?" Shalbourne jeered.

"I shall probably slap that smile off your ugly face!" she retorted unwisely.

Shalbourne's black eyes flashed red. "Ugly, is it? Just remember, my lovely wife, that it is the face of the man who has condescended to elevate you beyond your station!"

"And what makes you think you are so far above me, my

lord?'' Isolde spit back. ''My father may have only been a simple clergyman, but . . .''

''Oh, yes. Do let us hear about this reverend gentleman.'' Shalbourne's eyes narrowed dangerously. ''Just remember, oh wife mine, that your tales can and will come back to haunt you if they prove to be false.''

''Oh!'' Isolde exclaimed. ''You are despicable! Well, ask Sir James Danforth if you doubt my word! I'm sure he will remember the Reverend Henry Marsh, who served in his parish for some fifteen years or more.''

''Ah, but will he remember you, I wonder?''

''I should certainly hope so, seeing as how his only daughter Mary was one of my best friends!''

''Let us, for the sake of argument, concede that your worthy parent was indeed a man of the church. How does this fact . . . ?''

''Oh, did I neglect to mention that *his* father, my grandfather, was Sir Randolph Marsh? That his mother, my grandmother, was Lady Harriet Stauton? And although my maternal grandfather may have started life as a shopkeeper's apprentice, he was eventually honored for his services to the crown as a merchant in the East India Company. Surely that makes me good enough for even the illustrious Earl of Shalbourne?''

''If—*if* all you say is true, then what in heaven's name possessed you to advertise in the newspaper for a husband?''

''I didn't!'' Isolde shouted at him at the same decibel level he had employed, then added more quietly, ''My cousin, Mirabelle, took it upon herself to do so. And more to the point, what in heaven's name possessed you to take a wife out of the newspaper?''

It was Shalbourne's turn to blush. ''I had my reasons.''

''My goodness,'' Isolde gasped in mock horror, ''can it be that no one else would have you?''

"That will be quite enough out of you, woman!" Shalbourne's eyes sparkled dangerously. "My God, if you were a man . . ."

"If I were a man, my lord, we would not be having this conversation!"

Shalbourne changed tactics. "What were you doing that night? In that neighborhood?"

"I had thought I had made myself clear at the time. I was there very much against my will. I gave you no reason to suppose otherwise." Isolde blushed as she acknowledged to herself once more that her encouragement of his attentions at the time might have misled him. "And what in the world made you think I was an actress?" She said the word as if it were some vile sort of reptile.

"It was all your damn talk about returning to the theatre, that's what! Tell me, what else was I to suppose?"

"You might have supposed that I was telling you the truth!" In her frustration, Isolde began to cry.

"Oh, lord, it needed only this," Shalbourne said disgustedly, producing a handkerchief.

"I'm sorry. I don't need that, thank you," a dignified Isolde said as she wiped away a few tears with a gloved finger. She lifted her chin, set her mouth, and began, "I know you will probably want to have this marriage set aside."

"Ye gods, will I?"

"And I want you to know that I shan't stand in your way."

"You won't, will you?"

"But I would ask that you wait until after my birthday next month."

"Oh?"

"Yes. I shall no longer be obligated to answer to my guardian after that time as I am due to inherit a very large income."

"An income?"

"Yes." Isolde's eyes narrowed suspiciously. "Rather a large one."

"Go on. This becomes more fascinating by the minute."

"You needn't think I shall give any of it to you," Isolde said petulantly.

"Who asked you to?" Shalbourne retorted, sounding like an equally spoiled child.

"Well, I shan't pay to be rid of you, either! Especially since you are obviously so keen to rid yourself of me."

"What makes you think that?"

Isolde gasped. "Why, what you said to Lord Denbigh."

"I spoke a great deal of nonsense to George. Which comment in particular led you to suppose I wanted to be rid of you?"

"Oh! You are impossible! Contemptible! Monstrous! Oh, I can't think of anything bad enough to call you!"

"Charming." Shalbourne folded his arms across his chest, impervious to her insults.

"I should never have told you about my inheritance! If you think you'll see so much as a penny of my money . . ."

Shalbourne's bark of laughter cut short her tirade. "You mistake, my love. It's not your money I'm interested in."

"I find that difficult to believe!"

"Tell me, my dear, just how much is your 'fortune' worth?"

"Ah, ha! I knew you were interested in the money!"

"How much?"

Something in his tone made her heart leap in fear and she squeaked a reply in a voice she might have used if he had produced a pistol. "Two thousand a year."

Shalbourne's mirth knew no bounds.

"What is it?" Isolde asked hesitantly.

"Oh, God, I shall die laughing! She accuses me of fortune hunting for a paltry two thousand a year!"

"Well, I'm glad you find it so amusing, sir."

"Amusing?! My God, it's the best bloody jest I've heard in months! My dear girl, I think you should be aware that there is a lot more than a few thousand pounds at stake here. I'm talking about a sum to the tune of fifty to sixty thousand!"

"Fifty to sixty . . ." she repeated faintly.

"A year," he added grimly.

"Goodness." Isolde was stunned by the sum. It was more than she could comprehend.

"You may only have need of a husband for a few weeks, my lady, but I have need of a wife for a great deal longer than that. In fact, I begin to think it will all work out for the best between us. You shall be my revenge."

"Your revenge?"

"Yes. I don't think you are at all what Auntie Jane had in mind when she delivered her ultimatum, but I begin to believe you are more than a match for her any day." With that pronouncement, he leaned back, closed his eyes, and endeavored to fall asleep.

Isolde, on the other hand, found sleep evaded her. Her brain was in turmoil, her thoughts jumbled and disorganized. She was no longer sure what his lordship's opinion of her might be—at worst, a doxy, at best, a termagant, she surmised. She was filled with questions, especially regarding this mysterious Aunt Jane and why he had to marry to please her. However, even if she had had the courage to frame her questions, she had no desire to broach the subject and thereby awaken him. She writhed uncomfortably when she remembered their previous exchange and wondered how she had found the temerity to say what she had to such an intimidating opponent.

While he slept, she studied him and decided that his was not such an ugly face after all. The scar was long, certainly, but it gave him a rakish air that was not entirely unbecoming. She, too, eventually fell asleep, to dream of a knight in shining armor with a scarred face named Tristan who threw her over his saddle, shouting "Let Aunt Jane rescue you now!"

It was rather late when they pulled into an innyard. Shalbourne awoke in a vile temper, and his string of expletives and curses, most unintelligible to his wife, awakened Isolde. She noted the fact that he was not so agile in descending from the coach as he had been upon entering it. Also, his movements as he walked toward the inn were stiff, and he favored his leg more than she remembered seeing him do in the past. Isolde followed in his wake and ventured to inquire if they were stopping for the night.

"Yes," Shalbourne said nastily. "You didn't expect to reach Nottinghamshire in one day, did you?"

Isolde, who understood that his contentious demeanor arose from physical misery rather than anything she might have done, bit her tongue and restrained from making any sort of retort.

Mine host bowed low when they entered, his obsequious attitude arising from a previous acquaintanceship with his lordship. As he showed them into their private parlor, he congratulated the newlyweds and informed them that his wife, an excellent cook, would have their dinner ready before they could shake a stick. Also, if they should require any assistance, since they had neglected to bring along their personal servants, the chambermaid (his daughter) and the boots (his son) would be more than happy to be of service. He then bowed again and backed out the door, leaving them alone.

Shalbourne, who was never at his best after sitting cramped for hours in a coach, stirred up the coals in the grate and lowered himself painfully upon the chair near it.

"Damn," he muttered and fell to rubbing his leg.

"Are you feeling poorly, my lord?" Isolde asked solicitously.

"What do you think?" he almost roared at her. Then, as a paroxysm of pain crossed his features, Isolde, not to be put off by his ill humor, went to his side and asked in a kind accent, "Is there aught I can do to ease your discomfiture, my lord?"

"There is nothing anyone can do!" he barked at her.

"Then . . ." Isolde, concerned at his obvious suffering, began.

"No, I retract that. You can shut up and leave me alone," Shalbourne said ill-naturedly.

"Well!" Isolde finally lost her temper. "That shan't be any hardship, to be sure!" She stomped to the opposite side of the chamber where she threw her bonnet on the window seat and almost ripped off the buttons on her spencer as she tried to remove the garment.

"Isolde," Shalbourne called her name softly, "you will want to come near the fire if you are as bitterly chilled as I."

Since she was cold, she advanced to the fire and sank into the chair opposite him, but her face remained stormy. Shalbourne took note of her angry countenance and grinned. "Actually, I can see that you are not chilled at all but quite heated. No, no, my dear." He laughed and raised a hand as she took a breath to speak. "Don't mind me. I know I am the very devil of a fellow after such a long confinement in a bumpy carriage and quite frankly, all I want at the moment is my dinner—not conversation."

It was as close to an apology as she was going to receive and she was not unaware of what it must have cost him. She decided to be tolerant and not waste her unwanted sympathy on him.

When their meal came, they ate it in virtual silence. As soon as the covers had been removed and the waiter had silently taken everything but the wine bottle and two glasses, Shalbourne asked politely, "Would you like for me to ring for the maid? We have a long day ahead of us tomorrow and I'm sure you would like to retire early.''

"Shall we arrive at our destination tomorrow, my lord?''

He shrugged and poured himself another glass of wine. "I expect.''

"I—I don't wish to be inquisitive, my lord.'' Isolde nervously rolled the stem of her wineglass between her fingers. "But do you mind if I ask where we are going exactly?''

"Good Lord! You are trusting, aren't you?'' Shalbourne murmured in wonderment. "Either that, or a naive fool. Of course you may ask. We shall be going to Shalbourne Manor, my main seat, which is not too distant from Allerton in Nottinghamshire.''

"Thank you, my lord,'' Isolde said. "I think I shall retire now.''

Shalbourne rose when she did and pulled the bell for the chambermaid. When the innkeeper's daughter arrived, a short, dumpy girl with lank blond hair and a ruddy complexion, Isolde took shy leave of her husband. He grinned at her discomfiture, took her hand, and kissed it, wishing her good night. She blushed and murmured her reply softly, then turned and fled with the chambermaid upstairs.

It had not occurred to Isolde to wonder about where her husband intended to sleep until the garrulous chambermaid mentioned that he had got the chamber next door. "And a finer set of rooms you won't find this side of Grantham.'' She continued, not noticing the play of emotions her prattle had produced on her ladyship's face. " 'Course, we don't have the quality staying here often, mind, but still, we knows what they like and what they expects, your ladyship.''

She continued in this vein while she brushed out Isolde's long brown hair and then braided it into a single plait. The girl giggled as she threw the nightdress over Isolde's head and she made the mysterious remark, "Not that you'll be needing this tonight, mi'lady."

Isolde frowned at the girl. "Whyever not?"

"Oh," the chambermaid was quick to apologize. "I'm sorry, mi'lady. I didn't mean to be cheeky."

This only served to increase Isolde's confusion, since she had not asked her question to quash the girl's impertinence, but rather to elicit information. Unfortunately, the chambermaid became silent, since she had perceived Isolde's remark as chastisement, and made a hasty exit. Isolde thoughtfully tied on her close-fitting nightcap and then crawled into bed, still not comprehending the girl's mysterious remark. She couldn't imagine what was meant, and so shrugged and immediately put it out of her mind. She noticed that the sheets had already been warmed, a pleasant surprise and an unexpected luxury in this country inn, since even her uncle had thought such practices extravagant and unnecessary. She blew out the candle on the bedstand and snuggled under the covers.

She had no idea how much later it was when she awoke with a start, but the fire had burned down until it was only a glow in the grate. The inn was quiet and still and Isolde suspected that the hour was well past midnight. Just as she was wondering what could have caused her to awaken, she heard a noise from next door. She deduced that her husband was just preparing for bed and heard a few muffled whispers from that chamber. A door shut and then footsteps receded down the hall as the boots retreated to his chamber in another part of the building. She heard Shalbourne as he paced briefly in his room. His cane striking the floor as he walked was too distinctive to be ignored. Finally, he stopped and Isolde began to drift back to sleep.

Then she heard Shalbourne's peculiar gait as he walked down the hallway. In a state between waking and sleeping, she wondered idly where he was going.

She jumped when she heard the soft knock on her door. "Who is it?" she asked in an agitated voice.

The door opened and Shalbourne entered. "Only I, madam. No need to fear."

He closed the door behind him and locked it. "You should learn to lock your door, my dear. Especially in a common inn."

"So it would seem!" Isolde retorted as she sat up, drawing the bed clothes up under her chin. "What are you doing here, sir?" she demanded as her heart thumped uncontrollably.

"I have come like any dutiful husband to bid his bride good night," he said as he made his way across the room to sit on the edge of the bed next to her.

"You have already done so. There was no need," she said breathlessly and backed away slightly.

"I hope you find the accommodations to your liking. I realize that this is not the most elegant of inns, but I have always found it clean and the service adequate."

"Yes, it's very nice, my lord." She stared wide-eyed at the point where his dressing gown fell open at the neck. She was both shocked and intrigued by the sight of his partially exposed chest. Never before in her life had she seen so much of the naked male anatomy, and Shalbourne's was made even more fascinating by the view of another scar much like the one on his face that began somewhere past his left collarbone and extended downward into the folds of his dressing gown. She could tell that wherever there was scar tissue, the dark hair (of which he seemed to have an abundance) would not grow.

"Is there something the matter, Isolde?" Shalbourne suppressed the smile quirking his lips.

"What? Oh! Oh, no!" She blushed, realizing that she had been staring. Plucking nervously at the quilt, she looked downward and said, "Actually, the inn is vastly superior to any I am accustomed to, so there is no need to apologize. Now, I—I must bid you good night, my lord. You said yourself we had a long journey ahead of us tomorrow.''

"Don't you think it might be proper for you to call me by my Christian name now that we are wed?''

"Perhaps, my lord." Isolde blushed anew. "If I knew what it was you preferred. Not Tristan, I assume. Edmund, perhaps, as your friend told my cousin?''

"No. Gay.''

"Oh," Isolde said, then stuttered out, "Gay!" since he was obviously waiting for her to say it.

Shalbourne smiled, then asked as he touched her nightcap, "Tell me, Isolde, why do you sport such a monstrosity as that? Not at all becoming. There. That's much better.'' He deftly untied and removed the offending object before Isolde could protest.

"My lord!" She said indignantly and endeavored to retrieve her property from his grasp.

"Why do you do that?" he asked, disregarding her struggles to redeem her cap.

"Do what, my lord?" Isolde asked, annoyed.

"Braid your hair in that fashion," he stated lightly.

"Because if I did not, my hair should be tangled quite beyond repair in the morning," she answered impatiently. "Now, sir, if you will return my cap, I shall go to sleep and I think you should do the same.''

He deliberately placed the cap inside his dressing gown, grinning at her. "I shall not hinder if you chose to retrieve it.''

"Oh, la, sir, if you have more need of it than I, I will gladly lend it to you. I fear, however, that you will find its lace and ribbons even less becoming on yourself than it was on me.''

"Most kind of you, my lady.''

"Good night, my lord," Isolde said with finality. She

then turned her back to him and laid down upon the pillows. She closed her eyes in the hopes that he would take the hint.

Shalbourne considered her for a moment or two as she lay upon the bed. He had drunk more after dinner than even he was accustomed to, which had given him the courage to enter his bride's chamber. After all, there was the second part of Auntie Jane's ultimatum to be considered. The wine gave him the audacity to reach out and loose her hair from the confines of that heavy braid.

Isolde flipped over to face him, an angry expression on her face. "What are you doing?" she demanded.

"I wanted to see what it looked like. It's quite long, isn't it?" Shalbourne said in explanation.

"Are you drunk, my lord?" Isolde asked curiously since she could perceive no other explanation for his odd behavior.

"Most likely," came his honest reply.

"I think, my lord, you should seek your couch and go to sleep." Isolde employed a tone she might have used with a naughty child.

"What?" Shalbourne asked. "Would you have me leave my bride on our wedding night?" Leaning across the bed, he took hold of her shoulders. "Did you think I would neglect so beautiful a lady as yourself? A very knave you must believe your Sir Tristan to be." He drew her closer. "The wound festers, my lady. And only you can administer the cure."

A mesmerized Isolde murmured, "Wound, my lord?"

"The arrow to my heart," he whispered, his lips next to hers.

"I would have you sleep, my lord," she whispered in an attempt to mask her fears.

"And so I shall," Shalbourne muttered softly. "Soon enough."

A family of butterflies took up residence in Isolde's stomach and her heart pumped as if she had just run up a very steep hill. It was certainly very pleasant to be kissed in the manner her husband was presently doing. However, it was when he pressed her back onto the pillows, sliding beneath the covers next to her, that she began to have serious doubts. She had spoken no less than the truth when she had told her cousin that she did not know what happened between a man and wife, and she wasn't at all sure she was prepared to find out quite so soon, especially with a virtual stranger. She came to the conclusion that the proceedings, no matter how intriguing, had best come to a halt when his stroking hand, which had heretofore confined itself to running up and down her arm, found its way to her breast.

"No!" she gasped, pulling away and clutching his wrist with her own small hand.

"No?" Shalbourne asked softly, fumbling with the drawstring at the neck of her nightdress.

"No!" A frightened Isolde squeaked, perceiving his intention only when he pushed the fabric down off one shoulder.

"No, Isolde?" Shalbourne whispered, emitting a short, quiet laugh. "I don't believe you really mean that."

"No! Don't!" Isolde pleaded. Thoroughly terrified, she struggled to get away but could not budge his weight from on top of her. "Stop! Go away!"

"Here, now!" Shalbourne grabbed her flaying hands and held them down above her head. "What's the matter with you? What are you . . . oofph!"

Isolde watched in astonishment as he rolled off her, doubled up and groaning. Well, she certainly hadn't expected her kick to be quite so effective; she didn't think she had hit him that hard with her knee.

"Good Lord, that wasn't necessary! You only had to tell me to stop!" Shalbourne complained.

"But I did!" Isolde exclaimed resentfully. "And you wouldn't!"

Shalbourne struggled to a sitting position, his face grim and forbidding. "What's the matter, madam wife?" he asked through clenched teeth. "Do you prefer to bestow your favors upon an unknown paramour in a closed carriage? Or is it simply that now that you have seen my face, and, of course, my lameness, that you find you can no longer stomach my embraces?"

He rose abruptly, and leaning awkwardly on his cane, began to leave the room. Isolde was too shocked to speak and so watched in silence as he turned the key in the lock and wrenched open the door. Stepping outside, he took one last look at her and added darkly, "I am most sincerely sorry, madam, that fate has seen fit to tie you to a cripple. My condolences!" With that, he slammed the door.

"Wait," she started and then found she was speaking to empty air.

Really, she thought, he might have at least stayed to hear her explanation! It wasn't that she found him repulsive, it was only that she was frightened and she didn't know him. Oh, dear, she groaned to herself, what did she know of this man, after all? And, God help her, in her haste to escape one distasteful marriage, had she plunged headlong into a worse? As if that were not enough to throw her into a state bordering on hysteria, she suddenly realized that she had just engaged in the action she had described to Mirabelle as that which produced children! What if she were now pregnant?!

With that elevating thought, she succumbed to the tears that had threatened all day and eventually cried herself to sleep.

Chapter Eleven

Wendall's arrogant assumption that Isolde would never have the courage or ingenuity to defy him had prevented him from discovering that the bird had flown until almost twenty-four hours after the event. Of course, the duplicity of his own daughter had not helped matters from Wendall's point of view.

On Friday evening, he had returned to his home and been informed by his fluttering spouse that Isolde had locked herself into her room. Wendall's immediate reply had been "Well, hang the young hussy! If she is fool enough to think such a ploy will change my mind, then let her go without her supper for her pains."

He had not attended his wife when she further reported that Isolde refused to answer any of her aunt's tentative inquiries. From years of habit, Wendall allowed this curious bit of information to flow in one ear and out the other. After all, when he had solicited his daughter for more information, Mirabelle had very helpfully invented a conversation that had occurred between the two girls through the locked door.

Therefore, it came as a nasty surprise the next morning when investigation into the matter proved not only that Isolde's door had been locked from the outside but also that the only thing her chamber contained to evidence her presence was a small note addressed to her uncle and lying on the pillow of her bed.

It read:

> *Dear Uncle,*
> *By the time you read this, I shall be married and on my way to the country with my husband. Do not try to follow as I have no intention of changing my mind in this matter and I doubt you would find me. Be assured that my husband is a gentleman and unknown to you. You shall hear from me again at the appropriate time. Yours, etc.,*
> *Isolde Marsh.*

Short and uninformative, the note produced an immediate reaction in its reader, a reaction that prompted his wife and daughter to fear for his life. He turned a bright, scarlet shade and his breath was expelled in short gasps through clenched teeth. A roar of anger began somewhere deep in his large chest and when it finally released, the windows shook.

Clutching the note in his hand, Wendall's eye was caught by the notation at the top of the page that read "Friday Morning." He roared a second time and turned his crazed, glittering eyes on his daughter.

"Friday morning?" he spluttered. "She has been gone since yesterday morning? You!" He pointed an accusing finger at Mirabelle. "You told me you spoke with her last evening! Well, Miss! What do you have to say for yourself?!" He punctuated this query by grabbing his daughter's arm and shaking her soundly.

Mirabelle gulped. "I'm sorry, Papa."

"Sorry! Is that all you have to say for yourself?" Wendall startled his audience of family and servants by throwing his daughter to the floor of his errant niece's bedchamber. "What more do you know of this, you ungrateful brat? Do you know who this scoundrel is that she has run off with? Tell me this instant!''

He stood over her, an avenging fiend, intimidating and terrible in his wrath. Mirabelle began to sob. ''I'm sorry, Papa.''

''Oh, dear, Wendall, please . . . oh, dear, you're frightening the poor child. Is this really necessary? I'm sure, that is, Mirabelle would never . . . not on purpose, would you, dear? You didn't, well, perhaps, tell your Papa an untruth?'' Mary helped her sobbing child to a nearby chair while Wendall dismissed the servants with another shout.

''What are you hanging about for? Get back to your duties! God knows, I don't pay the lot of you to stand about gaping at your betters!''

''Oh, Mama,'' Mirabelle addressed Mary Hackett. ''I meant it for the best. And he was ever so nice, not at all like Harold.''

''Who? Who, you unnatural child!'' Wendall demanded as Mirabelle leaned closer to her mother's protecting embrace.

''If you know something, Mirabelle, that is, I'm sure Papa will not be angry with you. It wasn't your fault. Just tell us what you know,'' Mary urged gently.

Mirabelle hiccupped on a sob.

''Get on with it!'' Wendall growled. ''I am almost out of patience with you, young lady. Tell me who the bastard is she's eloped with!''

Mirabelle gulped. ''His name's Gaylord Edmund Leighton and he's the Earl of Shalbourne.'' Once started, she raced onward, giving him all the facts she knew, including the name of the church where the heinous event had taken place, as well as the name of the vicar who had performed the scandalous wedding. ''It's not as if Isolde's disgraced herself or us,'' she said fearfully. ''And, oh, Papa, he really is an Earl, so that makes my cousin a Countess, so that makes it all better, doesn't it?'' She finished on a pleading note.

"A Countess." Mary breathed in awe. "Are you sure of this? After all, Mirabelle, you've never mentioned before . . . I mean, how in the world did she come to meet him?"

"Blast and damnation!" Wendall paced the room in nervous anger. "You say she's gone and married an Earl?"

"Yes, Papa," Mirabelle said meekly.

What followed was a series of discreet inquiries that elicited the unwelcome information that what his daughter had told him was indeed the truth. The one fact that galled Wendall above all others was that Gaylord Edmund Leighton did indeed turn out to be an Earl. Once this had been confirmed, his heart sank, since he realized that with a single, brilliant stroke, his niece had virtually tied his hands. As her guardian, if he were to seek an annulment for the hasty marriage, his friends would have laughed themselves silly. Only a fool would object to his "ward" marrying into the aristocracy.

Wendall was beside himself with fury. In an effort to curtail the inevitable gossip, he first sent notice to the guests that the wedding had been called off by mutual consent. The tale he gave was that, on closer inspection, the bride and groom had decided they would not suit. He further volunteered the information that his niece had retired to the country to visit friends, in the hope that the curious would remain aloof for a day or two. He could only pray fervently that a notice in the *Gazette* the next week would not completely undermine his efforts to keep the elopement quiet, at least until he could pave the way for a less shocking revelation of the facts. He then sent for Harold to break the news as quickly and as painlessly as possible.

Harold, baffled but still cheerful, was shown into Hackett's study as soon as he arrived. He had no suspicions as to what would greet him there and even began by saying, "Good morning, Mr. Hackett. What is this all about, sir?

You know I must be at the church in ten minutes but your man would not take no for an answer.''

"Good morning, Harold, my boy," Wendall interrupted him. "Please sit down."

Harold sank into the chair, a sense of foreboding sinking into his thick skull at his employer's solemn face and grave manner. The half-remembered sight of the stoic messenger and unsmiling servants started to have significance in the face of Wendall's manner.

"The most damnable thing has happened!" Hackett growled.

"Yes?" Harold squeaked as his imagination boggled at the unfathomable reason for this interview.

"Everything's ruined!" Hackett stared at Harold with a baneful glare. "And don't think I don't hold you partly responsible!"

Harold swallowed convulsively as he tried to review a catalog of possible infractions. He knew instinctively that his worst fear had probably been realized. Somehow, he had managed to alienate his patron and he could whistle Isolde's fortune down the wind.

"If you hadn't bungled the affair that night at the theatre, this would never have happened!" Wendall pointed an accusing finger at Harold.

Harold, resentful and hurt, said defensively, "I couldn't force her to like it, could I?"

"Yes, you could!" Hackett pounded his fist on the desk. "If you'd set your mind to it! Women always come 'round once you've had a tumble in the hay with 'em! It's in their nature, boy! I told you before, first they put up a bit of a fight, just so you know they aren't of easy virtue." He waved his hand impatiently. "Of course, that's all water over the dam now. The young snip's gone and eloped!"

Harold's mouth gaped open in surprise. "Eloped?!" he squeaked in consternation.

"I was so careful, too! Never letting her come in the way of anyone who might be persuaded to help her avoid this marriage! And I must say, Mirabelle's story of meeting him in a milliner's shop has a distinctively fishy . . ." Wendall coughed as he realized that his present line was hardly flattering to the young man seated before him. To cover his faux pas, he turned quickly and lowered himself into the massive chair behind the desk. "Ah, well, be that as it may, she's found someone else right enough! Seems she's gone and married that bastard Shalbourne!"

"Isolde's married to a Mr. Shalbourne?" Harold asked stupidly, all the while wondering if Mr. Hackett's objection to this Mr. Shalbourne was that he was born on the wrong side of the blanket.

"Not mister!" Wendall exclaimed. "Lord Shalbourne, mind you!"

"But how could he be a lord? I thought you said he was a bastard."

"Ignorant thick-headed fool! Haven't you ever heard the term used metaphorically before?"

Harold subsided into embarrassed silence.

"Now tell me," Wendall continued. "How the hell am I to object to such a match as that? Ummm? Everyone will think I'm mad to want to overset such a marriage. Very sneaky of the bitch. I could very easily have gotten an annulment if she'd gone and married a *Mr.* Shalbourne. But, oh, no, a mere mister isn't good enough for my hoity-toity niece. I expect she'll want me to refer to her as 'my lady' now. Ha! I'll see her in hell, first, by God! And now she's run off to some la-de-dah place called Shalbourne Manor in Nottinghamshire, as if matters weren't bad enough. How am I to face our friends with the fact that she's so dead to all propriety as to elope in this havey-cavey manner? Countess of Shalbourne, ha!"

"I guess any woman would rather be married to an Earl than me," Harold mumbled in a plaintive voice.

"There now, my boy," Wendall sympathized. "I know how you must feel. I feel terrible myself. After all, she's my niece, although I'm certainly glad I can say that there isn't any Hackett blood running through her veins! Ah, I had such plans for you, my boy! Knew you'd go far with that girl's money." Wendall coughed nervously. "God knows I would have liked to see you married to my Mirabelle, but she's already as good as promised to young Rutherford."

Harold didn't hear this last comment. "If ever I get the chance again," he said as much to himself as to Wendall, "I'll know how to repay the girl for this slight!"

"Do you mean it, boy?" Wendall sat up with tense hands, grabbing the edge of his desk.

Harold frowned as he considered the question. "Yes," he said and then added with more conviction, "Yes, I do."

Hackett laughed. "You are worthy of my confidence in you, my boy! Despite this stumbling block to my plans, with your cooperation, we could salvage them entirely." Wendall gave an enigmatic smile, began to chew thoughtfully on his finger, and gazed abstractly at a dirty spot on the ceiling. "Yes. Yes. Salvage them entirely."

CHAPTER TWELVE

There is always a certain inconvenience attached to the taking up of a new residence, and this, added to the inevitable awkwardness attached to a new marriage between virtual strangers, especially strangers who are not on speaking terms, had Isolde in a state that could only be described as overwrought. She had, during the long carriage ride to Shalbourne Manor, developed a pounding headache and a tendency to start at small noises. She was quite disgusted with herself for falling victim to what she considered the weakest of feminine characteristics, that is, a tendency on her part to resemble a watering pot. More than once she had to retrieve the handkerchief in her reticule. What was worse, every time she lifted the cloth to her cheeks to wipe away the moisture found there, Shalbourne shifted his position and audibly ground his teeth.

Arrival at Shalbourne Manor was a tremendous relief to both occupants of the cramped vehicle, until they realized that they were to be submitted to an even more subtle torture, the meeting and greeting of the household staff. Before they could retire to their respective chambers, they would be forced to run the gauntlet of well-meaning congratulations and introductions.

Every one of the servants had a particular trait they

wished to see in the new countess, but they were agreed that they would gladly give up their favorite hobbyhorse if my Lady Shalbourne could but succeed in curbing his lordship's famous ill temper and unpredictable starts. She was welcome to tie her garter in public or swear as colorfully as a sailor as long as she tamed the Gay Lord. They none of them believed she could, and all of them felt a twinge of disappointment at the sight of the bedraggled, wan creature that Simmons, the first footman, handed down from the coach.

As for Isolde herself, her first impression of Shalbourne Manor was not of a charming, warm-colored stone home built in the time of Charles II, but rather a formidable sea of people—all staring with bland or openly hostile expressions—set against a backdrop of the most imposing mansion she had ever beheld. Taking a deep breath to overcome her stage fright, she planted a smile on her face and set her mind to the task at hand.

"Mrs. Peters, the housekeeper" was Shalbourne's succinct introduction.

"My lady." Mrs. Peters sketched a curtsy.

Isolde extended her hand, which a surprised Mrs. Peters took into her own. Thinking Mrs. Peters was very much like one of the charity committee ladies in her father's parish, she decided to apply the same rules of diplomacy here that she had used then and said, "I hope that you shall be patient with me, Mrs. Peters, as I learn the routine of the household. I am afraid that life in my father's rectory did not prepare me to cope with such a large household without a great deal of tutelage."

Mrs. Peters, a God-fearing, churchgoing woman, was charmed. My lady's father had been a rector! A man of God! Not necessarily aristocratic but decidedly genteel. Isolde's star was on the rise. "Of course, my lady. I shall be happy to assist you in any way I can. 'Tweren't so very long ago that I was learning meself what you'll be learning." Mrs.

Peters beamed as she confided, "Indeed, mi'lady, started out as nursemaid to his lordship, Viscount Lindley, God rest his soul, and . . ." Taking note of my Lord Shalbourne's black look and frown, she stopped her effusions for the moment.

"And this is Sikes, my major domo and head butler. He is also with me in London."

"How do you do, Mr. Sikes?" Isolde extended her hand.

"My lady." Sikes unbent his stiff, upright position into a low, stiff bow over her hand.

"I shall rely on you as I will on Mrs. Peters to steer me correctly in household matters, Mr. Sikes. I should not like to upset your routine, either here or in London."

Sikes was pleased at this conciliatory attitude, as he had had visions of the lady being the type of encroaching mushroom who insisted on disrupting a perfectly run household with outlandish requests and changes. He gave one of his rare smiles to her and said more to her than the rest of the household had heard in years. "We shall endeavor to instruct your ladyship whenever she requests and we thank your ladyship for her faith in our ability."

Isolde hid a smile at his use of the royal "we," and her husband gave her a look filled with new found respect. Momentarily distracted from his bad temper, in a bemused tone of voice he introduced the temperamental French chef his uncle had hired almost three decades ago when he had arrived on England's shores, penniless and fleeing revolution in his homeland.

"Monsieur Pierre Gascon," Shalbourne said, indicating a small, grizzled man. "My uncle's . . . ah, my chef."

"Madam." Pierre gave her a courtly bow.

"Monsieur." Isolde inclined her head and smiled, then in perfect French, replied, "I'm pleased to make your acquaintance."

The voluble Pierre's small black eyes widened in surprise. Becoming very excited, he exclaimed in his native tongue, "But you speak the French!"

Answering in kind, Isolde replied, "Only a little, I'm afraid. A Madam Giselle d'Auvingny was for many years one of my father's parishioners and it was she who taught me."

"Your French, she is perfect!" A very pleased Pierre, suiting his actions to his words, then added, "Madam, I kiss your hand!" much to the astonishment of the rest of the staff, who had been unable to follow the conversation.

Shalbourne, who spoke French fluently, gripped her arm and pulled her along the line, muttering under his breath, "I shall have to look to my laurels if that flirtatious frenchie is to remain in my household."

And so they went down the line, Shalbourne introducing each in turn, Mrs. Peters supplying the name when his memory failed or a new face appeared. In each case, Isolde charmed and delighted the various members of her husband's household. When the end of the line had been reached, the outer door flung open and a young man came striding across the hall, a large spaniel at his heels, an apology on his lips, "Excuse me, my lord, my lady, I'm afraid I was detained in one of the outer fields."

"Jeremy!" Isolde cried in undisguised delight, a genuine, unrestrained smile on her face.

"Isolde?"

"Jeremy, whatever are you doing here?"

"Why, I am my Lord Shalbourne's steward. What in the world are you . . . ?"

"This is my Lady Shalbourne, Mr. Anderson," Mrs. Peters interrupted.

"My la—" he began, stunned.

"Oh, please, Jeremy! None of that from you."

"Good Lord, little Isolde Marsh, the Countess of Shalbourne! You've certainly come a long way since our school days together at your father's rectory!''

"So you already know my steward?'' Shalbourne asked, his black brows coming together in a scowl. The two small hands Jeremy had been holding were quickly dropped.

"Oh, dear, yes!'' Isolde turned her dazzling smile upon Shalbourne for a moment, little realizing the effect of such an expression on her physical attraction or the startling effect on Shalbourne, who had heretofore been deprived of the sight. Her eyes dancing and sparkling, she turned back to Jeremy as she remarked, "Indeed, Jeremy was the veritable bane of my poor father's existence.''

Jeremy, who was not unaffected himself by Isolde's sparkling looks, said, "Unfair, Isolde! You were as guilty as I in more than one prank. I recall in great detail one occasion when I was punished quite unfairly for having brought the kitchen cat's offspring into the classroom and hiding them in the drawer of your father's desk. What a caterwauling there was when your father opened that drawer and disturbed six sleeping kittens! The poor man was scratched all the way to his eyebrows when he unsuspectingly stuck his hand in searching for a pen. I remember that despite my vehement denial to having been a party to the crime, I was caned so soundly I couldn't sit for a week!'' Jeremy grinned and Isolde giggled.

The staff gathered in the hall had found this insight into her ladyship's character quite diverting, and as Shalbourne was stifling those servants who had been bold enough to join her ladyship's laughter with one of his frowning looks, Isolde exclaimed, "Fie, sir, such an unchivalrous attitude—'a gentleman always takes the blame for a lady and a gentleman takes his punishment like a man!' '' She quoted in a mock masculine tone.

"I swear, his words exactly!'' Jeremy laughed. "And no

more fair today than when they were first spoken. A gentle-man takes the blame for a lady's misdeeds, pshaw!''

"But you did help me," Isolde protested. "And I should have infinitely preferred your punishment to my own!" In a conspiratorial whisper, Isolde leaned forward and confided, "I was forced to work a sampler for my sins!"

"Ye gods! You?" Jeremy exclaimed. "As well ask the village blacksmith to set a stitch!"

Isolde's attention was caught by a cough behind her. Turning to regard her husband, the smile still in her eyes and on her mouth, Isolde exclaimed, "Oh, my lord! I am sorry. How rude of me! There is nothing more vexing than remi-niscences of which one has no part. It's just that seeing Jeremy so suddenly like this—"

"Quite," Shalbourne said drily.

Jeremy, recognizing the signs of a jealous husband's im-pending rage, hastened to add, "Of course, it's been a good many years since then, your ladyship."

"Jeremy?" Isolde frowned at him, questioning his for-mality.

"Come, my dear." Shalbourne took hold of Isolde's limp hand and tucked it into the crook of his arm. "You can remi-nisce to your heart's content on another occasion with Mr., ah, Anderson, is it? For now, Mrs. Peters is waiting to show us to our rooms. I'm sure you are in need of a rest after your journey."

Dismissing the servants still gathered in the hall, Shal-bourne followed in Mrs. Peters' wake, leaning heavily on his cane to gain the second floor. As they ascended the stairs, Shalbourne inquired in icy, polite tones, "And just when was the last time you saw my steward, my lady?"

"Oh, nigh onto two years ago now," Isolde answered, still surrounded by the euphoria of her unexpected reunion. "My father tutored Jeremy until he was sent to school at ten.

I only saw him on holidays after that, and not at all since I left to live with my aunt and uncle in London.''

"A handsome fellow, wouldn't you say?" Shalbourne asked with a deceptively casual air.

"Jeremy?" Isolde wrinkled her brow as if considering the question for the first time. "I suppose you could say Jeremy's person is pleasing enough, but it is difficult to think in such terms about a gentleman one has known since he was in short coats.'' She did not go on to add that Jeremy's brown locks and equally unprepossessing brown eyes did not compare well to tall, swarthy looks and intense, almost black eyes. Lady Jane had not been far off the mark in her assessment that the scar on Shalbourne's face would do him no disservice in the female eye. As for his limp, Isolde found its origin far more interesting than offensive. Oh, no, as far as Isolde was concerned, there could be no comparison at all!

The ensuing days were spent in a repetitious pattern. The bride would arise early and begin her lessons in managing a large household. The groom would rise late with a bad head, growl at his valet, and spend the afternoon closeted with his steward or various and sundry of his tenants in an attempt to acquaint himself with his estate. After partaking of supper together and saying good night, Isolde would retire to read herself to sleep, while Shalbourne would sit up once again until the wee hours of the morning drinking himself into a stupor. Although the household considered this odd behavior in a bride and groom, their sympathy was misplaced. They thought it despicable behavior in his lordship to reject his bride in such a fashion, little realizing that as far as Isolde was concerned, matters could stay as they were for quite some time to come.

The interviews with most of Shalbourne's retainers were characterized by a cordial, friendly atmosphere; not so those with Mr. Anderson, who fell victim to my lord's biting tongue. Jeremy, not to be intimidated, delivered several pompous and enlightening platitudes in return. The two gentlemen inevitably quitted the interview with an altercation of one kind or another on estate policy, neither gentleman wishing to broach the true topic of their differences (i.e., the fair Isolde), and often left in a towering rage.

On one such occasion, after being booted unceremoniously into the hall, Jeremy, shrugging his shoulders philosophically, inquired of the nearest servant after her ladyship. Upon being informed that she had been in the library when last seen, Jeremy quickly repaired there.

"Isolde?" he called gently as he closed the library door behind him.

"Here," came a disembodied sound from behind a settee.

"I might have known I'd find you here on the floor, covered with dust like a veritable hoyden!" Jeremy laughed at the picture presented when he ventured behind the couch. "You realize, of course that it might be considered beneath the dignity of the Countess of Shalbourne to sit on the floor while searching the lower shelves of her library."

"Oh, ho!" Isolde smiled. "Beneath my dignity, is it? Should I call in Simmons or one of the other footmen to retrieve books from the shelf while I sit in state near the fire and pass judgment? I can picture it now—'Oh, yes, thank you, Simmons, you're so kind but I don't think I care for that author, do you suppose I might see the next book on the shelf?' Stuff and nonsense! I'm sure I shouldn't have half as much fun. Besides, I have the most lowering suspicion that if I asked another to search the shelves for suitable reading material, my selection would be censored in the most odious, albeit well-meaning, fashion."

"And so it should be!" Jeremy sat on his haunches beside her. Gazing briefly at the shelf, he cried, "Ah, ha! Take this little piece for example! Just the sort of reading material I should expect to find in the library of the Gay Lord, but hardly suitable."

"Please, Jeremy," Isolde interrupted in a serious tone of voice. "Don't call him that."

"Eh? What?" Jeremy was momentarily startled and looked blankly at his companion. "Oh," he said simply as he realized. An uncomfortable silence fell between the two. "Damn it, Isolde, why did you marry him? I mean, why him?" Jeremy jumped to his feet and started to pace across the small room.

"Good heavens, Jeremy," Isolde tried to interject a light note as she, too, rose to her feet. "Why ever not? I . . ."

As she faltered, it was now Jeremy's turn to interrupt, "I thought we . . . I mean, surely we had an understanding?"

Isolde's eyes widened. "Surely not. I hadn't set eyes on you in over two years, Jeremy, until just a few days ago. You made no effort to seek me out. I didn't even know your place of residence, much less your occupation. We didn't exactly keep the post busy with our correspondence either. 'Our understanding,' as you put it, was no more than a speculative conversation between two young people who had known each other since the year aught."

"I was waiting until I had something to show for my labors," Jeremy said bitterly, running an agitated hand through his hair. "With your dowry, I could hardly offer less than . . . oh, well, I just didn't want to be thought a fortune hunter. I had intended to call on you after next season. I'll have almost a thousand saved by then. I thought . . ."

"It doesn't matter, Jeremy," Isolde said sharply. "I didn't know, did I? And circumstances change. People change. We would have been strangers then and your offer would have come too late. Perhaps if you had written more. Ah, well, no matter now."

Jeremy gave a sharp, bitter laugh. "No, you wouldn't have accepted me, would you? Egads, why should you when you are so obviously above my touch? A countess, no less! What cheek on my part to think you'd have looked twice at a poor land steward! Obviously, our social spheres have grown widely apart in the last two years. My God, your uncle must be flying high these days for you to have met and married an Earl! The business must have improved as well, because it's going to take more than a paltry dowry of two thousand a year to set this estate to rights! I never would have thought it of you, Isolde! To sell yourself to the highest bidder for a title!''

''If you are quite finished, Jeremy Anderson, you can be quiet and listen to me! It is true that we may have spoken in our youth of a match between us but you know, as well as I, that it was never settled and never seriously considered. Indeed, if you had given me so much as the slightest hint of your feelings, even up to two weeks ago, I should have welcomed your sentiments. But I am married to my Lord Shalbourne now and nothing can alter that. I intend to make the best of that situation, so I would appreciate it if, in the future, you would keep any comments that reflect unfavorably upon my husband to yourself!''

''Lord, you always were a firebrand, weren't you?'' Jeremy took her by the shoulders. ''Isolde, please. Don't be angry with me. I'm trying to accept the situation. Truly I am. I should never have mentioned my own feelings. I'm sorry. Please forgive me. You are right, of course. I didn't make sure of you and if I had . . . Well, as you say, it's too late now.''

''Indeed, it is.'' Isolde laid a gentle hand on his cheek. ''Poor Jeremy.''

Jeremy took her hand into his own, then turned his head and fervently pressed a kiss into its palm. Looking earnestly at Isolde, he said in a husky voice, ''Please just promise me that if he should ever make you unhappy or well, you know, be unkind to you, please know that I shall stand your friend,'' Jeremy concluded in a worried tone.

''Good God, do you expect me to beat her?'' came a lazy drawl from the doorway.

Chapter Thirteen

Isolde and Jeremy sprang apart in consternation when startled by Shalbourne's unexpected contribution to their conversation. Guilt was clearly written on their faces, although neither one could have explained exactly why.

"My lord," Isolde gasped.

"How long?" Jeremy enquired hoarsely.

"Quite an affecting little scene," Shalbourne replied. "I was especially moved by the part about standing her friend if ever she should need one." Shalbourne's bland expression changed, becoming positively demonic as he lifted one eyebrow and sneered, "Try to remember in the future, Mr. Anderson, that the little girl you knew at the parsonage is now my Lady Shalbourne and my wife. I suspect you should find it rather difficult to obtain another situation without the proper recommendations. Do I make myself understood, Anderson?"

Jeremy, whose countenance had flushed red when my lord had first spoken, was now paper-white. "Perfectly, my lord."

"Unless I am deceived, Mr. Anderson," Shalbourne continued in his most biting tone, "you have been dismissed once this evening to continue whatever it is you pretend to do on this estate. I beg leave to suggest that entertaining my wife is not one of the duties for which you have been employed. You may leave us, Mr. Anderson."

Jeremy gave a stiff bow. "Good night, my lord. My lady." Stiff-backed, shoulders set, jaw clenched, he exited the room.

Shalbourne turned and with a single, sweeping gesture slammed shut the door after Jeremy.

The hush in the room was clamorous in its eloquence. Finally, Shalbourne turned to look at Isolde and cut through the silence to say, "Whatever may have been acceptable in your previous situation, my dear Isolde, in future, try to remember your new position—and mine! I will not willingly give fuel to any backstairs gossip. And neither should you."

Isolde clenched the book she had picked out some ten minutes ago until her knuckles turned white. "You are insulting, my lord. And insufferably rude."

Shalbourne limped forward and took her chin between his long, shapely fingers. Isolde stiffened. "You are the Countess of Shalbourne now, and would do well to remember that. As for your Mr. Anderson"—Shalbourne's hand dropped—"perhaps it would be best if he found a new situation."

"You can't dismiss him," Isolde gasped.

"Can't?" Shalbourne asked incredulously. "Can't dismiss him?! I can do anything I damn well please."

Isolde blanched. "This is nothing more than a childish whim on your part. There is no reason to dismiss Jeremy."

"See that it remains so, my pretty wife," Shalbourne instructed. "I have been patient with you, madam, but be assured that I shall make you think me the very devil himself if you give me cause. I shall know if you have played me false. Ours may not have been the most ideal circumstances for a marriage, but I will not accept any excuse for being cuckolded, nor will I accept someone else's by-blows as my own!"

The sound of a hand making contact with a cheek rang out in the dimly lit, wood-paneled room. Isolde's voice shook with rage, "Of all the evil-minded, foul, disgusting . . . take your hands off me!"

"You try me too far, madam!" Shalbourne snarled, grabbing the tender flesh of her upper arms and pulling her forward. He leaned down and pressed his lips against hers in a punishing kiss. It was as if he would use that action to brand her as his own. The kiss ended as abruptly as it had begun with Shalbourne thrusting her away, saying hoarsely, "Go to your room before I forget that I was at least bred a gentleman."

Isolde scurried to her room to lick her wounds in private while Shalbourne limped to his study to drink himself into peaceful oblivion.

At teatime the next day, Isolde sat down with Jeremy to break bread and reminisce, ignoring my lord's unspoken order to stay away from her childhood friend. As she poured out the tea and plied him with cakes, she inquired after the health of his parents and other mutual friends from their village of Stretton. "You know," Isolde informed him, "I never saw anyone after I went on that visit to London two years ago. I was to have come home anyway within the week when my parents made that hasty and ill-advised trip to London. Their carriage lost a wheel in the middle of a crowded street, you know. It was an open carriage—you might remember the one. They . . . they were thrown from it and crushed by a passing wagon."

"I'm sorry, Isolde." Jeremy squeezed her hand. "My mother wrote as much to me."

"I wasn't with them. Of course, she would have told you that. They never made it to my grandfather's house. I still don't know what possessed them to come after me in that impetuous manner when the arrangements had already been made for me to leave town accompanied by my cousin,

Mirabelle, and a maid. My uncle insisted I was too distraught to go back to the vicarage to pack our things away, which is why I never had an opportunity to take my leave of anyone. Uncle Wendall went in my stead and closed out affairs. I . . . I'm sorry.'' Isolde surreptitiously wiped a few tears from her eyes. ''I don't know what's come over me. I've not discussed their deaths with anyone outside the family before.''

''Then I'm honored you chose me for your confidences,'' Jeremy said, taking another sip from his teacup. ''It's ironic, isn't it? Mother said your father had just performed a funeral the day before your parents took off for London. Almost as if they were fleeing the specter that event had conjured.''

''Yes, it was odd that they should run from Death's clutches, so to speak, only to arrive willy-nilly on his doorstep,'' Isolde agreed. ''Whose funeral was it? I never did learn and felt quite badly that I never had the chance to write the proper condolences.''

Jeremy shrugged and took another cake. ''Wasn't anyone you knew. A woman staying at the Red Lion died unexpectedly. She had been traveling by stage and didn't feel well, so she had stopped at the inn while the stage went on. They sent for your father when she requested someone to hear her deathbed confession.''

''How sad!'' Isolde was distracted from her own tragedy in contemplating another's. ''Didn't her family ever come to claim her or make inquiries?''

''No,'' Jeremy said. ''Couldn't find any relatives, so they buried her in the churchyard.''

''Poor woman.'' Isolde shook her head. ''How sad to be caught in a strange inn in a strange village, with no friends or acquaintances, and to die so swiftly and unexpectedly.''

''Yes,'' Jeremy agreed. ''Caused quite a controversy, it did. She was carrying a large purse and there was a great deal of dispute as to who was the appropriate heir.'' Jeremy grinned in remembrance. ''Old Harry Cheever made her a rather elaborate headstone in the hopes that he could make a large claim on the estate.''

Isolde found herself smiling in reply. ''That man! What he won't do for a shilling or two! And did he receive his largess?''

''No.'' Jeremy laughed. ''Old Man Huntley at the Red Lion charged an exorbitant 'death fee,' as he called it, and laid claim to the whole.''

''Death fee?'' Isolde laughed. ''What next?''

''Claimed it had upset his inn, given it a bad name. Besides, he felt he was bound to burn the sheets and the bed she died in as a precautionary measure, and so charged accordingly.'' Jeremy set down his cup and continued. ''Not that I believe for a minute that an old skinflint like Huntley would be so wanton as to destroy perfectly good furniture and linens just because the exact nature of the woman's illness was never really decided.''

''Yes,'' Isolde concurred. ''I expect he charged his 'death fee,' and never burned, much less replaced, that furniture and bedding.''

''Poor old Cheever,'' Jeremy said, his eyes shining. ''His headstone was never paid for and since the woman's name had been a long one, it cost him quite a bit in time and effort, first to last. All for naught!''

Isolde giggled. ''I shouldn't laugh, I know. It is nice to know, though, that the woman's name is preserved so that if anyone should happen by and recognize it, they might contact the poor lady's relatives.''

''Egads!'' Jeremy exclaimed. ''Someone should have explained that aspect of the case to Cheever. After all, he might have eventually gotten his fee out of some unknown relation of poor Mrs. Jessamina T. Biggelswade. God knows the name is unusual enough that if someone had recognized it, they would probably know where he might send his bill. As it was, he got drunk on Huntley's ale and destroyed the stone in a fit of pique."

"Biggelswade?" Isolde's cup rattled in its saucer. "Are you sure?"

"Lord, yes," Jeremy assured her. "I'm not like to have forgotten that name! Can you imagine going through life with such a one?!"

"No," Isolde agreed absentmindedly. "Can you imagine?" She slumped back in her chair, a stunned expression on her face. She wondered if this Mrs. Jessamina T. Biggelswade was any relation to her erstwhile suitor and if it was her Christian duty (hoping all the time it was not) to find out and inform him of the woman's death. Before she had come to any conclusions, however, they were interrupted by Shalbourne sweeping through the door.

"Just what the hell is going on here?" he demanded, his tone biting.

"My lord!" Jeremy jumped to his feet, his cup rattling precariously in its saucer.

"Good afternoon, my lord." Isolde smiled with chilly politeness. "Would you care to join us? Although I must warn you in advance that you might find the conversation a bit tedious, as Jeremy and I were discussing some of our mutual acquaintances and friends."

Shalbourne ground his teeth audibly and hissed at Jeremy. "Get out, Anderson! I wish to speak to my wife—alone!"

Jeremy cast an anxious look at Isolde, who smiled reassuringly and nodded her dismissal. Deciding that discretion was definitely the better part of valor in the present case, Jeremy bid a hasty retreat.

"You still haven't answered my question," Shalbourne said when the door had shut.

Isolde, outwardly unperturbed, began to stack used dishes and cups neatly onto the tea tray. Blinking at him stupidly, she said, "Oh? Well, goodness me, I could have sworn I had."

"Don't adopt that tone with me, woman!" Shalbourne took two long strides, reached for his wife's arm, and pulled her unceremoniously up from the chair. "I told you to stay away from that slimy toad!"

Isolde's reply was lost as Freckles, the late Lord Shalbourne's spaniel, who had heretofore been content to lie on the hearth rug, took exception to Shalbourne's actions. Barking in unusual excitement for a dog her age (and a great-great-grandmother, at that), she raced in circles around the couple and finally jumped from behind at Isolde's attacker. The vanquished Shalbourne crashed in an undignified heap to the floor, taking Isolde and the tea tray along for good measure.

"Oh, get off me, you great lumbering beast!" Isolde cried as she attempted to push the dog off her chest while it calmly disposed of one of the fallen cakes.

Shalbourne, who was entangled in her ladyship's skirts, a dog's tail in his nose, sneezed and swatted at the offending appendage. "Away, you fleabag!"

The dog nonchalantly stepped away from the two humans, missing not a lick in her mission to clean the floor.

Isolde, receiving a paw in her mouth as the dog moved on, was struck by the outrageous humor of her predicament. Giggling uncontrollably, she turned to look at Shalbourne, who was making an abortive effort to rise, and, catching his eye, she said in gruff tones between guffaws, "Off! You great, lumbering beast!"

Shalbourne stopped his struggles momentarily, an arrested expression on his face. His hands were on either side of her head, his lower limbs entangled with hers. With broken crockery around them, marmalade on his cheek, tea stains soaking into his shirt and her bodice, he, too, broke into a grin.

Isolde's heart skipped a beat at the transformation this change had wrought. His smile was irresistible, the sparkle in his eyes changed them from those of a brooding devil to those of a mischievous little boy.

"And here I thought it was the dog that you were referring to, fleabag!" Shalbourne broke into hearty laughter which she joined wholeheartedly.

As they gasped to catch their breath, the atmosphere between the two changed subtly. Their eyes met and held. Shalbourne, who had been careful to hold his weight away from her, relaxed against her and brushed a stray curl out of her eyes. With the thumb of his other hand, he rubbed a bit of marmalade off her cheek.

"Battle scars, my lady?" he asked, lifting the marmalade-covered thumb to his mouth and licking away the sweet sticky substance. "Let Sir Tristan tend your wounds," he whispered as he leaned his face closer to hers and placed his tongue on her sugared cheek.

Isolde did not fully understand her own reactions as her heart began to flutter and then race. She shuddered and closed her eyes, although it was certainly not a gesture of revulsion. Her hands fluttered as her heart had just a few seconds earlier and then found their way around his waist at the moment that his lips met hers.

Thus it was that Simmons discovered them when he entered to remove the tea tray. Gulping in consternation at the sight of his master and mistress prone on the floor amid shattered tea things, locked in what could only be described as a compromising embrace, he attempted to retreat silently. Unfortunately, his presence had already been sensed.

Shalbourne's head lifted and whipped around, his eyes piercing into the hapless servant. "Damn! Simmons, what do you want?" he barked and tried to lift himself off the floor as gracefully as his present position would allow.

Simmons, who had tried to model his own behavior after

the indomitable Sikes in the hopes of achieving a promotion, and who had previous to this occasion proved quite adept at never being flustered or at a loss for words, turned red as the coals in the grate. "Excuse me, my lord. I . . . I, that is." He choked and then continued in a strained voice, "The tea things, my lord. I thought the room unoccupied and came to remove them."

Shalbourne, now on his feet, turned to give Isolde a hand to rise. "Then do so. As you can see, there's been a slight accident."

"Yes, my lord." Simmons advanced hastily, bent to his knees and began gathering up broken pieces of china to cover his embarrassment.

"The dog, Simmons." Shalbourne's lips twitched as he held back a grin. To his own amazement, he was enjoying the absurdity of the whole situation. "She pushed her ladyship and me to the floor along with the tray."

"Yes, my lord," came a skeptical voice addressed to the tea-stained rug.

Isolde, whose discomfiture was almost as great as Simmons', announced stiffly, "I must go and change. If you will excuse me, my lord."

"By all means, my dear," Shalbourne answered gaily, kissing her hand before releasing her. "I shall have to do so myself momentarily."

As Isolde exited the room, she heard her husband remark, "Oh, by the way, Simmons, would you see to it that that 'fleabag' is not allowed back into the drawing room until she learns better manners." After a pause, he added with a grin, "I meant the dog, of course. Not my wife."

Simmons blinked and went rigid with shock as a chuckling Shalbourne quitted the library. "Of course, my lord," he added belatedly, shaking his head at the eccentricities of the quality and wondering if he would ever achieve the sangfroid necessary to become an under-butler.

The rest of the afternoon and the hours after supper passed agreeably for the newlyweds. In the hours before retiring, Shalbourne, who had reason to be cautious, forced himself to concentrate on wooing his wife as a suitor, rather than asserting his rights as a husband. If Isolde was a bit surprised to have her husband join her in the drawing room after their meal, she did not complain. The end of the evening saw the two retreating amicably, if not amorously, to their respective bedchambers, which could only be an improvement on the previous state of affairs.

The next morning was a Sunday, and Isolde, being the dutiful daughter of a clergyman who had already missed Sunday services twice, arose early to attend church, blissfully unaware that by such an action she was neglecting her duties as a hostess. In ignorance of the fact that her husband's aunt was looked for that day as well as Lord Denbigh (whom Lord Shalbourne had invited as a buffer for his formidable aunt's possible wrath when confronted with the bride), she had the servants arrange a carriage to take her to church instead of staying to greet her houseguests. Mrs. Peters, who was, sadly enough, equally uninformed, accompanied her.

While Isolde wended her way to church, Shalbourne partook of a late breakfast in his chambers. When finished, he decided that he had time for a quick gallop around the grounds before his friend and his aunt arrived. With this in mind, he dressed in buckskin breeches, riding boots, coat, and hat and descended to the stables. The cane he leaned on was the only jarring note in an otherwise perfect portrait of the English gentleman bent on a little equestrian exercise. The staff of the stable was no less startled by his lordship's request for a mount than it had been by her ladyship's unexpected summons for a carriage earlier. They were aware that my lord seldom rode—witness the fact that he had avoided doing so in the last two weeks—so most of the stock had already been exercised or sent to the farthest paddock when my lord came, demanding a suitable hack. Disdaining the first animal he was offered, Shalbourne chose to be mounted on a stallion of highly bred temperament that was housed in the far box.

"Are ye sure ye want to risk him, my lord?" asked one of the more stout-hearted grooms as he saddled the animal.

"Why ever not?" was Shalbourne's immediate reply, a touch of resentment in his tone. "Do you doubt my ability to hold him?"

Thinking "yes," the groom reluctantly answered, "No, my lord."

"Well, then, finish the job and I'll be off."

Offering to give Shalbourne a leg up, the groom was instead forced to stand back in uncomfortable silence as Shalbourne awkwardly attained the saddle under his own power. The groom could only admire his lordship's skill in containing the horse's antics, and clutching the cane that had been thrust into his hands, asked anxiously, "Ye won't be going too far, will ye, my lord?"

"Only to the stone bridge or thereabouts," came Shalbourne's vague reply. "I shan't wind the creature, if that's what you're afraid of."

"No, no, my lord," he was quick to deny. "Ye sure ye won't take no one with ye?"

"An escort, perhaps?" Shalbourne's eyebrow shot up.

The groom, who was not familiar with the danger signal that raised brow indicated, felt constrained to add, "Aye, my lord. To make sure ye come to no harm."

"Like a damned simpering schoolroom miss, I suppose, with my groom mounted and riding a sedate ten paces behind!" Shalbourne turned the full blast of his temper on the unsuspecting groom.

"No, no, my lord," the cowed groom tried to explain. "It's only if ye come to any harm. I didn't mean . . ."

But Shalbourne was not interested in his explanation, and pulling at the horse in a foolhardy fashion, he galloped out of the stableyard to put as much distance as possible between himself and his well-meaning servant.

Ignoring the scenery that was passing at an alarming rate, Shalbourne headed as if by instinct to the small lake his grandfather had commissioned Capability Brown to contrive on the estate. Set amid innumerable trees, its shores were decorated with the obligatory follies and temples. A picturesque stone bridge was thrown over the stream that had been diverted to create the scenery. This bridge, an interesting example of that school of architecture inspired by the Italian Palladio, was not entirely without its uses as it had to be crossed to gain access to the main gates. Clattering across the stone structure, Shalbourne made a sharp turn onto the path which ran perpendicular to the main drive toward the first of the follies, a Temple to Venus. By then, his burst of temper had been forgotten in the exhilaration of his mad gallop, and so he slowed his pace.

After almost an hour of riding and a complete tour of the lake and its scenery, Shalbourne was once more in sight of the main road and the stone bridge. Noting a carriage making its way toward the bridge, Shalbourne decided to wait and greet whoever it was. However, his horse, sensing that home, the stables, and his oats were near, objected to being forced to stand idle while waiting for the vehicle. Dancing, tossing his head and advancing a few steps onto the bridge, he attempted to demonstrate to Shalbourne that he had previously remained seated only on sufferance. Just when it looked like Shalbourne would win this test of wills, and not allow the animal to finish the distance to home, a shot rang out in the quiet.

The horse reared in consternation, taking exception to the bullet that had whizzed past his ears. The creature was panicked, and the coachman less than a hundred feet away was also having a time keeping his own team under control. The groom beside the coachman jumped to the ground and vacillated between running to the coach horses' heads, running to the aid of my lord or trying to ascertain whence the shot was fired. The coach lurched back and forth as the coachman jabbed at the reins. The door flew open and Isolde, in her Sunday finery, stumbled from the coach in time to hear a second shot.

What then took place before her horrified eyes seemed to occur in slow motion. Shalbourne clutched his left arm with his right hand, immediately losing his grip on the reins. The horse reared into the air and Shalbourne slid from his back like an inexperienced child. Landing clumsily on his bad leg on the parapet of the bridge, Shalbourne let out an anguished cry and writhed awkwardly to regain some balance on the narrow ledge. Isolde stood in frozen shock as she watched his battered, overbalanced body shift first toward the bridge's floor and then into the water of the lake.

The splash was greeted by Isolde screaming out "Gay!" and the arrival of a second coach, coming at top speed. Propelled into action, she picked up her skirts to an indecorous height, and ran down the bank to the water's edge. Ignoring mud and slimy water, as well as small patches of ice, she plunged in up to her knees, calling his name over and over.

The second coach made a sudden halt behind the first and Denbigh jumped out. He called to the groom at the head of my lady's coach, "You there! Go see if you can find who fired those shots! Tribbling, you go with him!" he shouted at his own groom, then set off at a run to the water's edge.

The sight that greeted his eyes made him want to laugh, his relief was so great and the picture presented so ludicrous. Shalbourne, dripping wet and covered with mud, with a variety of aquatic plants clinging to him, was standing in three feet of water. His wife, supporting him, was herself soaked to the waist, her bonnet hanging down her back, its ribbons wet and limp.

His mirth was dispelled immediately by the sight of blood on Shalbourne's upper arm. "What the devil!"

Shalbourne looked up with a jerky motion. "George! Where did you spring from?"

"Just arrived. Heard shots as I pulled into the gate." Then with a few quick strides, he walked into the water a foot or so and helped Isolde and Shalbourne out of the muck. "What happened, Gay?"

"God knows." Shalbourne shook his head. "Somebody's taken a dislike to me. Damned if I didn't think I was back in those cursed colonies again for a moment."

"Poacher?" Denbigh suggested.

Shalbourne was about to deny it vehemently, since after all, what self-respecting poacher wishing to retain his skin fired shots in broad daylight, when his eye was caught by Denbigh's silent signal and Isolde's white features.

"Probably," Shalbourne said tersely. "Damn, it's cold," he remarked further. "I think in the future, my lady, we should confine our natatorial activities to the summer months."

George produced a lopsided grin. "I've heard about people in Russia who cut holes in the ice and bathe in the cold waters."

"Ye God!" Shalbourne grinned in return. "You don't say?"

"Supposed to be remarkably healthy," Denbigh added.

"Nonsense," Isolde cut in. "I don't believe it. And if we don't return to the house immediately, we shall surely catch our death of influenza or worse!"

The three bedraggled flowers of England's aristocracy climbed into the nearest coach and made all speed toward Shalbourne Manor.

CHAPTER FOURTEEN

The arrival of guests is enough to throw the most ordered of households into disarray and the attempted murder of the household's head on the very day of those arrivals was enough to send Shalbourne's staff into a state reminiscent of Bedlam. The housekeeper was laid upon her bed nursing a mild case of hysterics. Maids and footmen scurried into each other in an attempt to provide a warming bath for the three principals. My lord's valets were pulling their hair out at the sight of wet, ruined leather boots and muddied breeches and coats. My lady's personal maid regretfully dumped my lady's best bonnet into the bin, since even the tweenie had rejected the opportunity to be its next owner. The cook burned his fingers in an attempt to brew his favorite posset for warding off chills. And Simmons, who had quite decided that promotion was looking less and less appealing, was left with the dubious honor of greeting Lady Jane and trying to afford some sort of explanation for the present state of chaos. As luck would have it, the arrival of the doctor, who had been sent for to attend my lord's arm, coincided with that of Lady Jane.

Indignant that neither her nephew nor his mysterious new wife had seen fit to greet her at the door, Lady Jane was positively beside herself at the cavalier treatment she received in comparison to the doctor.

Complaining bitterly, she demanded of a harassed Simmons to know the identity of that upstart who had been hailed and fêted for all the world like some royal potentate while she was left to cool her heels! Without waiting for Simmons' answer, she went on, "And inform that worthless nephew of mine that if this is any indication of the hospitality, to say nothing of the household management his bride is capable of, then all I can say is I hope that she is exceedingly beautiful. For otherwise, he is in for a very uncomfortable married life! And now, I should like to be conducted to my usual chamber and have a pot of tea sent along forthwith."

Following forlornly in her majestic wake, Simmons tried to direct the few remaining footmen as to the removal and disposition of Lady Jane's innumerable trunks. His explanation for the extraordinary events of the day was ignored by the sulking matriarch until she caught the word 'doctor.'

"Doctor!" Lady Jane demanded. "What's been going forth?"

"Why, this morning my lord was shot by a poacher."

"Shot?" Lady Jane fell back against the banister, blanching.

"Oh, no, my lady! I'm so very sorry! I shouldn't have told you in such a fashion. His lordship is quite unhurt."

"Unhurt?" Lady Jane's voice was faint and weak.

"Oh, yes!" Horrified at his own lack of tact, Simmons was profuse in his apologies. "I'm sorry, my lady. You mustn't worry. Indeed, when last I saw him, my lord was quite vocally arguing with my Lord Denbigh upon whether a doctor's services would even be necessary. Lord Shalbourne was quite adamant that it was only a flesh wound and not to be noticed."

"Humph!" Lady Jane started to regain some of her natural color. "How did it happen? Was the culprit apprehended?"

"Alas, no, mi'lady." Simmons shook his head as they resumed their progress upstairs. "Although it is thought that the poacher's shots originated from an area by the Temple of Apollo, nothing has been found to verify this yet. Indeed, the gamekeeper is even now searching the gounds." Simmons afforded a full explanation of the day's events to an astonished Lady Jane.

"Well!" Lady Jane cried at the end. "It's incredible! The man must be caught. Such a crime cannot go unpunished!"

Meanwhile, as Simmons escorted Lady Jane to her chamber, Isolde was informed that the doctor had arrived. She threw on an elaborately embroidered dressing gown over her numerous petticoats and chemise and told Susan, the maid who had been assigned duties as her dresser, that she would also attend his lordship. Just as Isolde placed her hand on the door handle, she recalled that she must ask the embarrassing question as to the exact location of her husband's rooms.

" 'Twould be faster to nip through this way, my lady," came a much puzzled voice as Susan indicated a door that Isolde had already discovered lead to a small closet. The door beyond, however, had been locked on her first and last exploring trip. She did remember hearing noises from the room behind it, a clear indication that it was occupied. Realizing that it must be a connecting door to my lord's chambers, a red-faced Isolde stammered, "Oh. Yes, of course. The excitement of the morning, you know . . ." She trailed off lamely and hastened through the door, not stopping to knock in her consternation.

As a result of her precipitate entry, Isolde was quite disconcerted by the sight that greeted her eyes. A stark naked Shalbourne, having just emerged from his bath, was arguing volubly with the doctor.

"Damn it, man!" he exclaimed impatiently. "It's just a flesh wound!"

"For all that, you were bleeding like a stuck pig not thirty minutes ago," Denbigh, dressed in a red velvet floor-length dressing gown, was clearly ranged on the side of the doctor.

"If you'll just sit on the bed, my lord," the doctor started. "I just want to make certain—"

"Damn it, George, if I wanted another damned valet, I'd hire one!" Shalbourne burst out irritably as Denbigh tried to cover his friend with a dressing gown, having caught sight of Isolde's frozen, wide-eyed figure in the doorway.

"Shut up, idiot," Denbigh said through clenched teeth.

Shalbourne ripped the dressing gown from Denbigh's hands and turned his back on the group only to be confronted by his very red-faced wife. To say that Isolde had led a sheltered existence at the rectory and subsequently at her uncle's was not putting it too mildly. Heretofore, aside from a small portion of Shalbourne's chest on her ill-fated wedding night, the only parts of the male anatomy she had seen uncovered were the face, the hands, and an occasional foot. She had not even had the benefit of a classical education in regard to the arts, so until she had arrived at Shalbourne Manor she had never been exposed to paintings or statuary depicting the female form, much less the male. Therefore, her innocent startled eyes were inexorably drawn from Shalbourne's face to his wide shoulders, thence to the barreled hair-covered chest and finally to his tapered waist, lean hips, and long legs. She was not so much disturbed by the scar which ran from one shoulder to his navel, or by the sight of his well-muscled thigh in comparison to the other scarred and mangled one, as by that part which was found between and clearly labeled him a man.

"Isolde!" Shalbourne hastily wrapped the robe he had grabbed from Denbigh around his waist in a makeshift fashion, leaving the sleeves dangling in a ridiculous manner, the collar on one hip and the hem thrown over the other. "What the hell!"

"Excuse me, my lord," Isolde's voice, thin and weak stammered. She swallowed and continued, "I wanted to find out what the doctor had to say. And to make sure you were well." Her voice tapered off to a whisper, "I'm sorry."

The doctor, sensing an ally and recognizing that this shy young lady must be the young hothead's wife, advanced eagerly. "My lady, if you could please persuade his lordship to sit for only a few moments, I could look at his wound and—"

"Oh, for God's sake!" Shalbourne exclaimed as he took a few limping steps and threw himself into the chair next to the bed. "Look at the bloody thing, if you must. Just do it quickly and go!"

Isolde, regaining some of her composure, went to the doctor's side to inquire worriedly, "Will he be all right?"

"Good God, woman!" Shalbourne's cry caused Isolde to jump. "I'm not going to cast up my accounts over a simple flesh wound! God knows, I've suffered worse in my day. Lord, look at this bloody scar on my chest if you doubt my word. Or, possibly, you'd like to make a closer inspection of my damned leg!"

The doctor, taking note of Isolde's hurt and mortified expression, patted her hand reassuringly. "Don't worry, my lady. Gentlemen are inclined to be fractious on such occasions."

"And don't talk about me as if I weren't in the room."

"There, now," the doctor said as he finished wrapping his more professional-looking bandage around Shalbourne's arm. "You'll do, my lord. Terrible thing, these poachers. A man isn't safe anywhere anymore. Ah, well, hasn't been the same since they killed the French Queen thirty years ago.

Now, if you'll just give me your wrist, my lord, I'll finish by bleeding you.''

"Like hell you will!" Shalbourne cried.

"But, my lord, the Prince Regent himself is a great proponent of the beneficial nature of bleeding!" The doctor waxed indignant. "Why, when the Princess Charlotte died only a few weeks ago, his doctor bled him of . . ."

"I don't give a tinker's damn what fool thing Prinney takes in his head to do, you aren't getting another drop from me!" Shalbourne interrupted.

The doctor heaved a great sigh and agreed against his better judgment. He warned it was only putting off the inevitable, as he would no doubt be vindicated on the morrow. "But we shall wait and see, my lord"—he sighed again —"if you insist."

Simmons chose this moment to knock quietly and then enter without being bid. "Excuse me, my lord. Ah, my lady!" he added, a bit startled at her presence in my lord's chamber.

"Yes, Simmons, what is it?" asked an impatient Shalbourne.

"Lady Jane, my lord, has arrived."

"Lady Jane? Damn!" Shalbourne exclaimed.

"Must have seen the announcement in Thursday's *Gazette*," Denbigh offered by way of explanation.

"Thursday's. What are you talking about, George?" Shalbourne demanded.

"The wedding announcement. I sent it 'round to all the papers early part of last week. Knew you'd forget. She probably saw it and hurried . . ."

Shalbourne interrupted, scorning such a possibility, "I told her myself! I may have neglected to make arrangements for inserting the news into the London papers, but I certainly took the time to write to Lady Jane regarding the marriage. She even wrote back to say she would be joining us today.

Although, she might have picked a better hour to arrive! Gad, George, you wouldn't believe what she said when I told her I was married already!''

"Who is Lady Jane?'' was Isolde's confused question.

"Why, my aunt, of course,'' Shalbourne explained, puzzled that she hadn't known this immediately.

"Oh, dear.'' Isolde pressed her hands to her cheeks, visions of avenging relatives dancing in her head. It had never occurred to her that Shalbourne might have relations who would object to his marriage. Summoning up reserves of courage that she hadn't known she possessed, she announced, "I'll be there at once, Simmons.''

"Isolde!'' Shalbourne's voice arrested her in midflight, his arm outstretched to her. Taking her hand into his and pressing it, palm up to his lips, he murmured, "Thank you.''

"For what?'' she asked unsteadily, breathless.

He smiled at her and her heart skipped a beat. "Why? Because you called me 'Gay,' of course. What else?''

She dimpled at his sally. "Excuse me, ah, Gay,'' she amended shyly. "I must change my dress before I go to your aunt.'' She left in a flurry of skirts and flying hair.

"My, my, Gay,'' Denbigh breathed after the door shut behind her.

"Just what do you mean by that remark?!'' Shalbourne demanded aggressively.

"Nothing, nothing,'' Denbigh grinned at his friend. "Just think you ought to admit I'm not half bad at matchmaking.''

Isolde, both fearful and curious about meeting her husband's aunt, had hastily thrown on the first gown she found in her closet. Stepping into the hall, she hailed the first person she saw, who happened to be a maid with an armful of sheets, and asked hesitantly, "Mary, isn't it? Do you suppose you might help me? I am looking for Lady Jane's rooms."

"Oh, of course, my lady." Mary laid her burden on a nearby table. "I shall be happy to accompany you there."

Traversing from the south wing to the north was not an easy task and Isolde was quite lost by the time they had passed through their fifth gallery and run up and down their second flight of stairs. Arriving at last at Lady Jane's door, she was taken aback when it was jerked open in response to Mary's tentative knock by a rather plain-faced, scowling woman somewhere between forty and sixty, looking for all the world like a crow who had just been chased away from a particularly choice field of corn.

"Lady Jane?" Isolde ventured timidly.

"She's resting now. What do you want?" The dark, somberly dressed creature demanded rudely. "Have you got the tea?"

"Tea? What? No, I'm sorry."

"Her ladyship asked for tea twenty minutes ago. Where is it?" Jenkins, Lady Jane's dresser and personal maid, demanded.

"Why, I don't know." Isolde had been put off her stride by Jenkins' behavior.

"What kind of household is this?" Jenkins shot at her sharply. "And what kind of maid's uniform is that?" Jenkins let her eyes pass disparagingly over Isolde's simple muslin gown.

Mary bobbed a quick curtsy and gave a smug smile to Jenkins. She was about to have her revenge for all the times that Jenkins had snubbed her in past visits. "Would you like me to see what has happened to Lady Jane's tea, my lady?"

Jenkins stood in open-mouthed surprise. "You're . . ." she began.

Isolde turned to Mary, ignoring Jenkins' imitation of a fish. "Thank you, Mary." Then looking back at Jenkins, she asked politely, "Do you suppose I might speak with your mistress now?"

"Yes, yes, of course," Jenkins became obsequious. "Come right in, my lady. Lady Jane is in the sitting room. Follow me."

"Is that my tea, Jenkins?" came a sharp voice as Jenkins opened the sitting room door.

"No, my lady. Lady Shalbourne to see you."

"Well, send her in! Send her in!" Lady Jane urged impatiently.

Isolde, following in Jenkins' footsteps, entered before Lady Jane had finished her demand.

"Well!" Lady Jane's voice held surprise and even a bit of unholy glee. Lady Harriet Marsh as I live and breathe, she thought.

"How do you do, Lady Jane?" Isolde extended her hand and advanced gracefully into the room. "I'm so sorry that I wasn't on hand to greet you, but I'm sure you understand, what with the excitement of the morning and all. I had not finished dressing myself, and, indeed, was with the doctor and my lord when the news was brought that you had arrived."

"Yes, yes, Simmons told me everything." Lady Jane waved aside her explanations and asked the question burning in her mind, "Tell me, my dear, are you by any chance related to the late Lady Harriet Marsh?"

"Yes," Isolde said baldly. "She was my father's mother."

Lady Jane beamed. "Your father's mother! And your father?"

"The Reverend Henry Marsh, your ladyship," Isolde said, almost defensively and a little defiant.

"A man of the cloth, was he?" Lady Jane, who did not remember any rumors regarding the gentleman, was pleased. "I can't say that I was acquainted with the gentleman, but I did know your grandfather, Sir Randolph, many years ago when I first made my debut." Lady Jane gave an inward sigh of relief. The letter she had received from her nephew had prepared her for the worst. Her own less than cordial reply had expressed displeasure and doubts at her nephew's actions. She realized now that he was just having a go at her when he had tried to pass off that banbury tale about choosing a bride through the medium of the *Chronicle*. "Goodness, I haven't thought about Sir Randolph or Lady Harriet in years! She was the old Earl of Langhurst's eldest, wasn't she?"

Isolde, who recognized Lady Jane's catechism for what it was, dryly confirmed this fact.

"And your mother, my dear? She was . . . ?" Lady Jane smiled benevolently. "I've forgotten."

"Miss Susan Challoner."

"Challoner. Challoner. Hmmm, I don't seem to be able to recall her." Lady Jane frowned in concentration.

"Miss Susan Challoner of Challoner's Spice and Tea Importers."

"Spice and tea!" Lady Jane gasped, then swallowed convulsively. "Your mother's family was in trade?" she asked in an appalled voice, much as she would have if Isolde's maternal relations had engaged in theft or murder.

"Yes." Isolde lifted her head proudly. "My uncle still runs the firm, since my Grandfather Challoner died two years ago. Indeed, I myself am due to receive an annual income from the firm of two thousand pounds starting on my next birthday as well as a lump sum of ten thousand as my dowry now that I have wed. So you can see, my lady, it is quite a successful venture."

"I'm sure it is," Lady Jane interrupted imperiously. "But you are the Countess of Shalbourne now and must take your proper place. It would never do for you to speak of your connections in trade. Your parents . . ."

"My parents are dead," Isolde stated without emotion.

"Ah, I'm sorry, my dear," Lady Jane sympathized briefly, then added more severely. "However, it would never do to allow a whisper of your trade connections to destroy your chances at the outset. If you conduct yourself as I say, I'm certain we will be able to open more than one door."

"I'm sorry if you don't find me good enough to be Countess of Shalbourne, my lady," Isolde said stiffly.

"No, no, my dear. You misunderstand." Lady Jane snorted. "Actually, I am more grateful than I can say that you are so very, well, presentable. And please, call me 'Aunt Jane' as your husband does." Lady Jane smiled.

"Aunt—Aunt Jane." Isolde complied hesitantly.

"And I shall call you Isolde. That is correct, isn't it?" Lady Jane asked. "Very pretty. Very unusual."

"Excuse me, my lady. Your tea has finally come."

"Ah, thank you, Jenkins. Lady Shalbourne and I will take our tea in here at once," the elderly lady instructed.

"I must tell you, my dear," Lady Jane began after they had been served with cups of tea, plied with cakes and biscuits, and then left on their own once again by the servants. "You should know that my hot-headed nephew must be handled with a great deal of tact."

"Yes. I'm sure you're correct there," Isolde agreed readily.

"Frankly, Isolde," Lady Jane said, eyeing that young lady skeptically, "a girl of your background could not possibly have been prepared to deal with a gentleman of my nephew's disposition."

"I assure you, my ah, Aunt Jane," Isolde informed her, "although my life has been a sheltered one, my lord's disposition in no way shocks me. Indeed, in many ways, he reminds me forcibly of some of the more adventurous and naughty boys under my father's tutelage. He indulges in mischief not so much out of a bad or evil nature as from the fact that he is heartily bored.''

Lady Jane beamed. ''Brava, my dear girl! You have gone right to the core of the problem on this one! If a man is satisfied at home, then he needn't look to others for his entertainment. I'm glad to see you aren't going to be missish about the women he may have entertained in the past.''

''Women?''

''Lord, yes. My nephew used to change his mistresses like other men change their sheets.''

Isolde smiled tremulously and the teacup in her hand rattled against its saucer. She wasn't quite sure how they had gotten on to the present subject, but when she had mentioned Shalbourne's boredom, it had not been his rakish, women-strewn past she had had in mind.

Lady Jane leaned forward confidentially and took Isolde's limp hand in her own. ''A bit of advice from an old woman, my dear, for what it is worth. If you want to bind a man to your side, never deny him your bed and, remember, there's no reason why you should not enjoy the experience as much as he does!'' She scowled. ''Most young ladies these days are quite nauseating with their die-away airs and their martyred attitude. Why, in my day, we knew how to enjoy ourselves! I should rather be accused of being lusty and licentious than sanctimonious and prudish any day!''

Isolde turned a fiery red and swallowed guiltily as she recalled the fact that she had been married for almost two weeks and that her husband had only sought her company once, on their ill-fated wedding night.

''Mind you, I'm no advocate for overstepping the bounds of matrimony to find your pleasure,'' Lady Jane continued. ''I have seen many a couple break their hearts over each other's infidelities.''

''Oh, I would never.''

''Of course you wouldn't, my dear,'' Lady Jane was

quick to reassure Isolde of her good opinion. "But you mustn't let my vile-tempered nephew imagine there has been any straying on your part, either. He would be madly jealous. The deplorable fact is that my nephew has the hot blood of a Latin in his veins from his Spanish mother, and he is often apt to think with his heart rather than his head." Lady Jane turned to pick up a small, bite-sized piece of cake. "Suffice it to say that trying to attach my nephew's affections by making him jealous will only serve to make matters worse. The only way to bind him, as I've already said, is to be a loving wife." She laughed. "Of course, I am also of the opinion that children make wonderful knots in those bonds. And I should like very much to be a great aunt as quickly as possible. There now," Lady Jane set aside her teacup after a short silence. "I've embarrassed you, haven't I?"

Isolde laughed nervously. In a small voice, she answered, "I don't know how we came to discuss this." She pressed her cold hands to her flushed cheeks. "Oh, dear, this is very difficult for me. You must know, Aunt Jane, that my mother died some years ago and that, well, my own Aunt Mary with whom I lived did not see fit to enlighten me. I am afraid I am woefully ignorant. How will I be able to tell if I am . . . Oh, dear. Do you suppose you could tell me? I hate to ask you on such a short acquaintance but . . ."

"You mean to say that that dissolute nephew of mine took your innocence without so much as a word of explanation?" Lady Jane was aghast.

"Please!" Isolde hastened to say. "You mustn't blame Gay. He couldn't have known that I was in such ignorance."

"Well, if you can be so quick to defend him, he must have gone about the business in a much kinder manner than I would have expected from someone of his temperament." Lady Jane shook her head. "But, then, I suppose his reputation as a rake and seducer must have some basis in fact. Still, I expect it came as a bit of a shock, so unprepared as you were.'' Lady Jane became very businesslike. ''Well, my dear, if no one has told you, then I suppose I must.'' Although she couched her explanation in as confusing terms as possible, Isolde did manage to get the gist of what was being said without revealing her own complete ignorance. She also came to the appalling conviction that there was not even the remotest possibility of her being pregnant as a result of what had occurred at that inn that night. From what she could gather, marital relations involved a greater degree of intimacy than she had ever dreamed possible. Her hands shook as she realized the narrow escape she had had, for to contemplate even the most preliminary steps that Lady Jane described in connection with Harold Biggelswade was enough to produce a sick lump in the pit of her stomach.

''And now, my dear,'' Lady Jane interrupted Isolde's thoughts. ''You can tell me your plans for your guests this Christmas.''

''Guests?'' Isolde exclaimed. ''Plans?''

''Yes, certainly.'' Lady Jane proceeded to rattle off a list of twenty to thirty of the local gentry who were apparently, according to tradition, invited for a dinner every Christmas Eve.

Isolde reeled at the shock. However, Lady Jane was by no means finished. ''How do you plan to decorate the Hall? Are you prepared for Boxing Day? Do you have enough supplies on hand for any unexpected visitors from the neighborhood? I'm sure that as soon as word is out that you and Shalbourne are now receiving, there will be an endless stream of bride visitors. And, of course, aside from the formal dinner, Shalbourne Manor has always held a ball at this season. There is a dance for the tenants and villagers as well, but you need only put in an appearance.''

Lady Jane continued to outline the things that had been

done at Shalbourne Manor for many years past and those which she expected Isolde would want to continue. "Actually, my dear Isolde," Lady Jane added conspiratorially. "That's the main reason I wrote Shalbourne that I would be here earlier than I had originally planned. Reading his letter concerning your nuptials, it suddenly struck me that you might not know exactly how to go on and that you would need my guidance."

Isolde could only shake her head numbly in mute agreement to this obvious understatement. She was quite overwhelmed by Lady Jane's plans and expectations. She was just beginning to understand what being my Lady Shalbourne entailed, and was finding the prospect a daunting one.

CHAPTER FIFTEEN

A creative hostess can always deal with disaster. If the cook overseasons the meat or a footman serves the red wine with the fish course; if the dessert has been saturated with soured cream or if the under-butler drops soup into the lap of a guest; the courageous hostess can and will overcome. However, trying to explain an absent host was taxing creativity to the limit.

Earlier in the day, the inevitable tension which arises from the advent of some thirty-six guests for dinner had communicated itself to the entire Shalbourne household. The end result was that "words" had been spoken between two of its members over the luncheon plates. When my Lord Shalbourne announced his intention of riding out to meet his steward and inspect a tenant's roof on the far corner of his estate during the afternoon, returning in time to dress before his guests were expected, Lady Jane promptly instructed him not to dilly-dally on his errand.

"I am more than six, dear aunt!" had been Shalbourne's nasty-toned reply. "And I am perfectly capable of ordering my life efficiently without anyone's help, thank you!"

"See that you are!" had been the uncowed response, and the two parted company on less than cordial terms.

It wasn't until Isolde had descended to the drawing room

after dressing for their Christmas Eve dinner that she found out that Shalbourne had not returned from his errand. Before Mr. John Littleton and his household arrived, Lady Jane and Lady Shalbourne had been telling their guests that my lord had been delayed while inspecting his estate and would be down shortly to greet his guests, asking their indulgence in Shalbourne's name for his tardiness. Unfortunately, the sentence Mr. Littleton chose to tack on to his introduction to the new Lady Shalbourne soon put paid to the ladies' hopes that their excuse might shortly prove to be a true one.

"My dear Lady Shalbourne, you are quite charming!" Littleton had grinned amiably and kissed her hand in a gallant fashion. "Why Shalbourne should choose to spend the afternoon drinking toasts to the health of every man in the Bird-in-Hand taproom, I shall never know! I know that if you were my bride, I should never spend my time thus!"

"Drinking in the Bird-in-Hand taproom?" Lady Jane's eyes narrowed suspiciously. "What are you talking about, John?"

Mr. Littleton looked genuinely distressed. "Ye gads, have I set the cat among the pigeons? I assure you, Lady Jane, I exaggerate. He only drank one or two tankards that I know of." Littleton's expression of chagrin would have been comical if Lady Jane had not been so angered or Isolde so distressed. "I am a poor friend indeed to have left him in such a condition when I knew you must have been looking for him momentarily." He lowered his voice conspiratorially, "Not feeling quite the thing, is he? Well, that Fraser of his is a good man and will have him right as a trivet in no time. I'm sure he'll be down to join you shortly!"

The two ladies smiled weakly at this further revelation, hoping devoutly that Mr. Littleton was right in his assessment that Shalbourne had already returned and was even then being dressed for dinner by his valet.

After the entire Littleton party had been properly introduced, a short lull descended before the next group embarking from their coach could enter. Lady Jane seized the opportunity to hiss angrily at Isolde, ''It's all defiance! That's what it is! He knows how important this is to me—to us! And now he intends to mortify me by insulting our guests! If he does deign to give us the dubious pleasure of his company, he'll probably be dead drunk! Oh! That boy! Just when I thought he might be attaining some measure of maturity! Why, when he was so determined to inspect that roof today, I thought sure this was a sign.''

A confused Isolde felt compelled to defend her absent lord, ''But I thought you were angry with him for making that inspection today? Surely you can't condemn him for the action one moment and then . . .''

''For his concern for his tenants' welfare, no.'' Lady Jane explained through a pasteboard smile which was directed at her approaching guests. ''For insisting on assuming his responsibilities today and then sneaking off to that low tavern instead! Why, you're looking lovely tonight, Lady Peverell.''

It was unfortunate that Mr. Anderson was the next guest after the Peverells to be announced since his words of greeting unwittingly lent fuel to Lady Jane's fire. ''I am sorry to be so late, ladies. However, I waited as long as I could for his lordship at McCauley's farmhouse before I finally gave up. I knew I had to dress for your dinner and, as luck would have it, this would be the day my horse missed its footing jumping McCauley's fence. I'm afraid the fall's made me a bit stiff, and . . .''

''Are you telling me,'' Lady Jane interrupted his apologies to demand, ''that that desolute nephew of mine never met you at all this afternoon?!''

Jeremy, uncertain whether it was too late to cover for his employer but more uncertain whether he even wanted to, spoke hesitantly, "I'm sure his lordship has a good reason for not meeting me as we'd arranged."

Lady Jane snorted. "A very good reason, I should expect. Too drunk to get there, I suppose."

A horrified Jeremy, seeing the stain creeping over Isolde's cheeks, halfheartedly attempted to defend Shalbourne, "Oh, no, my lady! I'm sure his lordship must have just mistaken the time for our appointment."

Isolde was never so grateful for anything in her life when Mrs. Peters chose that moment to present her with a domestic crisis. Her feelings were entirely too ambivalent for comfort. On the one hand, it looked very much indeed like Shalbourne had chosen to defy his aunt in a most childlike fashion by doing exactly as he pleased with his afternoon. On the other hand, if he really had intended to go on to meet Jeremy to inspect the roof, his not showing up could mean he was dead in a ditch somewhere. She frowned wryly to herself at the thought. Dead drunk, she supposed.

Dinner, which could not be delayed any longer, was one of the worst meals Lady Jane and Lady Shalbourne had ever had to endure. Their excuses for Shalbourne's absence stuck in their throats and made eating impossible. None of their aristocratic guests would have been so rude as to question the veracity of Shalbourne's sudden illness which prevented him from coming to table. However, more than one bit of hushed laughter was followed closely by a surreptitiously pitying glance when John Littleton's story of having last seen Shalbourne in his cups at the Bird-in-Hand made the rounds.

It wasn't until much later in the evening, when the last lingering guest had departed and only the two ladies were left in possession of the drawing room, that Simmons was able to make his report. Contrary to the ladies' certain belief (and fearful hope) that his lordship had returned in too disgusting a condition to greet his guests, his lordship, according to Simmons, had not returned at all.

"Not here, you say?!" Lady Jane demanded incredulously of a nervous Simmons.

Isolde, who had spent most of the evening angry, felt a shiver of fearful concern creep up her neck. "Not here?" she echoed, but in an entirely different tone of voice. "Oh, Aunt Jane, something must have happened!"

Lady Jane's frown boded no good for her absent nephew. "Thank you, Simmons. You may go. Oh, and tell the other servants they may retire as well. I don't expect we shall see Lord Shalbourne this night."

"Aunt Jane," Isolde began as Simmons slinked from the room, grateful that Lady Jane's wrath had not been directed at him. "Don't you think we should organize a search party?"

"Certainly not," Lady Jane answered gruffly. "Shalbourne has probably chosen to put up at the Bird-in-Hand for the night. He will no doubt use his inebriated condition to account for his insulting us and his guests this evening. Go to bed, my dear. I am sorry as I can be for your embarrassment this night. However, you can be sure my nephew will pay the price!"

Isolde, seeing that further argument would only serve to increase Lady Jane's displeasure, chose to keep her worries to herself. She reluctantly bid Lady Jane good night and retired to her rooms.

Sleep evaded Isolde. She tossed and turned, reliving the nightmare of her guests' departure and the sly, superior and pitying looks she had received. One moment she was convinced Lady Jane was right, that Shalbourne had drunken himself into a stupor and stayed at the Bird-in-Hand to sleep it off. The next, she was convinced that he was in trouble and needed her help. It was almost two hours after she had first laid down on her bed that she heard the noise.

Isolde sat bolt upright in the bed, startled out of the uneasy sleep into which she had drifted. Listening intently, she heard somebody moving laboriously down the corridor. Isolde clamped her mouth in grim lines. From the unsteady gait and bumbling steps, she was forced to conclude that Lady Jane was right. Her husband was drunk. Roaringly so as the vase of flowers on the small table at the top of the stairs crashing to the floor made witness. Thrusting her feet into the slippers beside her bed and throwing on the wrapper hung over a nearby chair, she quickly lit the candle on her mantelpiece with a taper. Damn him! she thought to herself, forgetting the language of a lady, "I lie here and worry about him for *hours* and all that's the matter is that he's drunk! Disgusting!"

Racing to the door, she stepped into the hall in time to see Shalbourne stumble over his own bed chamber's threshold not ten feet away. Isolde thought she heard an oath which was followed immediately by a loud crash.

"Damn!" Shalbourne ejaculated quite distinctly.

Isolde, propelled into action, held her hand so that her candle was protected from any wayward drafts. Following in Shalbourne's wake, she called out softly from the threshold he had just vacated, "My lord?"

Another oath, the sound of a hesitant step and then Shalbourne emerged from the shadows into the small circle of light from her candle.

"Yes, wife?" Shalbourne asked through clenched teeth.

"Oh, dear God, what happened?" Isolde demanded as she made out his features.

"Naught but a small blow to the head." Shalbourne threw off into a dark corner what was left of his cravat. "Do you suppose you could trouble yourself to light a few more candles, so that we might 'curse the darkness,' so to speak?"

"Yes, yes, of course," Isolde assured him. "You'll have to tell me where they are, though."

"If you could lend me your arm . . ." Shalbourne left the sentence unfinished as she hurried to his side. Using her as a support, he directed her to his dressing table where he pried the candle from her nerveless fingers and lit the ones found there. Leaning closer to the mirror mounted on the back of the large piece of furniture, he mumbled, "Ye gods, what a lump. Didn't break the skin, though, which is more than the rogue who did this can say."

"But what . . . who . . . ?"

"A footpad, my love," Shalbourne replied as he shrugged out of the tattered remnants of his wet coat. "Damn, it's cold out there!"

"But where? When?" Isolde seemed only capable of sputtering interrogatives.

"Would you believe practically on my own bloody door-step? The bastard attacked as I was riding out to meet Mr. Anderson after I had left the Bird-in-Hand. In broad daylight, too! Left me to rot in the woods just beyond the west paddock. God knows, if it hadn't been such a deserted and overgrown spot, or if my horse hadn't panicked, he would never have gotten away with his nefarious scheme. I did manage to draw blood on him, though."

"How?"

"The sword stick in my cane. Quite a handy little device. A shame he decided to steal it as well as my mount. Would you mind wringing some water through that for me? There's a love. Ah, damn, my head hurts. Yes, that's fine. Just fold it up and I'll place it on my head. Ah, thank you."

"He took your horse?" Isolde asked incredulously. "And your cane?"

"Yes, damn him. Stap me, I was fond of that cane! I am most happy to say, though, that most of the blood you see on

me was his. I might have come about after I'd run him
through with my sword stick if my damned horse hadn't
knocked me into a low-hanging branch. Felled by a single
blow! Knocked me out cold!''

"Oh, Gay, I'm so sorry.'' Isolde's expression displayed
lines of anxiety. ''Shouldn't I call Fraser to prepare a hot
bath for you? If you've been lying unconscious in the cold
all this time, you're sure to be frozen through.''

"No. Too late for such antics. 'Sides, wasn't lying on the
wet ground that was so bad. It was the walk home without
my cane. I could use a brandy, though.''

"I'll go get it.'' Isolde picked up her candle once again
and moved swiftly for the door.

"Darling,'' Shalbourne's voice was lightening into amusement now that his ordeal had ended and he was receiving the
proper amount of sympathy and attention. ''That's what we
have servants for.''

"Oh, but your aunt sent them all to bed. She was persuaded you wouldn't have any need for them tonight.''
Isolde looked shamefaced. ''I'm afraid she believed you had
put up at the Bird-in-Hand for the night.''

"John tell you I was there dealing with Lushington, did
he? I might have guessed.''

"Oh, but, Gay,'' she hastened to add, ''I just knew you
wouldn't have done without sending word that you weren't
coming. Especially when you knew we would be having
guests. I was worried sick.''

Shalbourne was touched by her show of faith and
trust—also her naivete. He was honest enough to admit to
himself, if not to her, that he had been sorely tempted to
stay at the Bird-in-Hand and get thoroughly disguised, as
well as entertained by the lovely barmaid, just to show
Lady Jane he was not to be dictated to anymore. His
cheeks stained redder than they already were from the
cold as he recalled his childish behavior, glad that he was

at least not to blame for missing his appointment with Mr. Anderson. He coughed. "Ah, well, you're right there, of course. I would never have purposely set out to embarrass you in such a fashion."

Isolde smiled brilliantly at him. "I'll just nip down to the library for the brandy decanter. Is it the red-colored stuff or the white?"

"Actually, it's the brown."

"Oh, yes."

Isolde raced off. While she was gone, Shalbourne took the opportunity to throw off his remaining soaked garments and shrug into a warm dressing gown. Just as he was tying the belt, Isolde came back without warning.

"Here we are." She closed the door awkwardly behind her. "There was even a glass sitting next to it. Wasn't that fortunate? Now, you just hop into bed and I'll give you some of this," she instructed as she set the decanter, glass, and candle beside his bed and pulled back the covers.

Shalbourne allowed himself to be led to the bed and tucked in, his dressing gown still on, as he had no wish to embarrass his wife with a display of what he had on—or rather, did not have on—underneath.

"Here," Shalbourne coaxed, and patted a spot beside him on the bed's counterpane. "Sit while you pour."

Isolde didn't hesitate, all the while concentrating on the task at hand. "There you are. Now, drink up."

Shalbourne did as he was told without argument.

"It must have been awful for you." Isolde shivered expressively. "I should have been scared out of my wits. You might have been killed!"

"I think that's what he thought—that he had murdered me. Or, rather, that my horse and that tree had! He certainly left me to die of exposure!" Shalbourne held out his glass for another bit of brandy which Isolde filled absent-mindedly.

"How horrible!" Placing a cool, slim hand on his forehead, Isolde asked anxiously, "You're not catching a fever from it, are you?"

"Lord, no," Shalbourne said softly and gently took the hand on his forehead into his. "I've the constitution of a horse. It will take more than a few hours in the cold to dispatch me." He placed the now empty glass on the table beside him. Then, taking the decanter from her, he placed it beside the glass. Taking her hand once more into his, he raised it to his lips, his eyes never wavering from her own. Mesmerized by his steady gaze, Isolde gulped and burst out, "Oh, Gay, are you sure you have sustained no injury?"

Ignoring her question, Shalbourne whispered huskily as he took hold of a handful of loose hair, "I see you've stopped wearing that odious cap."

"What . . . . Oh, I, ah . . ." Oh, dear, was she forever doomed to stutter when speaking to the man? "I just didn't think about it tonight." Isolde nervously tried to shift away. The natural embarrassment of being in such a circumstance began to assert itself as she realized for the first time that she was seated on her husband's bed dressed only in her night-gown and robe.

"Because you were worried about me?" Shalbourne leaned toward her, placing an arm about her shoulders to pull her near and his hand under her chin to lift her face to his. "I'm flattered by your concern."

The kiss that followed was gentle and sweet, as if Shalbourne was trying not to frighten the birdlike creature in his hands.

"I—I suppose I should go to my bed now," Isolde suggested tentatively in a hoarse whisper. The hands clutching convulsively at his lapels belied her words.

"Stay, love." Shalbourne brushed a strand of hair from her cheek. Weaving his fingers through the heavy mass on the nape of her neck, he punctuated his words with slow, penetrating kisses. "Stay and make me warm. I was almost murdered tonight and I need you." On that final word, he gently pushed her unresisting body down on the bed next to him.

CHAPTER SIXTEEN

Convinced that the mysterious poacher of almost a fort-night ago and the base footpad of the previous evening were one and the same criminal, Lord Shalbourne was anxious to lead the hunt to find "the scurrilous bastard!" He firmly expressed this view as he tried to avoid the well-intentioned ministrations of his household. The excitement of Christmas morning was lost in the face of the outraged sensibilities, vengeful thoughts, and horrified speculations that every resident, employee, or hanger-on at Shalbourne Manor felt and expressed to varying degrees.

It wasn't until well into that afternoon that Shalbourne was given an opportunity to investigate the matter further. He and, of course, Lord Denbigh, with all the excitement of a pair of lads searching for pirates' buried treasure, had seized the first chance they could to set out in search of clues. When Shalbourne returned from that expedition, he slammed the front door in a towering rage, a cane in one hand, an old-looking sack in the other.

"Simmons!" he shouted at that hapless individual who had been hovering in the hall hoping for a glimpse of the newest chambermaid.

"Yes, my lord," he stuttered.

"Send Anderson to me! At once!" Shalbourne shoved his

hat and gloves into his startled servant's hands. Simmons decided not to mention that it was Christmas Day and that Mr. Anderson might prove difficult to run to ground.

Shalbourne then stalked into the library as quickly as his cane and limping gait would allow. Slamming the door behind him once again, he went straight to the decanter on the desk, threw down the sack he clutched next to it, ripped out the decanter stopper, and then slopped the contents into a glass.

"Gay?" Isolde's voice startled him into spilling some more of the brandy on to the Aubusson rug. He whirled around, his fierce stare noting for the first time that she sat in the library's most comfortable chair. Isolde rose with a shy smile on her lips and took a few steps closer. "How was your ride?" She bit back a grin and asked in her best indulgent mother tone, "Did you find anything?"

Shalbourne glared, shrugged, and turned his back on her. He downed the drink in his hand in a single gulp. "Who? Who could hate me that much?" he growled. Turning back to face his startled wife, he continued. "My footpad last evening was just too coincidental for comfort, coming so hard on the heels of that poacher less than a fortnight ago. Quite disconcerting, Isolde, to know I've an enemy who wishes to put a period to my miserable existence. And for the life of me . . . no, forget that, a bad choice of phrase. For the love of God, I cannot imagine who could dislike me quite that thoroughly."

"You're really serious in believing it was no simple poacher Sunday last who mistook his prey. You really think it was a murderer who missed his mark," she stated in a wondering tone.

"Yes," Shalbourne answered grimly. "If I didn't know better, my first guess would've been a distant cousin anxious to step into my shoes. Being the last of one's line, however, does have certain advantages. Although she had never approved of me, I acquit Aunt Jane of trying to assassinate me. But who does that leave, I ask myself. An ex-lover? An ex-lover's husband? A disgruntled servant? A dissatisfied tenant? An ex-comrade in arms who didn't like me? God knows, even I have to admit I am not always the most popular of fellows. I damn near choked a man to death in Brook's less than a month ago. Why not him? Damn it, my best guess was that it was a madman who didn't like the color of my bloody hair!''

"Gay!" A hand flew to Isolde's neck as she clutched the book she had been reading to her breast. "You can't believe that *I* . . . !''

Shalbourne raised his brow in a skeptical gesture. His features twisted into devilish, harsh lines. "I was very keen on that ex-lover theory. Very keen.''

Isolde gasped. "Gay! What are you saying?''

"Ye gads! I should have seen it sooner!" Shalbourne made a swift movement and grabbed her wrist. The book fell unheeded to the floor. "Have you been planning it with the bastard all along? Was last night just an attempt to distract me?''

"Oh! How could you?" Isolde raised her other hand to slap him. He caught it in mid-flight. Pulling her forward, he twisted her arms behind her back until she cried out in pain.

"Was it all an act?" he demanded through clenched teeth. "Were you really a virgin, or are you just as well versed in the art of deceiving a man as the most common lightskirt?''

Isolde kicked and struggled in frustration. "How could you? How could you?" she screamed at him and promptly burst into tears of rage.

"Oh, God!" Shalbourne moaned and closed his eyes in pain. Letting go of her hands, he enfolded her in a fierce embrace, burying his face in her hair. "I'm sorry. I'm sorry. Isolde, please!" His voice shaking with emotion, he stroked her heaving shoulders. "Forgive me, please. Oh, God, that was a despicable thing to say!"

"Yes, it was!" Isolde sobbed, not yet ready to be mollified.

Shalbourne raised his head to look into her face. Placing one large hand on her cheek, he wiped away the falling tears with his thumb. "My aunt will tell you it is my Spanish heritage that makes me such a damned bloody jealous fool. Isolde, I . . ." he stopped as if he wasn't really sure what he wanted to say next. "Isolde," he whispered huskily and then swooped down to take her lips with passionate fervor.

Her head swirled as she gripped his shoulders, her sobs forgotten. Her knees weakened and she felt once again the tingling sensation that she had experienced just last night. At that moment, she knew she loved him and would forgive him anything.

Shalbourne broke off the kiss as suddenly as he had begun. Holding her in a strong embrace, he gave a soft laugh and said into the ear nearest his mouth, "If I continue in that vein, Simmons will no doubt discover us once again in a compromising position." He pulled back and smiled at her. Limping to the chair she had just vacated, he sat down and pulled her onto his lap.

Isolde giggled as she relaxed her head on his shoulder. "And this is not compromising, my lord?" She slapped playfully at the hand which was boldly progressing toward her rounded derriere.

"Not in the least," he assured her with a tender smile. Sobering, he frowned. "I knew you weren't really involved. I'm sorry you had to be the recipient of my nasty temper, but I have only just discovered that your friend, Mr. Jeremy Anderson, is the culprit who tried to kill me."

A shocked Isolde struggled to sit up. "No!" she gasped. "What possible reason could Jeremy have had?"

"The oldest reason there is—jealousy."

"No!" Isolde exclaimed again.

"My dear Isolde, it's obvious the man is in love with my beautiful wife!" Shalbourne's smile did not reach his eyes as he stroked her hair.

"Oh, Gay," Isolde admonished him. "You're letting your imagination run away with you. Jeremy knows I have no interest in him other than friendship. And, besides, surely you would have recognized him as your assailant yesterday?"

"Not necessarily," Shalbourne said abstractly as he ran the events once again in his mind. "The fellow was enveloped from head to toe. His hat pulled down over his eyes, a large muffler around his face, which would account for my not recognizing the voice, and a shabby greatcoat which he could have picked up anywhere."

"Yes, that's all very well and good," Isolde played devil's advocate to Shalbourne's theorizing. "But that doesn't *prove* it was Jeremy. Certainly you would have recognized his horse at the very least!"

"No," Shalbourne absent-mindedly played with her fingers as he tried to recall more details. "My assailant was afoot. That, combined with his costume, makes it very difficult for me to give an accurate assessment as to his height and weight."

Isolde, who had been cogitating with equal fervor, snapped a finger and cried, "Of course! It couldn't have been Jeremy!"

Shalbourne shot her a skeptical look.

"No, really, Gay," she said, catching the glance. "Think about it. You said yourself last night that you stabbed the man with your sword stick before your horse ran you into that branch. Except for a bit of stiffness last night, Jeremy seemed fine at dinner.''

"Stiffness?" Shalbourne demanded. "What's that about Anderson experiencing some stiffness?"

"Nothing to notice," Isolde replied calmly. "It seems my cow-handed friend took a tumble jumping a fence yesterday and . . .''

"Where?"

"I don't know. I think at your tenant's farm."

"No, damn it! Where was he hurt?" Shalbourne clenched her fingers.

"Gay!" Isolde said indignantly. "You're hurting my hand.''

"Where, Isolde? Where was he hurt?"

"Well," Isolde chewed on her lip thoughtfully. "He seemed to be favoring his right side a bit."

"It was him!" Shalbourne exclaimed. "It had to have been! The fellow took my hit on his right side!''

"Good lord," Isolde breathed in horror. "Oh, but, Gay"—she shook her head and said—"Jeremy could never have made it to dinner with a stab wound.''

"Why not?" Shalbourne demanded. "I couldn't tell you how bad it was. Maybe it was only superficial. He may have bled buckets all over my shirt but that doesn't mean he wasn't still mobile.''

"That still doesn't prove . . .''

"Not by itself, no," Shalbourne agreed. "But coupled with the evidence in that sack." He pointed at the rucksack he had dumped on the desk and shrugged.

"What is . . . ?" Isolde asked, fearful the answer might prove that Jeremy was indeed the culprit.

"It contains two dueling pistols."

"Dueling?"

"To the best of my knowledge, there is only one prey a man hunts with a dueling pistol."

"Good Lord!" Isolde's eyes widened in shock. "Do you suppose they might . . . ?"

"Belong to the poacher that shot me Sunday last?" Shalbourne emphasized the word "poacher" in a skeptical fashion. "Yes, I'm absolutely sure of it."

He went on to explain that he and Lord Denbigh had come upon his gamekeeper Matlock while out seeking clues. "He asked me if Anderson had given me the 'message' yet. Needless to say, I was at a loss."

"Message? What message?" Isolde enquired.

"I'll come to that presently," Shalbourne told her. "It seems Simmons took my order to heart to have that spaniel —Freckles—you remember?"

Isolde shook her head in assent.

"Well, Simmons gave her to Matlock after that fiasco with the tea tray. Matlock, being an enterprising fellow, conceived the notion of taking the bitch out to patrol the grounds. Unfortunately, the stupid beast has been indulged and petted all her life, so it was a bit much to expect her to begin her hunting career at the age of eight even if her ancestors have been bred for centuries for just that purpose! Anyway, according to Matlock, she made a good show of wagging her tail, sniffing the ground, and hauling him about in the prescribed zigzag pattern. Matlock himself admitted, though, that it probably wouldn't have produced any results if it had not been for the rabbit that popped out of a hole right under Freckles's nose."

Isolde giggled. "I can just picture it! Freckles was probably more curious about the strange creature she'd discovered than interested in hunting it down!"

"Exactly," Shalbourne grinned in reply. "Anyway, the silly bitch pulled Matlock headlong into a hedge of thorns before he let go of her lead. His cries for help brought one of the stableboys, and between the two of them Matlock was released with both the maximum number of scratches and the greatest possible damage to the rose bushes. In clearing away some of the thicker brambles, they discovered something rather curious, an abandoned rucksack which contained two dueling pistols.''

''You say he found the rucksack under a rosebush?'' an incredulous Isolde asked.

Shalbourne shot a frowning look at his wife. ''Don't interrupt, love. But, yes, it was under a rosebush, to answer your question. We then went back to Matlock's cottage to see the pistols.''

Once there, Shalbourne told her, it had been the work of only a few moments for the rucksack and its contents to be produced and examined. The pistols proved to be amazingly clean and showed no signs of rusting. Although the guns proved to be empty of any shot, they did have traces of powder still clinging to them, giving every indication of their having been recently employed.

Isolde jumped up at this point in his narrative and demanded to see the weapons.

Shalbourne reluctantly rose and walked to the desk, where he pulled one of the pistols from the sack. Testing the weight of the weapon in his hand, he remarked grimly, ''You do realize, don't you, that they couldn't have been under that bush *before* the 'poacher' shot at me. The night before, you'll recall, a thunderstorm broke out practically above the house. If nothing else, the flints would have been quite ruined. And look at the rucksack. Unremarkable, I admit. Except that it, too, has obviously not spent an evening in the rain.''

''When did you say he discovered them?'' Isolde asked as she timidly touched the pistol's barrel.

''The Tuesday after the Sunday I was shot. He told Anderson about it immediately, and was quite pleased that even after almost eight days, I hadn't come to see them for myself. I think he was hoping he might be able to keep them. I think this proves my theory, don't you?''

"What? Just because Jeremy neglected to tell you immediately about the guns? He might have placed no importance on them and . . .''

"Come now, Isolde,'' Shalbourne scoffed. "Even if Anderson weren't responsible for them being under that rosebush—which I'm sure he was—wouldn't you think any intelligent human being would have questioned their significance?'' Shalbourne laughed without humor. "No, Isolde, he knew their importance right enough.''

"Gay, you can't condemn a man as a murderer just because he didn't give you a message.''

"It wasn't just the message. He's the only one with motive *and* opportunity. The day before I was shot, when I came back to interrupt your tea party, I made it clear that he was to leave you alone. He made his resentment equally clear. The next morning he must have followed me out when I went riding. After he shot me and saw that Denbigh's groom was making chase, he ran, dropping the sack with the guns in his flight. Then Matlock found them by a fluke and gave Anderson a message to me about his curious discovery. Anderson realized he had to try again before I got the message, so he arranged to meet me at McCauley's farm. On the way, he accosted me disguised as a footpad. However, his scheme went awry once again when I stabbed him first. He didn't stay to make sure I was dead, but merely assumed I must be. Then, as cool as can be, he went to last night's dinner with that cock and bull story to account for his wound. Damn it, Isolde! It all fits!''

"Good Lord, Gay!'' Isolde frowned. "You know as well as I do that your story is full of holes! Jeremy could never . . . !'' She left the sentence unfinished as she exclaimed, "Now, those pistols, though! They might be able to tell you who the culprit *really* is! Done to special order, aren't they? Far above the touch of any steward.''

''But that's just it, Isolde. I know exactly where those pistols came from. And I don't mean Manton's, either.'' Shalbourne's hands tightened convulsively around the pistol in his hand. ''You see, they are mine.''

CHAPTER SEVENTEEN

Shalbourne allowed Isolde to persuade him to be merciful with Mr. Anderson to avoid any scandal that would result. Although it galled him that Anderson persisted in protesting his innocence, Shalbourne contented himself with merely dismissing his steward rather than pressing for an arrest and trial.

As a result of that dismissal, Shalbourne gave himself wholeheartedly to taking up the reins of his estate. His days were filled with the latest farming techniques and animal husbandry, his nights, with becoming more acquainted with his wife. Denbigh cut short his visit in early January, expressing the opinion that the Gay Lord was well on his way to becoming a very "Dull Dog!" Lady Jane, on the other hand, was pleased with her nephew's progress. She left the newlyweds to their own devices in February, instructing them to come to her in London in mid-March so that Isolde could be properly introduced to polite society.

When spring came and Isolde had still not received any reply to the numerous letters she had penned to her cousin Mirabelle, she persuaded her husband to take up Lady Jane's invitation. Besides, Isolde wished to consult with Shalbourne's man of business about the inheritance she should have received in January.

Her first action upon returning to town was to call on her Aunt Mary and cousin Mirabelle. Unfortunately, her Uncle Wendall, who she discovered had intercepted her letters, came home early and kicked Isolde out of his drawing room, forbidding her to enter the house ever again.

It was a depressed Isolde who dressed that next evening for her first party. Lady Jane had arranged the much coveted invitations to the ball given by Lord and Lady Jersey at their home, Osterley Park, on the outskirts of town.

The three occupants of the coach on the way to the ball were startled, to say the least, when a shot rang out as the Shalbourne coach journeyed to Osterley Park. A voice, muffled by an enveloping scarf, shouted above creaking leather and stomping horses, "Stand and Deliver!"

The coachman, pulling at his horses' mouths with jerking motions, was cursing himself because he had not seen fit to include a blunderbuss or a guard as part of the traveling plans that evening. As a result, there were only himself and a single unarmed groom with the coach aside from its three occupants. It was his opinion that they were hardly in a position to argue with two armed ruffians, so he considered it expedient to do as the scoundrels demanded.

Enfolded into bulky coats and scarfs, with hats pulled down over their foreheads, the mounted highwaymen loomed as menacing creatures of prey. Only their eyes and pistols reflected any of the moon's light. One, who appeared to be the leader, stayed on his horse, his two pistols trained on the coachman and the groom. The other dismounted and wrenched open the carriage door.

"Out! The lot of you!"

Shalbourne, not to be daunted, descended with as much sangfroid as if they had just arrived at their destination, and a liveried servant now held the door rather than a rogue in an ill-fitting coat. "Happy to oblige, my good man. Nothing like a stroll in the moonlight to break up the monotony of a long journey, eh?''

His words were falsely inane, his gestures slow and measured. Handing the ladies out of the coach, his mind was only half on the task. His sharp, militarily trained eyes were quickly making an assessment of his enemies' weak points. As he saw it, the leader, mounted as he was, had the decided advantage over all of them. However, if his very nervous partner, and he was *very* nervous, as Shalbourne noted from the way his pistols shook unsteadily in his hands, could be in some way incapacitated, there might yet be hope to retain both his purse and his self-esteem. For Shalbourne considered it a personal affront that the ladies he was escorting might have cause to question his ability to protect them.

''That's—that's far enough!'' the nervous one stuttered, and stepped back to set another foot of distance between himself and his victims.

The two ladies, the ball they were going to forgotten, clung together in frightened silence. Shalbourne, standing between them and the nervous criminal, remarked politely, ''I suppose you'll be wanting our money and our jewels.''

''Yes . . . yes.'' The man sounded grateful for Shalbourne's quick understanding. ''Or your life,'' he added as an afterthought.

''Of course,'' Shalbourne answered drily. Really, the man was a buffoon! It hardly seemed worth the effort to protest this robbery! With his adrenaline flowing fast and furious, his form challenged comparison when he loosened the sword stick from his newly purchased cane. The nervous robber would probably have seen no more than a flash of cold steel in the moonlight before it ran him through if Shalbourne had not tripped ignominiously because of his limp.

In addition, at that exact moment the mounted highwayman, tiring of the game and with a clear view of Shalbourne, simply pointed his gun and cold-bloodedly fired.

Lady Jane screamed. Lady Shalbourne cried out her husband's name in an anguished voice, and the mounted rogue gave a cry of triumph as he saw his lordship fall. The horses stirred, stamped, and neighed in reaction. The nervous excuse for a criminal, his frightened eyes staring at the fifteen inches of steel that had almost entered his craw, fainted dead away. There was the sound of breaking glass and the reek of laudanum in the air as he hit the ground, but no one had eyes for anything but the fallen Earl.

"Gay! Gay!" Isolde knelt beside her husband's still form. She could have sworn that no bullet had touched him. Turning him onto his back with a burst of unlooked for strength, she gasped in horror. "Gay! Oh, darling, speak to me! You can't be dead!" The light was uncertain but she still knew blood when she saw it. Pressing her hand to the side of his head, she reacted instinctively, as if her feeble attempts would staunch the flow from that source. "A handkerchief! Somebody! Please!"

"You've killed him!" Lady Jane was hysterical. "You've killed him! I'll see you hang for this! I swear to God." She ran to the mounted leader and grabbed his boot. He kicked viciously, throwing her to the ground. "Shut up, you stupid old cow. Or I shall kill you as well."

"How dare you strike a lady!" the coachman shouted ineffectually as he tried to calm his horses.

"Gay! Gay, don't be dead. Please don't be dead," Isolde pleaded softly, as the tears from her eyes dropped onto the head in her lap, mixing with the blood which trickled slowly down his lordship's face. The elegant blue gown was soaked with blood but Isolde didn't care. She was oblivious to anything but the need to stop the bleeding.

No one had thought to grab the fainting man's guns, so that now, when he slowly returned to consciousness and sat up with a groggy look and swaying body, he was the first to notice the two pistols lying on the ground next to him. It took him only a moment to realize where he was and that the danger had still not passed. Grabbing the guns, he scrambled as best he could to his feet.

"Idiot!" The mounted criminal rode his horse a few feet to close the gap between them. Kicking at his partner in the same way he had kicked Lady Jane, he growled, "Get your horse, fool! And get the girl, too! Oh, no, you don't, my fine friend!" This last was addressed to the groom, who had been inching along his perch on the coach to jump at the mounted culprit. With the pistol pointed at his head, the groom settled back into his seat without a murmur of protest.

The nervous man staggered to his horse, took a few deep breaths, grabbed the reins, and walked back to Isolde's kneeling form. Without regard for her or her fallen husband, he grabbed her arm and pulled savagely upward. "Forget him! Ain't nothing you can do for the bastard now."

"Murderer! Murderer!" Isolde swung at him with her free arm. "Let go of me!"

"Here, now stop that, ya silly bitch. I ain't no murderer. It was self-defense. He would've killed me if he'd had the chance. 'Twas a fair fight as far as I kin see."

"Fair fight?" The coachman was outraged. "It certainly weren't! And so I'll tell the Bow Street Runners, you just wait and see if I don't!"

"What are you doing? Put me down!" Isolde kicked and scratched ineffectually as the man threw her first over his shoulder and then, with a bang that knocked the breath from her lungs, over the front of his saddle. Stowing the pistols in his large, capacious pockets, he jumped onto his horse. "Here! Stop moving around like that!" He cuffed her on the side of her head with a large hand.

"Ready, nitwit?" his disgruntled partner asked.

"Ready."

"What are you doing with her ladyship?" the frightened groom demanded in a squeaky voice.

Ignoring the question, the highwayman growled, "Just so you won't get any ideas about following." He fired a shot from his second pistol, killing the closest of the horses and plunging rest into chaos. They turned and rode off until even the sound of their horses' hoofbeats was a fading memory.

Isolde felt battered and bruised by the time they halted next to a vehicle which was pulled off the road some four or five miles from where they had left the Shalbourne coach. She couldn't fathom why the two highwaymen had chosen to bring her along. Neither did she care particularly what they might choose to do with her. There was only one thought that kept running through her head, over and over again. "Gay is dead. Gay is dead." Finally, even those words were meaningless, and the pain deep in her chest from unshed tears was her only reality.

She felt numb, and allowed them to bundle her into the waiting carriage without protest. Although they hadn't bound her, she didn't think to try an escape. Her mind had ceased to function properly, and such a measure did not even occur to her. She heard them moving about as they tied their horses to the back of the coach. After only a moment, they appeared in the coach's doorway, and the one who appeared to be the leader growled to the other as he held out his hand, "The bottle."

"Bottle? What bottle?"

"The laudanum, featherhead!"

"It broke."

"What?"

"It broke. When I fell. Can't you tell? I reek of the bloody stuff. Was a stupid idea anyway," he grumbled.

"Of all the muttonheaded fools!" the leader exclaimed.

"I couldn't help it!" the other whined.

Isolde sat forward with a start. Up until that point she had not been paying attention to their argument, but that phrase caused a jolt in her memory. No attempt to disguise his voice could conceal those complaining accents! "Harold Biggelswade!" she exclaimed.

Harold threw aside his hat in disgust and pulled down his enveloping, stifling muffler before thinking to deny her statement. "Yes. It's me," he began to mutter defensively. "But how you came to guess, I can't . . ."

"You fool!" His partner growled as he jabbed his fist into Harold's stomach. "Now she knows for certain who you are! She was only guessing!"

Isolde peered at the leader filling the doorway. With a sudden motion, she leaped forward and whipped off his hat before he could back out of her reach. Then, grabbing at the scarf with her other hand, they struggled for a moment or two, her body leaning precariously out of the coach.

"Damn your eyes, bitch!" he cried as he threw her off onto the coach's floor. However, it was not before she had managed to inch his scarf down past his nose.

Coming to a sitting position, she watched in fascinated horror as he pulled the scarf back up. "Uncle Wendall!"

He spat out an expletive, and with a resigned gesture, abruptly pulled the scarf the rest of the way down. "That's right, niece. It's me."

"But why? What did you think you were doing? Playing at Highwaymen like a couple of overgrown schoolboys?" Isolde's voice rose on an hysterical note. "How could you?! And now my husband is dead!" she wailed.

"Shut up!" Wendall stepped up to the coach, grabbed her arm, and slapped her. "Sit in the seat and be still, damn you!" he instructed. Then turning to Harold, he cursed, "God damn fool! See what comes of breaking that bottle! If we'd gotten the laudanum down her throat, she would never have guessed our part in this! What the hell caused you to faint like that anyway?''

"I couldn't help it!" Harold yelled back. "Didn't you see that blade? I've already tasted his steel once, and don't care to again! Why, he almost killed me!''

"But he didn't! My God, I'd have thought you would have expected such a trick, seeing as how you'd already fallen for it once! And more to the point, you lost the bloody bottle by falling down like you did!''

"It's not my fault," Harold said sullenly. "We could've knocked her out with a pistol butt—like I wanted to from the first.''

"Fine! Lovely!" Wendall exclaimed. "But you bloody well didn't even do that much, did you?''

"Well, nothing was stopping you from doing it, either." Harold defended his actions, or lack thereof.

"Aye, but you bloody well didn't give me a chance, did you, before you were introducing yourself like ye was an old hen at a damn tea party! You weren't standing next to this coach two seconds before you told her who you were!''

"I did not!" Harold was indignant. "She guessed!''

Wendall had no answer for this and so chose to ignore it. He twisted around, and before throwing his considerable bulk into the coach next to Isolde, he told Harold, "Well, we'll just have to go on from here. Get up in the box and drive back to Burton Crescent as we'd planned.''

"But what are we going to do now?" Harold asked as he stood in the doorway, one hand resting on the open door's handle.

"You do realize this means a complete change of plans! I wouldn't have credited it!" Wendall said with biting sarcasm, his condescending voice reducing Harold to the status of simpleton.

"I s'pose you'll think of something," Harold said in a disgruntled voice and then looked at the ground. Almost, he wished Wendall wouldn't think of something, if only because Harold resented Wendall's superior attitude and would have liked for him not to be quite so very clever for once.

Wendall grabbed the door out of Harold's hand. "Well, then, up on the box with you. And, remember, take us to the tradesman's entrance. Don't want everyone in the neighborhood to see us pulling up to the front door and taking my lovely niece inside." With that, he slammed the door shut and settled back to wait for Harold to begin tooling the coach back to the Hackett townhouse.

"You don't seriously think you're going to get away with this, do you?" Isolde hissed at him from her perch opposite in the carriage. "I'll see you both hang for the murderers you are, if it's the last thing I do!" Isolde grabbed the strap next to her, as the coach lurched forward.

"I've had just about enough of your back talk, girl!" Wendall seized her arm and shook her before throwing her back into her corner. "You may think that because you happen to be a countess, you can threaten me, but there ain't no way I plan to hang for this! No how!"

"How do you propose to escape? I can't imagine how you thought this nefarious scheme of yours could work at all. Just what was all this in aid of anyway?"

"Why, niece, it's very simple." Wendall leaned back in his seat and crossed his arms on his large chest. "Once you were a widow, you would have married Harold as I had wanted you to do last November."

"You shot Gay on purpose, didn't you?" Isolde exclaimed, horrified at the realization that he had not simply been protecting Harold from the stiletto.

"Of course. I must say that his high and mighty lordship, attacking Harold as he did, made it look a great deal better than it might have done. So nice to have had his cooperation. Will sound much more plausible in the ears of the authorities when that sanctimonious old woman tells that tale than it would have if I had shot him without provocation. Really, my dear, he played right into my hands. I've always been lucky that way, though. Why, even this scheme tonight, for example. I should never have thought of it if you hadn't mentioned the ball to your Aunt Mary yesterday.''

"You must be mad! And why should I have consented to being the bride of one of my husband's murderers?''

"For the very simple reason that you would not have known that your groom was one of them. We might have gotten away with it, too, if you'd taken the laudanum as you were supposed to.''

"I can't see how a few drops of laudanum would have changed anything,'' Isolde said.

"Ah, but if you had been drugged, as we had planned, you would never have known who your kidnapers were.''

"You could not have kept the knowledge from me forever,'' Isolde pointed out.

"Why not? When your 'kidnapers' applied to me for a ransom, how were you to know that your loving uncle, who had paid such a large sum to have you returned, was one and the same as the man who took you in the first place. With the help of the sleeping draught, you would have been kept in ignorance until Harold and I had managed to 'rescue' you, as it were. Really quite an ingenious scheme, if I do say so myself.''

"It might well have been. But I don't see how you propose to get away with it now. For I do know who you are and if you think I shall keep quiet, you are very much mistaken. As for marrying Harold Biggelswade . . . ! You must be completely insane.''

"I've been thinking about that,'' Wendall said mysteriously. "I am not yet of the opinion that all is lost. There is still a way to salvage this night's work, if I will but put my mind to it.''

"Well, your attic's to let if you think there is any way for you to avoid hanging! Unless you plan to kill me, too. I have no intention of keeping quiet."

"Ah, but that's just it, missy. As you've so shrewdly pointed out, you shall have to die as well."

Isolde gasped. "You're quite mad!"

"Not in the least," Wendall stated calmly. "It is unfortunate that I can't just kill you here and now. But, if you should die without first marrying Harold, your fortune will descend to your Aunt Mary and then your cousin, Mirabelle. If Mary could be persuaded to leave your share to Harold instead of our daughter, it wouldn't matter. However, she would not consent to do so without an excellent reason, and I am not prepared to give her one. Really," he added in disgust, "for such a mouse of a woman, she can be remarkably stubborn!"

"And so if Harold marries me first, my half of Challoner's will be his without further complications, is that it?"

"Why, yes." Wendall was pleased at her quick understanding. "Quite selfish of Mary, really. But how could she be made to understand that I want my chief clerk to have so much of the firm's profits?"

"Then all this is Harold's doing!" Isolde gasped in surprise, having always discounted Harold as any sort of threat to anyone. "Is he blackmailing you then? Is that it? Have you made some sort of promise to him that if I marry him, that will be payment enough?"

"Don't be absurd," Wendall scoffed.

"Please, Uncle, tell me," she said with a sympathetic note in her voice. "I shan't condemn you if the blackguard is forcing you to do this. After all, once he gets his hands on my money, what's to prevent him from murdering me and marrying Mirabelle as well to get the rest?"

Wendall's face broke into a slow grin. His shoulders began to shake in silent chuckles. From there he progressed to a few quiet giggles until he was guffawing and laughing in great gulping breaths.

"I don't see what's so funny," Isolde said indignantly.

"Oh, lord!" Wendall wiped away the tears of laughter with a large white handkerchief that he had pulled from his inside coat pocket. "Don't waste your sympathy, my dear niece. I can assure you that any plots or schemes to insure Harold's share in the family fortunes are quite my own doing. And your worries about Mirabelle are quite misplaced. Harold would no more dream of marrying her than he would of marrying, well, his sister. If he had one, that is."

"You are quite demented! I can't credit that you are really serious!"

"Oh, I'm serious, right enough. Never doubt that," Wendall assured her, no longer laughing. "Not that I shan't be sorry to kill you. I shall. It would have been much simpler if your demise hadn't become a necessity."

"But you can't! You mustn't!" Isolde felt a cold shiver of fear creep up her neck as it finally penetrated that he was in earnest.

"Can. And will," Wendall said as calmly as if they were discussing the weather. He then fumbled under the seat until he produced a length of rope. "And, now, my dear, as much as I regret the necessity, I shall have to bind your hands and gag you, just in case you should decide to make any sort of outcry when we arrive at my house. It would never do for the neighbors to get the impression that you were reluctant to accompany us inside. And Harold has already informed me of your propensity for screeching when crossed."

Isolde struggled against this plan of action but Wendall proved much stronger than she. When the coach came to a halt some fifteen minutes later, she was bound and trussed up like a Christmas goose, unable to make any sort of sound. The silence of the mews behind the houses on Burton Crescent was broken by the sound of a window sash being thrown back. A few brief shouts were exchanged while Wendall pushed aside the curtain on the coach's window an inch and peered out. "Ah, here we are now. And if I don't mistake myself, that is Jonathan Coachman leaning out of the window in his room above my stable! Bloody hell!"

The door opened and Harold stuck his head in. In a furtive whisper, Harold said, "Jonathan's up and about. He saw us drive in. Said he'd be down in a trice to stable the horses for the night. What should I do?"

"Damn!" Wendall cried. "If he sees her with us, we're sunk. You distract him while I take her inside."

"How am I to do that?" Harold groaned.

"Bloody fool! I've been saddled with a flaming idiot!" Wendall complained to no one in particular. "I don't care. I can't think of everything! Just don't let him see us go in."

When Wendall heard Harold greet Jonathan and ask him to look at the lead horse because he thought it had thrown a shoe, Wendall grinned and whispered, "There's hope for that lad yet. But I suppose, sooner or later, blood will tell."

Harold had chosen the horse that was farthest away from a view of the townhouse's back stairs. The steps descended to a door which led directly into the kitchen, housed in the basement. While Jonathan was occupied inspecting the feet of the horse, Isolde was pulled roughly from the coach's interior. Stumbling down the stairs, she was propelled through the door and across the darkened kitchen, unable to do a thing to stop it.

Once inside, Wendall dragged her resisting body across the kitchen, and down the hall, which was lit by one candle that wavered as they passed it in their progress up the back stairs. Stopping at the top of the stairs, he cautiously opened the green baize door and peeked around it. Ascertaining that the hall was empty except for a candle or two, he pulled her up the main staircase and into the dark library at the top. Pushing her into a chair, he stirred the coals in the grate, and with a taper, lit the branch of candles on the mantel. Turning his back on Isolde, he started to move across the room to light the candles near his massive desk.

Isolde, whose legs had not been bound, took the opportunity to jump from her chair and race to the open door.

"Oh, no, you don't, my pretty!" Wendall's grip on her hair pulled her up short. He threw her back on the hearthrug and growled. "That wouldn't do you no good anyhow. Ain't nobody home. Your Aunt Mary and Mirabelle are at a lecture this evening with the Rutherfords. As for the servants, I gave them the evening off and most of them seem to have taken advantage of that fact. Can't think why Jonathan's still here and not down the street at his favorite tavern. But, no matter, he didn't see you and I'll make sure it stays that way."

Harold appeared at that moment in the doorway. "Jonathan's taking care of the horses. Now what do we do?"

"You stay here with her," Wendall instructed him. "And watch her careful. She's already tried to run away once. See you don't take your eyes off her."

"Here! Where 'er you going?!" Harold demanded in a nervous squeak.

"Ass!" Wendall shook off the hand that Harold had laid on his arm. "I'm just going upstairs to my wife's room. It occurs to me that we might still come about if I can but find a bit more laudanum."

"But why?" Harold asked in an anguished voice.

"Because, idiot, if we are still to put her up in the attic bedroom until I can be contacted by her kidnapers and pay the ransom, much less have her participate in a marriage ceremony, she'll have to be kept quiet. Tying her up won't be enough. If she's in an insensible stupor, she'll be cooperative enough. I'm not taking any more chances. Now, stay here! I'll be right back.'' With that, he slammed the door and headed up the next flight of stairs.

CHAPTER EIGHTEEN

Mirabelle had just fallen into a restless sleep when she heard a thud in the room below her own. Blinking awake, she strained her ears. Her heart began to race when her listening was rewarded by the muffled sounds of an angry voice. Sitting up cautiously in her bed, she debated whether to get up and investigate. With the steps thudding on the stairs coming ever closer, she whipped the covers over her head and lay as still as she could. Her heart in her throat, she was convinced that some villain was headed straight for her room and that if she kept quiet, he wouldn't see her and would go away.

When the sound of a door being opened penetrated through the quilt wrapped about her ears, she guessed that whoever it was had entered the room next to her own. Mirabelle forced herself to attain some semblance of calm and tried to consider who it could be. Throwing the covers back cautiously, her hands trembling slightly, she picked up the tinderbox next to her bed and lit the candle found beside it. Her bare feet made no sound as she crept across the room to look at the ormolu clock on her mantel. "Only nine-thirty!" she thought to herself, almost dropping the candle at the implications of that thought. "Too early for Mama to be home and Papa said he wouldn't be back before midnight!''

The blood drained out of her face and she felt faint. That meant that she wasn't just being fanciful! The person she now heard rummaging about in her mother's bedchamber was a burglar! Mirabelle stuffed a fist in her mouth to stifle the involuntary scream that started up her throat at the thought. She knew, too, that she was alone in the house. Jenny had said, as she tucked Mirabelle into bed, that she was going to go back to her husband's rooms above the stable. Mirabelle had to get to their quarters before the robber decided to search her own room and discovered her there! She threw on her silk wrapper and picked up her slippers. Blowing out the candle, she turned the handle slowly and cautiously pulled open the door. The creak of the hinges sounded like a cannon to Mirabelle, and so she stopped when she was able to just squeeze through the aperture. Tiptoeing, she held her breath and began to slowly walk down the stairs. Just as she'd got to the last step and was beginning her slow trek down the next set of stairs, a voice from inside the library broke the silence and caused her to freeze. Ducking down, she pressed up against the railing of the stairs for cover and began to pray fervently as the library door flew open.

"Thought I heard something on the stairs," she heard Harold Biggelswade grumble.

Almost she stood up and revealed herself. Only Harold! That meant that the person she heard in her mother's room was her father, since he and Harold had been out together. How stupid of her! "Really, Isolde would have been quite amused at me," Mirabelle smiled and thought to herself. "Talk about an overactive imagination!"

Harold had neglected to close the library door and so Mirabelle was able to hear quite clearly a voice that shocked her into silence. Isolde? Here? After what Papa had said to her yesterday about never darkening his door again?!

"You can't want to be a party to this, Harold," Isolde exclaimed. "If you're caught, my uncle will say it was all your idea, and he won't raise a finger to prevent you from hanging. Kidnaping and murder are not frivolous matters, Harold, and sooner or later, you will pay for allowing yourself to be persuaded."

"Shut up! Shut up!" Harold yelled at her. "I should never have taken off that gag! I thought you would be grateful for the chance to be able to breath more easily. But not you! Oh, no! Ungrateful bitch! I'm still bleeding where you bit me, too!"

"It's your own fault for trying to kiss me as you did!" Isolde retorted. "I hope your lip is so swollen you can't eat for a week! I'd have scratched your eyes out as well if I hadn't been bound as I am!"

Mirabelle's mind whirled. Kidnaping! Murder! And if she understood correctly, Isolde was tied up, a captive in her father's library!

"I shan't be sorry when you die," Harold said like a petulant child. "You're nasty-tempered, that's what you are!"

"Stop that!" Mirabelle heard Isolde exclaim, followed by the sound of ripping fabric.

Mirabelle couldn't hear Harold's murmured reply but Isolde's next words gave her a pretty good idea of what was happening. "Don't you dare touch me, you filthy beast!"

Mirabelle didn't know what she could do, but she knew she couldn't stand idly by and watch Harold hurt Isolde. Before she had a chance to move, though, her father's voice called from the top of the stairs.

"Harold! Harold!"

Mirabelle ducked back down near the floor. She could hear Harold get up and move to the open doorway.

"What is it?" he asked in a guilty voice.

Wendall's reply was interrupted by a piercing scream for help.

Mirabelle heard her father curse, and then say, "What the hell are you doing down there? Get that girl gagged! Do you want her to inform the whole neighborhood of what's going on here? If you don't shut her up, I swear, I'll murder you as well as her!"

Her father! Her own father really was party to this horrible plot! Mirabelle did not wait to hear Harold's reply. Moving swiftly but silently, she flew down the stairs and through the green baize door at the bottom under cover of Isolde's screams. Racing through the kitchen, she emerged into the mews, stumbling and sobbing. Seeing the lighted stable, she ran inside.

"Here, Miss Mirabelle!" Jonathan stopped in the midst of combing one of the coach horses. "What's the matter?!"

"Oh, Jonathan!" Mirabelle wailed. "It's awful! Perfectly horrid!"

"There now, missy." Jonathan had come over to the shaking figure just inside the stable doorway and awkwardly patted her on the back. "It ain't so bad. You have a nightmare or something? You're not alone in the house anymore, you know. Didn't you hear your father come in?"

"That's just it," she gasped out between sobs. "My . . . my father . . ."

"What is it?" Jonathan was now alert. "What's happened? Your father hurt? Where is he? I'll go to him at once."

"No!" Mirabelle screeched and grabbed his arm. Her fingernails dug into his flesh and she exclaimed frantically, "No! Don't go in there!"

"But, Miss Mirabelle."

Mirabelle took a deep breath. She knew that if she gave

into hysterics now, she would only make things worse. Her sobs stopped but the tears continued to roll down her cheeks.

"Don't go, Jonathan," she said in a determined voice. "You must do as I tell you. It's very important. Life or death."

"But—"

"No!" she yelled, then said more calmly, "No. I can't explain. But you must do as I say. Saddle a horse and go to my Lord Shalbourne's house in Mount Street."

Even as she said the words, Mirabelle knew that it was the most logical decision. Lord Shalbourne would know what to do. Isolde was his wife and his responsibility. Besides, she knew without a doubt that she and Jon Coachman would not be able to put a spoke in her father's wheel without some sort of help. In her naivete, she was convinced that Shalbourne had only to appear and her father would be cowed into doing as he was told.

"Tell Lord Shalbourne that Isolde is here."

"But, Miss Mirabelle, whatever would your cousin Isolde be doing here? How could she have gotten into the house? The front door is locked and I been here with me eye on the back all evening."

"She must have come with my father and Harold. Oh, please, don't ask questions! Just go and get his lordship! They're going to kill her!" Mirabelle's sobs returned. "I heard them say so myself! Oh, please, don't you see? You must go quickly! Before it's too late!"

Jonathan was still not completely convinced. But, he reasoned to himself, if I ride to his lordshp's house and find Miss Isolde home, I can always persuade her to return and calm down Miss Mirabelle. And if Miss Mirabelle is right. Well! Jonathan set his mouth grimly. I wouldn't put it past that blighter Hackett to threaten his niece that way. Especially considering the way he's treated me and my Jenny all these years. Either way, a trip to Shalbourne House was clearly in order, as Isolde's husband would certainly want to be informed about any threats made against his wife.

"I ain't had a chance yet to unsaddle the horses your father and Mr. Biggelswade took with them tonight. I'll use one of them. Just you go upstairs and wait with Jenny. I'll be back before you can shake a stick."

"Oh, thank God! Thank God!" Mirabelle was happy to give over some of the responsibility.

When Jonathan arrived at Shalbourne House, he was glad to see that the house was ablaze with lights. This, along with the presence of the other horse, at least indicated that someone must be home. He walked reluctantly up the front steps and timidly lifted the knocker.

The door swung wide immediately and the awesome personage that confronted Jonathan demanded, "Is the doctor with you?"

Jonathan was taken aback. "No," he said hesitantly. "I ain't seen no sawbones. I come to see Miss Isolde . . . ah, her ladyship. From Miss Mirabelle."

"I'm sorry," that lofty gentleman answered. "Her ladyship is not at home." He began to close the door.

Jonathan swiftly stuck his foot in the door. "Here, now, you ain't got no call to turn me away. I said I came from Miss Mirabelle to see her ladyship and if she ain't here, I got an important message for his lordship."

A voice called from the top of the stairs inside the house. "Is that the doctor, Sikes?"

"No, your lordship," Sikes called back. "It's a, ah, gentleman asking for her ladyship."

Jonathan stepped inside behind the unsuspecting Sikes and advanced to the bottom of the stairs. Looking up, he told the shadowed figure at the top, "Jonathan Greene, your honor, what's coachman to Miss Isolde's . . . ah, her ladyship's . . . . Oh, it's you, Lord Denburgh. Miss Mirabelle sent me."

"Mirabelle? Mirabelle Hackett?!" Denbigh exclaimed, ignoring the fact that Jonathan had mangled his name. "What can she want?"

"Ah, well," Jonathan looked down at his shuffling feet and twisted his hat in his hand. "She said I was to tell his lordship that Miss Isolde, ah, her ladyship, is at her house and that her father, Mr. Hackett, says he's gonna kill her. I know it sounds daft, my lord, but if Miss Isolde, ah, her ladyship could just come herself and calm down Miss Mirabelle, I'd be ever so grateful."

"What's that?" Denbigh raced down from the top of the stairs and grabbed Jonathan's arm. "Miss Isolde. Damn, now you've got me doing it! Her ladyship is at her cousin's, you say?" Denbigh demanded.

"Ay, my lord." Jonathan looked askance at the man who held his arm. Had everyone gone moonstruck mad?

"Denbigh!" Another figure appeared at the top of the stairs. "What the hell is going on down there?"

"A miracle, old boy, a miracle!" he called back. Then, dragging Jonathan up the stairs with him, Denbigh laughed heartily and exclaimed, "You sent for me to help you look for the devil! But, Gay, he's come to find us instead!"

Jonathan looked at the other gentleman and gasped. He was startled to see Lord Shalbourne, tall, dark, and foreboding, dressed only in a shirt, unbuttoned waistcoat, black silk knee-breeches and stockings. His entire outfit was covered in blood, and a bandage set at a raffish angle across his forehead seemed to indicate his injury had only recently been bound up. Jonathan's eyes fell for a moment on the jagged scar across the man's cheek and he wondered if my lord had just come away with his second souvenir from a duel.

"Speak up, man! Speak up! Do you have something important to tell me!" Shalbourne demanded gruffly.

"Miss Mirabelle sent me, your grace." He swallowed convulsively. He had never realized Shalbourne was such a fierce looking fellow, and his lordship's attitude made Jonathan lose all confidence in the possibility that what Mirabelle said was true. "Miss Mirabelle was mighty upset, your honor. She's gone moon mad, she has. I just thought if Miss Isolde, ah, her ladyship was to come back with me and show Miss Mirabelle that she were all right, she would leave off her tale."

Denbigh, impatient for the story to come to an end, finished it for the slow coachman. "That's just the point, Gay. Mirabelle says Isolde is there! At her uncle's house! And that he plans to kill her!"

"Is it possible?" Shalbourne muttered to himself, then turned swiftly on his heel. Racing down the hall, he almost knocked over Lady Jane, who had just descended from the third floor.

"Young man, what are you doing out of bed? And why aren't you undressed yet?"

Shalbourne ignored her and entered his study. Without a break in his stride, he stalked over to the desk and pulled open a drawer. Removing a wooden case, he opened it and produced a dueling pistol. Grimly, he began to load the weapon.

Lady Jane shrieked. "What are you doing? You shouldn't even be up! You've lost a lot of blood."

Shalbourne, intent on his task, did not look up. "Would you be so kind, Denbigh, as to send for my valet to fetch my shoes and a coat of some sort? I think I shall make a call on my wife's uncle."

"Are you mad?" Lady Jane wailed.

Jonathan, who had appeared at Lady Jane's elbow while

awaiting further instructions, agreed, "Aye, my lady, they all seem to be moon mad tonight."

She ignored this sage observation and started to exclaim, "But your wound . . ."

"Is only superficial." Shalbourne finished the sentence for her. "I may have bled like a stuck pig, but the bullet just grazed me, and only stunned me momentarily. You would do better to attend our poor coachman belowstairs. I think he really suffered more when that bastard shot the horse. There, that should do it," he said as he finished loading the second pistol. "Ah, thank you, Fraser. I see you've brought my top coat as well. Quite provident of you." Shrugging into first his coat, then his Garrick, he stuffed the two pistols into his pockets and stepped into the shoes Fraser held for him. Speaking to Denbigh, he remarked, "I believe you have a horse here, George."

"Yes," Denbigh said, hesitating.

"Then I hope you don't mind if I commandeer it."

"Now, see here, Gay, I can't let you ride out of here like hell for leather when . . ."

"I should like to see you stop me, George." The savage sparkle in Shalbourne's eyes defeated Denbigh's arguments before they born. "Thank you, Fraser," he said, taking his hat from his valet's hands, and adjusting it on his head with difficulty because of the bandage.

"What is going on here?" Lady Jane demanded. "Where do you think you are going? Lord Denbigh," she exclaimed, hopeful of finding an ally, "Perhaps you can talk some sense . . ."

"Auntie Jane." Shalbourne came over to the elderly lady and took her hand. Kissing it lightly, he bowed and then, straightening, he looked Lady Jane in the eye and said, "You are a wonderful lady and it's not that I don't appreciate your concern, but do, please be quiet!" With those words, he limped out the door, calling for Jonathan to come with him to lead the way to the Hackett townhouse.

Recovering from her momentary shock at his defiance, Lady Jane's strident voice called after him as she leaned over the railing, "What do you want to see Isolde's uncle for anyway? What is the meaning of this? Shalbourne!" she yelled in a most unladylike fashion as he stepped out the door which Sikes held open. "Stop this instant! I demand you come back here." In a scandalized tone, she asked one final question, "Gaylord Leighton, you can't seriously mean to go riding in your evening breeches!"

Chapter Nineteen

After Jonathan had clattered out the stable door, Mirabelle stumbled up the stairs to his and Jenny's apartments. Jenny, surprised to see her mistress in such a state, gathered the hysterical Mirabelle into her arms, soothed her, and plied her with tea laced with the Irish cure for all ills, whiskey. After fifteen minutes of incoherent conversation, when Jenny was finally made to understand just exactly what was happening in the house, the light of battle entered her eyes.

"And you mean to tell me you left Miss Isolde alone with that blighter?" Jenny cried. Shaking her head sagely, she announced, "Well, we'll soon take care of that, we will!" She wrenched open the door to the stairs.

An overwrought Mirabelle grabbed Jenny's arm to prevent her leaving. "Where are you going?"

"Now, now, Miss Mirabelle. You'll be right snug in here. Ain't no one going to know where you are. Just you wait here fer my Jonathan an' his lordship. I'm going to give that Harold Biggelswade a piece of my mind!" Jenny, who had been indulging a bit in "false courage" all evening, sallied forth, swaying only slightly, and disappeared into the darkness.

Isolde, gagged once again, had spent a nerve-racking fifteen minutes since Wendall had shouted down the stairs.

Harold, suitably chastened but peevish, paced, sat, growled, bit his nails, played with the gun he held, and paced some more. When they heard movement once again in the hall, Harold jumped up from his perch on the library step where only moments before he had stopped to rest. Knocking his gun to the floor, he squeaked, "Well, it's about time, Hackett."

"And just what do you think you're up to in here, Mr. Harold Biggelswade?" Jenny filled the doorway like an avenging angel. "Saints preserve us! Miss Isolde! What's this knave been doing to you?" Clucking her tongue, she bustled into the room and marched to Isolde's side, ignoring Harold as he fumbled to retrieve his gun.

"Lordy, lordy, Miss! What have they done to ye!" Jenny reached behind Isolde's head and removed the gag.

"Oh, Jenny." Tears filled Isolde's eyes.

"Here! Hey! What are you doing?" Harold skipped from one foot to the other and waved his arms.

Jenny rounded on him. "That's jist what I be wantin' to be askin' ye!"

"Oh, Jenny, you don't understand what danger you're in! My uncle," Isolde began.

"That's right! She ain't going nowhere till Hackett gets back!" Harold interrupted, although with the loss of his gun, his threat had lost some of its impact.

"Here, now, lamb." Jenny patted Isolde kindly on the shoulder. "Ain't no call to work yourself into a stew, help's on the way."

"Thank God." Isolde lay back in the chair, eyes closed in relief.

"What?" Harold screeched and ran around in a small circle. "No! No! I don't believe you!"

Spying his gun under a chair, he dived for it and came up blowing like a fish on land. "Who?" He pointed the newly found weapon at Jenny. "Who's coming 'sides you?"

Jenny cast a disdainful eye at the gun. "Humph! Don't you point that thing at me, Harold Biggelswade! My Jonathan'll be here soon enough."

"Jonathan!" Harold laughed hysterically in relief. "That old woman! I left him stabling the horses and whistling some inane tune. Whiskey on his breath! You'll be lucky if he ain't fallen down into a dead drunk by now on some bale of hay! And that's the great Sir Galahad you're expecting to show up. God, I'm going to be sick laughing!"

Jenny frowned at Harold. "Ye'll be laughing out 'tother side of your mouth soon enough! Jonathan's done gone for his lordship, Miss Isolde's husband."

"Oh, no." Isolde fell back in the chair once again while Harold gave a bark of triumph and an evil grin.

"Won't be finding any help there, I should think!" Harold danced about the two ladies in glee.

Jenny, who had bent over Isolde when she'd fallen back in despair, looked up at Harold's continuously moving figure. "Jist you settle down there, Harold Biggelswade. You'll be making Miss Isolde dizzy with your dancing and prancing about like that. Now, Miss Isolde," Jenny said solicitously. "You jist sit forward a bit and I'll untie those nasty ropes."

"You don't understand, Jenny," Isolde wailed as she allowed Jenny to push her limp body forward and begin work on the ropes. "Gay"—she choked on a sob—"Gay. They've killed him!"

"Now, now, missy, you're jist gettin' hysterical fer nothin'." Jenny worked at the knots.

"Here! Stop that!" Harold bounced up to the two.

"Don't you wave that gun in my face, you young puppy!" Jenny instructed him and pushed the gun away.

Harold stuck his nose in Jenny's face. "You think his high and mighty lordship's coming to rescue you, don't you? Well, he ain't! 'Cause he's dead, I tell you! Dead!''

Isolde moaned and Jenny gasped. "Why, you . . . oh, how dare you speak sich lies, upsetting my Miss Isolde like this!"

"It's true, Jenny," Isolde cried. "Oh, God help me, but it's true!" Isolde brought a hand forward and pointed out a dark stain in the folds of her dress. "This is his. . . ."

"Lord above—blood!" Jenny's eyes widened in horror. "Why, you . . . you . . . oh!" Jenny stopped in frustration as she searched for a word to call Harold. "Well, you kin be mighty sure if what his lordship has been kilt, they'll still be those at his house mighty interested in who mighta' done sich a turrible thing! And they'll be here right enough with me Jonathan before you kin shake a stick and that's a fact!"

Harold blanched during this speech. "No! Jonathan's out back, I tell you, stabling the horses. He can't be—"

"Ha!" Jenny laughed. "He went off some time ago and I expect he'll be back soon enough! If not with his lordship, then with Bow Street Runners, make no mistake!" With that threat, Jenny turned back to Isolde.

Harold, who wanted to preserve his one shot for when he might really need it, laid aside his gun and picked up a volume of Shakespeare, undoubtedly for the first time. He used it as a club, rapping Jenny on the side of the head. Jenny crumpled into a heap on the floor.

"Oh, God, what have you done?" Isolde cried.

"She talked too much," Harold muttered.

The door swung open. Wendall was confronted with the sight of Isolde sitting on the hearthrug, his maid's head cradled in her lap, and Harold standing over them, a large volume in his hands. "What's going on here?" he bellowed as he slammed the door behind him.

"You!" Harold flung the volume onto the chair Isolde had just vacated. Dancing across the room with a bouncing, heavy gait, much like an aroused gorilla, he continued, "This is all your fault! Well, I ain't taking it no more, you hear me? No more! She says Jonathan's gone for help! She says he's gone to his bloody lordship's house, damn you! And he's going to be bringing the Bow Street Runners down on us any minute! Well, I ain't staying to find out, you hear me? I ain't staying!''

Wendall started to speak, ''Now, look here, my lad, there's no call—''

''No! You shut up! You just shut up, you hear me? This was all your idea! Well, I don't want no part of it anymore, you hear me? It was going to be real easy, you said. All I had to do was shoot at him from a bunch of trees, you said. Weren't nobody going to see it weren't no poacher. Well, that girl, that Mary, knows, I bet! That one what I had to be nice to in order to steal the guns. I had to promise her marriage, I did, in order to get into that gunroom. Well, she'll remember me right enough!''

''Oh, my God,'' Isolde gasped as she listened to this speech. ''It was you who shot at Gay. And you were the cruel young man who took advantage of that maid at Shalbourne Manor. Why? Why?''

Harold turned on Isolde, his eyes red with the demon that possessed him. '' 'Twas his idea!'' He pointed an accusing finger at Wendall. ''All his idea! I was to use his lordship's own gun, I was, and what better way to get hold of one than to court one of the maids? Well, I hated it! I hated it!''

Harold snatched up the gun he had laid aside on the library steps and pointed the gun at Wendall. ''And if that weren't enough, you told me I had to try again. He had to be dead before I could come back to Challoner's. Well, he damn near killed me with that bloody sword of his! And how was I to know he weren't dead? I were bleeding to death and there weren't no way a normal human man coulda' survived the blow that branch gave him!''

''Calm yourself, Harold.'' Wendall advanced into the room.

Isolde, who had been following this latest speech, a hand at her throat, now exclaimed, "You! You were the footpad that attacked Gay on Christmas Eve!"

"Hold your tongue, you fool!" Wendall shouted at Harold. "Do you want her to know everything?!"

Harold, panting and gasping like a man who had just run a four-minute mile, swung the gun at Isolde, then back at Wendall, then back at Isolde as he did his odd dance step toward the doorway. "I ain't staying, you hear me!" he announced. "I ain't staying! You promised me 'twould be easy this time! You promised me there weren't no way it could go wrong this time! Well, it has, and now, everybody knows what we done." Harold's eyes widened in his mottled red face. "No! No! Everyone knows what you done! I didn't kill him! You did! And I ain't going to hang with you, you hear me! My God, you done killed a bloody peer of the bloody realm! They won't even consider transporting us—we'll swing on the nubbing cheat, for sure!"

Wendall fixed his stern features on Harold's face and said calmly, "You are becoming distracted for nothing, Harold. Now, give me that gun."

"No!" Harold squeaked and then backed away. The gun he trained in Wendall's direction shook visibly. "I'm leaving, you hear me. I'm going to America. Ain't no one going to find me there."

"Harold!" Wendall's deep voice rang with authority. "Now you put that gun down and—"

"No!" Harold took a few nervous steps forward and then back, continuing his odd, partnerless dance. "Where's your money, Mr. Hackett? I want what's coming to me and I want it now!"

Afraid that the nervous palsy in Harold's hand might cause him to set off the pistol accidently, Wendall assumed a soothing manner. "In the desk. The bottom drawer, if you must know. But, Harold, this is madness."

Waving the gun with both hands at Isolde, Harold ignored Wendall's plea and instructed, "You! Isolde! Go to the desk. Get the money box!"

"Now, Harold." Wendall took a tentative step forward as Isolde swiftly laid Jenny's head on a cushion she'd grabbed from the chair next to her. Jenny made a snorting noise and murmured in her sleep.

"You stay back!" Harold swung the gun at Wendall again.

"All right, Harold," Wendall said in a conciliatory tone as he retreated to one side of the desk. He had never seen the menacing creature waving the gun at him before. Isolde, who had, swiftly opened the bottom drawer of the desk and removed the wooden box.

"It's locked," she announced.

Keeping the gun trained on Wendall, Harold sidled across the room by doing a fancy two-step, reaching behind him and picking up the volume of Shakespeare on his way. "Set it on the floor," he instructed Isolde, never taking his eyes off Wendall.

"What . . ." Isolde began.

"Set it on the floor, damn you!" Harold shouted.

Isolde hastily complied.

Raising the volume to the highest distance his hand could reach, he dropped it on the wooden box. The old wood splintered at the hinges.

"Now, open it," Harold instructed Isolde once again. She dutifully pried open the box.

"The money!" Harold exclaimed. "Give me the money!"

Isolde removed two large stacks of bills and a bag of coins. Harold took one shaking hand from the gun and stuffed the first stack of bills in one coat pocket and the other stack in the opposite pocket. The coins he pushed through the small opening at the waist of his pants. "Not exactly what you promised me," Harold growled at Wendall. "But should pay me passage right enough."

Wendall tried to reason with him once again. "Harold, you're not being rational."

Harold did his sideways two-step back toward the door. "Ha! I'm being smart for the first time in a long while."

"Harold!" Wendall spoke sharply. "Stop this right now! You know I've always taken care of you, haven't I? Haven't I? Gave you a job when you first came to London, didn't I? Didn't your own mother send you to me? She trusted me."

"Shut up! Shut up! I ain't listening to you anymore!" Harold stamped his foot like a child indulging in a tantrum.

"You speak more respectful to me, boy!" Wendall, who had reached the end of his tether, shouted back.

"Why?" Harold sneered. "Why should I? 'Cause you're me ruddy boss? Well, you ain't no more, 'cause I quit!"

"Harold, you will do as I say!" Wendall blustered.

"No! No! Why should I?"

"Because I'm your father!" Wendall shouted back.

Dead silence fell at this shocking statement.

Harold, first frozen into immobility, began to shake again. Swinging his head back and forth in denial, he whispered hoarsely, "No . . . no . . . I've always hated my father! You . . . you . . . I . . ." Tears filled Harold's eyes, his skin flushed and he screamed, "You ruined my mother's life! You lousy stinking bastard! You raped her!" He began to cry in great, gulping sobs. "I'm going to kill you!" He raised the gun, shaking.

"No!" Wendall denied. "Jessamina lied if she told you . . ."

"Jessamina!" Isolde took a step forward, bringing her closer to Wendall and opposite Harold. "Harold!" she cried, distracting him. "Was your mother a woman named Jessamina Thorpe?"

Harold was momentarily dazed. He looked at Isolde as if he had forgotten she was in the room and couldn't imagine why she was there at all. "Yes," he said, puzzled. "But she always called herself Mrs. Biggelswade. Just to be more respectable-like.''

"Oh, my God!" Isolde breathed. Turning on Wendall like a fury, she accused, "You! You killed my Uncle James! You murderer!''

"I did not!" Wendall tensed, with two now out for his blood. " 'Twas a fair fight! A duel!''

"He was shot in the back! You call that a fair fight?''

"I couldn't let him tell Challoner!" Wendall defended himself. "He'd of killed me. Mary . . .''

"Oh, my lord and savior," Isolde cried with dawning horror. "My parents knew! They knew! And that's why they came running to London so precipitously two years ago.''

"Aye, they knew all right. That silly bitch, Jessamina, told your father everything before she died at that Inn.'' Wendall clenched his teeth and grunted. "They came here looking for Mary. They were going to tell her . . .''

"They came here first?" Isolde gasped. "They came here first before going to Grandfather Challoner's? Then you . . . oh, lord, you must have killed them, too!''

"I didn't!" Wendall whined. "I didn't. I just tampered with their wheel a bit. London traffic killed them, not me!''

"My God!" Isolde's horrified eyes were trained on the monster standing only a few feet in front of her. "Where does it all end? With me? With Jenny? With Harold? Your own son? Will you have to kill him, too?''

The door burst open behind Harold. Harold went flying on his face, the gun sliding from his grip across the wood floor and coming to rest under a bookshelf.

A voice Isolde thought she would never hear again snarled, "Don't anybody move!''

Isolde swung round, ignoring his command, tears of joy springing to her eyes. "Gay! Oh, thank God.''

Wendall, seeing his chance, moved remarkably fast for

one of his bulk and years. Grabbing the letter opener sitting on the desk next to him, he put a strong arm around Isolde and pulled her back against his chest as a shield, just as she started to take a step toward her husband. Holding the letter opener, which resembled a flat, sharp dagger, to her throat, he spoke to Shalbourne, "I thought I'd killed you."

Before Shalbourne could frame a suitable reply, Jonathan pushed past him and started toward Jenny's still figure near the fireplace.

"That's far enough!" Wendall barked out.

Jonathan froze, noticing for the first time that Wendall stood at the other end of the room with a daggerlike object at Isolde's throat. "Jenny," Jonathan croaked as she moaned and tried to open her eyes. "What have you done with my Jenny?"

Harold scrambled to his feet and crouched up against the library steps in the far corner away from the others. "Just a book. Just hit her with a book." With the loss of his gun, he'd lost all his bluster as well. He curled up next to the steps into a fetal position, rocking back and forth.

"You won't get away with it, Hackett," Shalbourne announced. "Let her go."

Wendall tightened his hold on Isolde's neck. She dug her nails into the arm trying to choke her. Wendall pushed the tip of the letter opener into the expanse of tender, white flesh exposed above Isolde's evening dress. "Put down those barkers," he told Shalbourne through clenched teeth. "Or I bury this chiser in your lovely wife's bosom."

Shalbourne's fingers tightened convulsively on the two pistols in his hands. "Let her go," he growled again.

"Put down your guns!" Wendall's voice went up an octave in frustration and the letter opener drew a small drop of blood.

"Gay." Isolde's wide-eyed look and pleading voice were his undoing. Shalbourne slowly set the two pistols on the small table next to where he was standing.

Wendall grinned. "That's better." Dragging Isolde before him, he started toward the door.

Shalbourne stared into his wife's eyes as if he could communicate some urgent message that way. He watched in helpless silence as Wendall pulled her closer and closer to the door, Isolde tripping over her feet as she came.

When they pulled even with Shalbourne, Wendall couldn't resist stopping briefly to laugh. "I guess I'll just have to give up trying to kill you. You're just too stubborn to die! But Isolde here . . ."

Shalbourne made a menacing noise that began somewhere deep in his throat. Like a mad dog, he jumped at the couple, grabbing the hand that held the letter opener and forcing it back and upward away from Isolde's skin.

Isolde, not to be outdone by her husband's intrepid behavior, sank her teeth deep into the other arm that held her close to Wendall's chest. Wendall howled and dropped his hold on Isolde.

Isolde ducked under Wendall's arm, allowing Shalbourne to launch full force at Wendall. The two men fell backward out the doorway and onto the stair landing, silently grappling. An uncertain light from the library illuminated the fierce expressions on their faces as Shalbourne, banging Wendall's wrist against one of the wooden stair rail posts, forced the letter opener from his opponent's grasp. Then, Wendall, in a desperate burst of strength, struggled to his feet.

Aiming a foot at Shalbourne's gut, Wendall was pulled off balance as Shalbourne grabbed his leg. In an attempt to regain his footing, Wendall sank his fingers into the bandage wrapped around Shalbourne's head. Shalbourne jerked his head back. Coming away with handful of cloth, Wendall lost his footing altogether and lunged headlong down the stairs.

Wendall screamed as his body pitched downward. There was the sound of wood splintering when he hit the railing.

The scream died suddenly as he thudded to the next landing with a sickening crunch.

Shalbourne impatiently wiped away a drop of blood that trickled down from his freshly opened wound. Breathing heavily, he struggled to his feet and leaned against the now gaping railing. Calmly, he remarked, "I suppose we should find out if he's alive."

"Gay," Isolde whispered, her voice choking on a sob. "Oh, Gay." She hurled herself at him, throwing her arms around his neck. Shalbourne staggered but didn't mind. Reaching up, Isolde pulled his face toward hers. "Oh, Gay, darling! When I thought you were dead, I wanted to die, too!" Shalbourne was startled but cooperative when she pressed her lips against his. After only a second of passive participation, Shalbourne took over, his hands tightening their grip on her arms as his mouth probed passionately and intimately. Oblivious of their audience, the two clung locked in an embrace which gave vent to their pent-up emotions.

CHAPTER TWENTY

When the outer door next to Wendall's still form rattled as
someone tried a key in the lock, Isolde and Gay broke apart,
distracted by the sounds.

Before anyone at the top of the stairs had a chance to
move, Mary Hackett pushed open her front door. "It was
very nice of you to escort me home." She addressed someone behind her and then almost tripped over her husband.
"Oh!" she exclaimed.

"Miz Hackett?" Peter Rutherford followed close behind.
"What is it? What's wrong? Lord!" he cried, seeing
Wendall's battered and broken body at their feet.

"Aunt Mary!" Isolde gasped.

Shalbourne's hold on Isolde stiffened. "His wife?" he
asked grimly.

Isolde nodded mutely.

Mary looked wildly around, first at Peter, than at the fig-
ures at the top of the stairs.

Peter moved forward and knelt. "I'm sorry, Miz Hackett.
I'm afraid his neck's broke."

"Oh!" Mary's hand fluttered to her throat and she sank
gracefully into the chair next to the door that the footman
usually occupied. "Oh! Wendall . . . dead? Oh, dear, oh,
dear, oh, dear."

Peter stood and moved to her side. Taking her hand to pat it, he started, "I'm sorry, Miz Hackett."

"Oh, thank God!" Mary cried and promptly burst into tears. "It's over . . . it's finally over. He's dead! Thank God!"

"Miz Hackett?" Peter looked at her as if she had gone stark, staring mad.

"Oh, I'm sorry, Peter." She smiled crookedly as she wiped her face with shaking fingers. "You think that's odd, don't you? But he made my life a misery for thirty years, and Mirabelle was the only good thing that came out of my marriage. All I can think is, thank God it's over!"

She looked up from the shocked face beside her to the shocked faces at the top of the stairs. "Oh, good evening, Isolde. Is this your young lord?" she asked as if there were nothing out of the ordinary in their present circumstances.

Isolde started down the stairs. "Aunt Mary, I want to explain."

Mary Hackett very calmly stepped over her husband's still form as if it were no more than a sleeping household pet. Climbing the stairs, she met Isolde halfway. Tucking her niece's hand into the crook of her arm, she started up the stairs again. "You must introduce me to your husband, my dear. I've never met an Earl before."

Shalbourne limped to the edge of the landing and solemnly confronted the ladies. "I'm sorry, madam, about your husband."

"Why, thank you." Mary stepped on the landing and looked up into the faces looming before her. "That's very kind of you. Although unnecessary." She smiled sweetly at him, the resemblance between her and her beautiful daughter never more evident.

"You must understand," Shalbourne said, standing stiff and erect. "It was self-defense."

"My husband fell down the stairs. It was an accident,"

Mary said as if she were explaining to a roomful of grammar school students.

"But," Shalbourne began, wanting to confess.

Mary fixed her gaze on him. Her soft blue eyes hardened to agate. She enunciated each word distinctly and slowly. "My husband fell down the stairs. It was an accident."

"Where is Mirabelle?" Mary asked curiously after a moment of silence, as she looked from one to the other.

"She's in me rooms above the stables," Jenny, leaning groggily on her husband, answered from the library's doorway. "Leastwise, she was when I left her."

"Oh?" Mary reflected. "Quite wise. We mustn't let Mirabelle see her Papa until he is properly laid out."

Jonathan jumped down the stairs at her words. "She's right there, Mr. Rutherford. Can't leave him here for Miss Mirabelle to see."

"Oh, no, of course not," Peter agreed emphatically.

"Won't you come into the library, your lordship?" Mary asked Shalbourne politely. "Please do sit. Did you know that your head is bleeding?" Mary asked as if she were inquiring if he knew the sky was blue. She indicated the wing chair by the fireplace. "There. That is the most comfortable chair in the room. Whatever is that cushion doing on the floor? Ah, well, no matter."

Shalbourne, leaning heavily on Isolde, complied with her request.

"Goodness, what is this?" Mary asked herself as she noticed the broken money box and large book next to it on the floor. She glanced up as the sound of whimpering broke the silence. "Harold? Whatever is the matter, dear? You really mustn't sit on the floor like that. You'll get your clothes all wrinkled."

"No." Harold came briefly out of his stupor to stare wild-eyed at the faces around him. "No!" he screeched again and then, jumping to his feet, he ran madly out the library door, down the stairs, and through the front door, going past Jonathan and Peter without a glance for their burden.

"Well!" Mary exclaimed as she picked up the broken money box and book. "I suppose he remembered an urgent appointment. Someone has been reading Shakespeare I see. I wish people would remember to put away their things when they are done with them." She shook her head sadly and sighed at the perversity of those who were so inconsiderate as to leave their discarded toys for someone else to pick up. "Jenny," she addressed the maidservant hovering in the doorway. "Would you make us some tea, dear? Oh, and could you get— Oh, well, never mind. I have a handkerchief that should do quite nicely as a bandage for his lordship's head, and I really think that what is most needed at the moment is some tea."

"Yes, mum," Jenny looked askance at her mistress and spoke hesitantly.

"Oh, and, Jenny," Mary added as she flung off her bonnet. "Maybe you could go to Mirabelle and send her in now that the excitement is over. Thank you, my dear."

"Aye, mum." Jenny was just as glad to make a hasty retreat.

Mary started to struggle with her coat. Isolde jumped to her aunt's aid. "Why, thank you, my dear. I never could do that properly by myself."

Peter Rutherford appeared in the doorway. "It's done, Miz Hackett. We laid out Mr. Hackett in the parlor."

"Why, thank you, Peter. Won't you come in and meet my niece's husband, his lordship? Oh, don't get up, my lord. Peter won't mind." Mary waved a hand at Shalbourne to keep him in his seat. "Peter, why don't you pull up that chair for Isolde and then one for yourself? Oh, before I forget. My lord, this is Mr. Peter Rutherford. He is engaged to my daughter, Mirabelle, whom I understand you already know."

"Ah, yes." Shalbourne bit back a grin. "I've met Miss Hackett."

"Peter's an apothecary," Mary supplied helpfully.

"Ah, how nice," Shalbourne said uncertainly.

"Perhaps, Peter, you would be the best one to take care of his lordship's head!" Mary dug in her reticule and produced a handkerchief. "After all, it is your profession, sort of, isn't it?" She handed the dismayed Peter a small lace-trimmed square of lavender-scented cloth.

"Oh, that's all right, Mrs. Hackett." Shalbourne hastily grabbed the cloth from Peter's limp fingers. "I can take care of it myself. See. Almost stopped."

When Mirabelle joined them a few minutes later, she could hardly believe her eyes. Isolde, her dress torn and blood-stained, was sitting on the arm of her husband's chair and swinging her leg, one arm around her husband's shoulders, the other lying in his lap, her hand clasped with his. His lordship looked like he'd been through another war, but didn't seem to care. His greatcoat had long since been removed and lay in a bundle at his feet. He wore an odd outfit consisting of an elaborately embroidered peach-colored waistcoat, black satin knee breeches, and an elegant shirt (collar and cravat long since gone.) A lace handkerchief had been tied around his head with the blue ribbon from her mother's bonnet. Peter was sitting in a chair opposite inspecting a rather lethal-looking dueling pistol and her mother. . . ! Her mother was standing precariously at the top of the library steps, searching the shelves and chattering like a magpie.

"Oh, hello, my dear. Won't you join us?" Mary scrambled down the steps, her search forgotten.

Explaining as kindly as she could, Mary told her daughter that there had been an accident and that Wendall had been killed in a fall. The next ten minutes were taken up with ministering to Mirabelle. She was soon brought out of her doldrums, though, since, like her mother, she had never held any particular or profound affection for the man who had been her father. By the time Jenny appeared with the tea tray (which Jonathan obligingly carried for her), the room was once again filled with light-hearted conversation.

An urgent knock on the front door sent Jonathan flying down the stairs to see who it was "before they break it down," as Mary put it. Opening cautiously, Jonathan was confronted by the sight of Lord Denbigh brandishing yet another pistol, Fraser hugging my lord's forgotten cane/sword stick, and Lady Jane clutching a poker.

"Well, man!" Denbigh shouted at Jonathan. "Where are they?"

Jonathan threw open the door. "Come in," he said, exasperated. Nothing would amaze him at this point! "Come in and join the tea party." He indicated the door at the top of the stairs with a jerking thumb. "In there. Cackling like a bunch of old hens." Shaking his head, he muttered, "Moonstruck mad, that's what they 'ere. All gone moonstruck mad."

"Reinforcements have arrived!" Denbigh announced cheerfully, assessing that the situation confronting his eyes was hardly a dangerous one.

"Late as ever, I see, George," Shalbourne answered in much the same tone. "Good Lord, who have you got with you?"

"Oh, come in!" Mary Hackett couldn't have been more pleased if the Prince Regent himself had arrived. "Do come in. Are these friends of yours, Gay?" Mary asked politely. She and Shalbourne had progressed to the intimacies of first names very swiftly.

"Lord, yes, Aunt Mary." Shalbourne struggled to his feet. "This disreputable fellow is my best friend, George

Archibald Ashton." He added with a wink and a stage whisper, "*Lord* Denbigh!"

"Oh, goody!" Mary clapped her hands. "Another lord! Is he an earl, too?" she asked hopefully.

Denbigh shook his head ruefully. "No, I'm sorry, ma'am. Only a viscount."

"George, may I present Mrs. Mary Challoner, formerly Hackett, Mirabelle's mother," Shalbourne continued. "And Aunt Jane! How nice! I certainly didn't expect to see you! Good gracious, Fraser! Did Sikes or Simmons or perhaps one of my other servants come as well?"

"No, I'm afraid not, old chum," Denbigh laughed. "Only Fraser. Couldn't rouse the rest of the household on your behalf. Not a popular fellow, Gay. No one else seemed to want to help rescue you."

"Rescue?" Mary laughed. "How absurd!"

Denbigh turned to her and bowed over her hand. "Certainly it was absurd, madam. Who in your beautiful clutches would want to be rescued?"

Mary giggled. "Oh, my lord."

Shalbourne then introduced his aunt. "Lady Jane Tiverton, Mrs. Challoner, formerly Hackett."

"Oh!" Mary cried. "A real lady! How nice. And Gay has told me ever so much about you! I'm so pleased to meet you. Oh, but, please, come in, come in. Sit down." Mary urged.

"Ah, Fraser. How thoughtful of you to have brought my cane." Shalbourne took the item from his valet's numb fingers.

"Why formerly Hackett?" Lady Jane piped in, this point puzzling her no end.

"Oh," Mary announced seriously. "I've decided to drop my husband's name." She added confidentially, "He was not a very nice man, you know. Besides, as Mrs. Challoner of Challoner's Spice and Tea Importers, I shall command much more respect. And, it sounds so much nicer. And, of course,'' Mary chirped in, gazing fondly at the young couple on the couch. ''Mirabelle shall be Mrs. Rutherford soon, so she shan't be a Hackett anymore, either. Oh, dear,'' Mary chewed thoughtfully on her fingertip as a thought occurred to her. ''I wonder if we are obliged to wait a full year after Wendall's funeral to have the wedding?'' Mary chewed thoughtfully on her fingertip. ''What do you think Lady Jane?'' she asked, deciding her ladyship was the most socially cognizant person present.

''Who is this Wendall, anyway?'' Lady Jane wanted to know before passing judgment.

''My husband.'' Mary shook her head sadly at Lady Jane. ''He's laid out in the parlor,'' she added. ''He fell down the stairs. And, now, we're having a wake!'' Mary smiled happily. ''Jenny tells me it's an old Irish tradition. Although I don't properly understand all the details. Anyway, it seems that they hold a party after someone is deceased and talk about him and tell stories or whatever. Only I don't think we will need any stories for this wake. We'll just have the party part. And Jenny has brought us the most delightful tea! Do take some with us,'' Mary urged her more aristocratic guests. ''Jenny says she's put a secret Irish ingredient in it. She says they always drink it at wakes.''

Denbigh, allowing himself to be plied with a cup of the concoction, took an experimental sip. ''Hmmm. Yes, I see.'' He gave Shalbourne a wry glance. ''That would explain a lot.''

''George,'' Shalbourne addressed the young man who had settled on the top of the library steps, sipping as quickly as he could at the whiskey-laced tea.

''Yes?'' Denbigh answered.

''Did you bring your carriage?''

''Oh, really, Gay!'' Denbigh sighed loudly. ''First you steal my horse and now you want to steal my carriage!''

Shalbourne grinned. "I'll send it back for you just as soon as her ladyship and I reach home." He held his hand out to Isolde who took it without hesitation.

"Oh, go on! Rob me blind!" Denbigh said. "After all, what are friends for?"

"Here, young man!" Lady Jane noticed Shalbourne and his wife were trying to exit. "Where do you think you're going?"

"Home." Shalbourne looked at his wife's face as he raised her hand to his lips. "To bed."

Lady Jane, who had already imbibed a full glass of spiked tea, agreed delightedly. "Oh, yes, do. Good idea, Shalbourne. Must have an heir, you know, before I change my will."

"That foundling hospital can have your bloody money, Aunt Jane," Shalbourne stated good-naturedly.

Lady Jane snorted in disbelief.

"All I want is to be alone with my wife," he added.

Isolde looked shyly at her husband and whispered to him, "Your aunt wants you to have an heir very much, doesn't she?"

Shalbourne grimaced. "Yes."

Isolde spoke in a louder voice, for the benefit of the room at large. "But, Gay, you may yet have an heir."

Shalbourne laughed. "Well, I certainly hope so. Eventually."

Isolde grinned, still looking only at the man who held her hands in his. "Would about seven months time be soon enough?"

Shalbourne's jaw dropped. "What?"

Lady Jane chortled with unholy glee. "Oh, it worked! It worked!"

"What worked?" Mary asked politely.

"My ruse worked!" Lady Jane giggled again. "Told him

I'd changed my will and left all my money to a foundling hospital in Grantham."

"Yes?" Mary asked, confused but interested.

Lady Jane bent over with laughter. "But that's just it! I never did!"

"What?" Shalbourne rounded on his aunt.

"Never could." She grinned inanely at her nephew. "You think I'd risk leaving the Earl of Shalbourne penniless, boy? Then you don't know me very well!" Lady Jane cackled again. "And that's just exactly what I was betting on!"

"Good God!" A shocked Shalbourne gasped his astonishment. "You mean, I never had to get married? Fall in with your schemes at all?"

"No. Never." Lady Jane grinned from ear to ear.

"Why, you." Words failed Shalbourne. His eyes turned dark with anger. His jaw clenched and his hands tightened their grip on what they were holding.

"Gay?" Isolde reminded him that it was her poor fingers that he was crushing.

Shalbourne glanced at his wife. His features softened. He burst into laughter, raised Isolde's hand to his lips once more and addressed Lady Jane, "You termagant! I ought to kiss you!"

"I knew a wife would be the making of you!" Lady Jane announced smugly.

When Lord and Lady Shalbourne finally escaped their well-wishers' loudly voiced congratulations, and found themselves alone in a darkened carriage heading toward home, a shy, uncertain silence fell between them.

"So," Shalbourne eventually managed to say. "There'll be another Leighton soon to plague the world, will there?"

Isolde nodded shyly. He grinned at her. "Isolde," he began softly. "My lady . . ."

"Yes," she whispered back, her heart pounding in anticipation of she knew not what.

"Having slain the dragon."

Isolde, recognizing the dialogue, asked, "What dragon?"

"Aunt Jane, of course."

"Oh, you!" Isolde laughed and struck him lightly on his broad chest. "Seems to me, she defeated you and not the other way round!"

"How can you say that? Anyway, fair lady, I would claim my reward." Shalbourne pulled her pliant body closer.

"Oh!" Isolde pulled back and sat up suddenly. "I must tell you! Uncle Wendall and Harold were responsible for . . ."

"Later," Shalbourne murmured as he raised her chin with one hand and pressed his lips against hers.

After a pleasant few minutes, Isolde broke away and murmured, "But, Gay, I must tell you . . ."

"Later!" Shalbourne growled.

"But—"

"Woman!" Shalbourne exclaimed. "Would you please tell me what could possibly be more important at this moment than for your husband to make love to you?!"

Isolde smiled and ran a finger lightly down his beloved scar. He was right! Explanations and a plea to reinstate Mr. Anderson could wait yet awhile. "Nothing," she replied. "Except to say that I love you."

Lord Shalbourne spent a very agreeable evening convincing his wife that the feeling was entirely mutual.

True romance is <u>not</u> hard to find.. you need only look as far as FAWCETT BOOKS